A Sovereign for a Song

The daughter of a Durham miner, Annie Wilkinson now lives in Hull where she works full-time as a health visitor. *A Sovereign for a Song* is her first novel.

Annie Wilkinson

A Sovereign for a Song

LONDON • SYDNEY • NEW YORK • TOKYO • TORONTO

First published in Great Britain by Simon & Schuster UK Ltd, 2004
This edition first published by Pocket Books, 2004
An imprint of Simon & Schuster UK
A CBS COMPANY

3 5 7 9 10 8 6 4

Simon & Schuster UK Ltd
1st Floor
222 Gray's Inn Road
London WC1X 8HB

www.simonandschuster.co.uk

Simon & Schuster Australia
Sydney

A CIP catalogue record for this book is available from
the British Library

ISBN 978-1-84983-496-4

Typeset by SX Composing DTP, Rayleigh, Essex
Printed and bound by
CPI Group (UK) Ltd, Croydon, CR0 4YY

Acknowledgements

To all my family, and friends Rilba, Sue, Paula, Lisa, Elaine, Cythia, Robin and Joanne for their help and encouragement; to Linda Acaster and everybody at Hornsea Writers for truly constructive criticism; to tutors Daphne Glazer and Ian Smith; to all writers on the history of coalmining in England, above all to Robert Colls for writing *The Pitmen of the Northern Coalfield*, he will find many echoes of his work in mine; to a late, unknown reporter for the *Barnsley Chronicle*; to Mary Lloyd, her family and her biographers for the inspiration of her life; to all at the RNA; and to those literary midwives Judith Murdoch and Kate Lyall Grant, without whom the book would never have seen the light of day.

Prologue

'She's telling me she can't go on. She's overwrought – I've never seen her like this. What have you been doing to her, Charlie? Calm her down, for God's sake. She's on in half an hour. You know how to talk to her. Make her right, or you get no more bookings here. She's top of the bill. I can't go out there and tell them all she's not going on, I'd get lynched. They've paid for Ginny James, and some of them'll tear the place apart if they don't get her. I'm not paying her eighty quid a week for this.'

'All right.' Charlie put his bowler on the table and glanced in the mirror to smooth his thick red hair. His diamond cravat-pin glinted in the lamplight.

The manager's black eyebrows met in a scowl. 'I mean it. She goes on and gives them what they've come for, or I'll have the law on the pair of you. Breach of contract.' He raised a fist.

Charlie's cold, pale blue eyes appraised him. 'All right. Get out.'

The manager left, muttering curses. Charlie stretched

out a beautifully manicured hand and picked up the half empty brandy bottle.

'Not twenty years old, and a drunkard. Disgusting in a woman. How much of this have you had?'

'Not enough to make me feel any better.' She was slumped over the dressing table, slightly tipsy and very truculent.

'Any better than what?'

She raised her head. 'Any better than dirt. You're driving me mad, Charlie.' Their eyes met in the mirror. She looked away and saw the tremor of her hand as she lifted it to put on the greasepaint. 'You're the one who drove me to drink. You think I'm made of stone. You treat me as if I'm nothing but a lump of flesh. You're not here because you want to be, you're here because that bloody man sent somebody running to fetch you because I'm not fit to go on and keep the audience happy. How can I when I'm not happy myself?'

'What nonsense. Joe Grimaldi was the most miserable man alive, but he could make an audience laugh more than anyone before or since.'

Her mouth twisted, and her eyes suddenly filled with tears. Charlie changed tack, became placatory.

'Come on, pull yourself together now. A good little trooper like you never lets her public down, and you love your audiences as much as they love you, Ginny,' he soothed.

She brought her fist down hard upon the table. 'Shut up, shut up, shut up arguing me down and smoothing me down and shutting me up! Why won't you ever listen?

You don't care a damn about me. I'm nothing but livestock to you. I'm something you trade, and if you weren't trading me here, you'd be trading me on the streets.' Her voice rose to a shriek before she turned back to the mirror and continued her agitated application of make-up with a hand she could not keep still.

'Lower your voice, Ginny. Of course I care, and of course I'm listening.' He stooped to kiss her neck.

She shied away. 'No, you don't care, and you're not listening. You're smoothing me down, and trying to tame me, but you can't tame me this time, Charlie, I'm past being tamed.' The hand slipped, and a red streak disfigured the side of her mouth. 'Now look what you've made me do. It'll all have to come off again. I'm past everything. I can't bear any more. You're murdering me inside.' The tears began to flow in rivulets from her reddened eyes and nose, and she dabbed at them with a handkerchief, completing the ruin of the greasepaint.

He sighed. 'All right. I am listening, truly. So tell me, what can't you bear?'

'Why are you asking me? You know what I can't bear,' she cried. 'You know it, but you'll still make me do it. I can't. I can't, Charlie. I'll have to have this child. It's too late for her to do anything now. If you loved me, you wouldn't let her near me.'

'Be quiet, Ginny. Do you want the whole theatre to know your business?' He hesitated for what seemed an age, then said, 'All right. All right then, I promise she won't come near you. Honour bright. Come to Charlie.' He held out his arms for her.

She made no move towards him, but lifted her hands in a gesture of hopelessness. 'Honour bright. You always say that when you're lying.'

'I'm not lying.' He shook out the folds of a monogrammed handkerchief and handed it to her. 'Blow your nose, little hinny. I seem to recollect doing this once before, when you were weeping for the onions in Helen's kitchen. Do you remember?'

She blew her nose, and gave him a watery smile, but the tears still gushed from her inky black eyes. 'And you wrapped it up and put it in your pocket, and you said I was cruel. But you're the cruel one. I was happy then, in Annsdale, working at your sister's and going home to me mam. I was proud, an' all. I got mad sometimes, but I never cried, and look at me now. Look what you've done to me, Charlie.'

She dipped her fingers into a pot of cold cream then rubbed it into her face and he handed her wads of cotton to remove the ruined make-up. 'You will marry me before the baby's born, won't you?' she whispered. 'Surely I'm earning enough now.'

Without hesitation this time he answered, 'Of course I will. I shall take good care of you. I will listen to you, Ginny, I'll listen very carefully, but we must leave it until we get home. You haven't much time, and it's very important for you to get ready to please your audience now. They're looking forward to seeing their Ginny on top form, and you mustn't disappoint them.'

He stayed with her while she washed her face in cold water and pinned her hair up into elaborate coils.

Another application of greasepaint did something to disguise her swollen eyes and blotchy complexion. As she put on the finishing touch, a blue silk hat trimmed with sequins and feathers he said, 'Remember what you rehearsed. Give them your best, and all will be well. Come and meet me in the bar after your turn and we'll go home together. Promise me you'll think no more about it until then.'

When she looked in the mirror, Ginny Wilde was gone. In her place was the second self, the zestful, devil-may-care Ginny James, star turn of the music halls, who had nothing to learn from Joe Grimaldi. After her last call, this lively and vivacious Ginny bounded on to the stage and delivered her goods with that dash and energy she had become famous for.

But after the act, when Ginny Wilde sat alone and afraid at the mirror with Leichner's greasepaint all removed, the memory of Annsdale Colliery and all she loved there stole over her like a fog of grief. Oh, she thought, and Martin . . . and Martin. How willingly would I change places with Maria, and lie still and quiet in my grave, if I could know I'd been loved half so much.

Out came the hairpins, and a mass of thick, black hair fell on to her shoulders, as unlike Maria's fine, blonde curls as could possibly be. Curls that had framed his poor wife's pale face like a halo.

Ginny stared unseeing at her reflection. 'Martin's a good man, the best,' she whispered, echoing her brother's words. The days she had spent under Martin's roof had been the happiest of her life. She picked up the brush, and pulled it swiftly through her hair, dismissing the thought. Useless, she told herself. Useless to think of that. She had fled Annsdale to protect them both from her father, and after three years of living with Charlie Parkinson, there was no going back. She was fastened to Charlie, cheat and liar that he was. She was stuck with him, and she meant to make damned sure he was stuck with her, and their child.

A fleeting, sardonic smile followed a frown. After all, it wasn't all bad. Charlie could make himself very agreeable when it suited him, especially between the sheets, and that was some compensation. 'I doubt if I'm fit to be a decent man's wife, now,' she murmured, pinning up her hair in a simpler style. A final smoothing down of her dress and she was ready to meet Charlie in the bar, determined, oh so determined to make the best of it.

But thoughts of Annsdale and happier days would keep intruding. Even the brutality had been no worse than what she faced now. The only difference was, it had all been on the surface there.

Chapter One

Oh, the pitmen are not bonny lads,
The pitmen are not bonny O!
If they re ever sae clean yet
They re black about the een
And I like them the worst o ony O!

Fifteen-year-old Ginny stood outside on a little wooden cracket, cleaning the front room window with a bit of string tied round the bottom of her long skirts to prevent the wind blowing them up to give any passer-by an eyeful. She bawled lustily at the top of her lungs, trying to goad her brother John, who was sitting in the kitchen drinking tea and complaining to their mother about his sore sides after a shift of pony putting.

Little Sally was on the mend. The fever had broken at last, and the household was beginning to get back to normal. With Lizzie and young Arthur out of the way playing street games with other children, the two elder girls were helping their mother tear into the backlog of work. Thirteen-year-old Emma was black-leading the fireplace, and their mother was getting on with the polishing.

'Sing on, Ginny, you're safe enough. I'm too tired to rise to it,' John shouted from the kitchen. She laughed, and changed the tune to 'The Putter's Lament'.

Aa cannet lift it, Aa cannet shift it,
Why it's enough to mak' ye cry.
Aa've chewed on till me arse is sair
Now Aa can't lift any mair.
Aa cannet lift it, Aa cannet shift it,
An Aa dinnet intend te try.
Aa's ganna put me gear away,
An' bugger off out bye.

'I'd like to see you try it,' shouted John, 'you want to try getting the coal away for a couple of demon hewers in a good cavil, with a pony that'll do nothing it's told 'til it's time to go back to the stable, and tubs that keep coming off the rails. You women! You don't know you're bloody born, man!'

She laughed again, and turned to see her father coming down the street dressed in his best suit, returning after an hour at the club. Black hair well brushed, suit pressed and shoes polished, he strode arrogantly along with his head up and shoulders back as if he owned the world. Save for the blackened scar that bisected one eyebrow, he might be taken for the owner of the pit rather than one of its hewers. He stopped to exchange a few words with one of his marrers who lived a couple of doors down the row, before walking on home, grim faced.

He slammed the gate hard enough to shake it off its

hinges. Bad omen. The set of his jaw and the glint in his eyes turned Ginny's entrails to ice. He passed her without a word and the door crashed shut behind him. She opened it again, and, picking up the stool and the bucket, followed him through the front room and into the kitchen.

He bent menacingly over John, who until he'd heard the door slam had been peacefully drinking his tea at the table. He looked up in alarm.

'Where are they, then?' Their father's voice was soft, controlled, raising the hairs on the back of Ginny's neck.

'Where are what?' John asked, all innocence.

'Alf Jackson's apples, that's what. Where are they?'

'I don't know. I know nothing about Alf Jackson's apples.'

'Mr Jackson to you.' Their father landed a blow on the side of John's head. 'What have you done with them?'

'Nothing,' protested John, voice now shrill, and face reddening at the accusation so that he looked a picture of guilt.

'Liar! You've eaten them. It's written all over your face. Why would he say you took them if you didn't? Why were you hanging about his fence earlier?'

Silence, followed by another blow to the back of John's head.

'Well?'

'I was taking a stone out of my boot.'

'And you thought you'd help yourself to his apples while you were at it.'

They watched in terror, Ginny in both fear and

loathing. Oh, how she hated her father. How she hated and despised herself for her powerlessness to stop him. She prayed to God to strike him dead and send him to Hell. Little Sally, still weak after pneumonia, began to cry and to cough. The interrogation continued regardless.

'Well?'

'What?'

'What? What? What have you done with his apples?' Her father's fury was coming up to boiling point, along with his determination to overcome John's resistance; to Break his Will, to Get to the Truth.

'I never touched his apples.' Shoulders hunched and arms covering his head, John tried to cower out of reach of their father's hammer fists.

'Arthur, for God's sake, leave him alone.' Face gaunt, their mother shielded her son with her own slender frame.

'Get out of my road. Your favourite's not going to get away with thieving.' He hurled her roughly across the room to crash against the mantelpiece. Without sparing her a glance, he took John by the ears and pulled him out of the chair before pushing him forward and kicking him violently in the small of his back, sending him sprawling. The skinny youth was no match for their father at the best of times and certainly not when exhausted after a day's putting.

'Upstairs. Get upstairs before I knock your brains out.'

John scrambled up as fast as he could go. Their

father deliberately and ceremoniously took off his jacket and waistcoat and hung them carefully in the front room before following John, unbuckling his belt as he went.

'Don't hurt him, Arthur, he's never touched anything belonging to anybody else in his life,' their mother begged, but neither she nor either of her older daughters dared try to stop him, not even hardy Ginny. They stood still and mute in the kitchen, staring at each other as they listened to scuffling and yelps from upstairs, and then to their father laying into John with the belt.

A furious knocking at the back door broke the trance, and Enid Jackson burst in. 'Mary Ann, tell your man John never touched the apples. It was me that lifted them when I took a bit of washing in, only that fool of a man of mine never saw me stoop to pick them up.' Enid, a fat and normally lethargic woman not built for running, clung breathlessly to the doorpost, and their mother was halfway up the stairs before she'd finished speaking. Enid gasped, 'I know what a temper your dad's got, so I came the minute Alf told me the mistake he'd made. He knew as soon as he came into the kitchen and saw the peel on the table. I was making a pie . . .' Her voice trailed off as she caught Ginny's eye.

'He ought to be more careful what he says about people. His loose mouth's just got our John a bloody good hiding.'

Enid's flabby features sagged even further. She sat down heavily on a kitchen chair and groaned. 'I got here as fast as I could.'

Emma put a comforting hand on the perspiring

woman's shoulder. 'It would have been a lot worse if you hadn't.'

A few moments later their father appeared. 'What's all this about, Enid?'

She repeated the story.

'Well, it's a bit late to come telling us all this, like. I've just given him a belting he won't get over for a week.'

'Well, I'm right sorry, Arthur, but Alf didn't realize until he came into the kitchen and saw the peel on the table. I wish you hadn't hit him.'

'Hit him!' exclaimed their father. 'I've nearly bloody killed him just like your Alf expected me to when he told me. And now he sends you round to make excuses for him. Bugger off home, Enid, and tell your man he's a liar and a coward, and he'd better watch what he says in future, or he'll get the next pasting. And tell him to get a fresh set of marrers while you're at it, or I will.'

'Well, Arthur,' said Enid, stung to a retort, 'Alf didn't tell you to beat the living daylights out of John, that was your idea. Happen you won't be so hasty in future.'

'Aw, get away home, woman,' repeated their father.

Enid left. Deflated, he slowly settled himself into his armchair. When their mother came downstairs, he met her look of anguish and reproach with one of defiance.

'Well? What the hell am I supposed to do when a grown man tells me he's had stuff stolen by me own son?'

'You could have listened to your own son, Arthur. Even a criminal gets a chance to speak in his own defence.'

'Aye, well, what's a kid going to say? He's going to deny it, whether he's done it or not. Who's going to take a kid's word against a grown man? Start doing that, and you'll have them doing aught they bloody well like.'

The atmosphere was leaden. Their father maintained a moody, sullen silence while their mother quietly gathered warm water and towel, and a clean shirt for John, and went upstairs. Emma studiously averted her eyes and avoided her father's gaze, but Ginny returned him a black and significant stare with an arrogance that matched his own.

'What the hell are you looking at?' he grunted.

'Nothing,' she said.

He picked up one of John's boots and threw it at her, but it fell short. The aggression had gone. He loved to feel himself in the right, and Ginny sensed that being so patently in the wrong weakened him in his own eyes. She felt herself safe from attack for today, at least.

'Well, look at something else, or you'll get a taste o' what he got.'

'Aye, I suppose so,' she said, 'you're good at that.'

'You'll screw your head off if you twist it much further,' remarked Ginny, watching John as he stood in front of the fire the following morning and looked over his shoulder into the mirror, trying to get a good view of his back.

'I know whose head I'd like to screw off. Just look at the bloody mess he's made o' my back, man. It looks as if it's covered in tramlines. An' I'll bet you anything you like he'll expect me to be at work tomorrow as if nothing had happened.'

'I don't think there's any doubt about that, so I don't think I'll take your bet,' she answered, stepping up to the mirror as he moved away, and brushing the long black hair she had just unravelled from its thick plait.

'Have you seen it, though?' He displayed his bruised back, and waited for her comment. When none was forthcoming, he went on, 'A day at work nearly killing yourself and when you come home, you get this. I can't work tomorrow in this state.'

Ginny shrugged helplessly. 'There's not a lot I can do about it, like.'

John started putting on his shirt. 'Well, there's something I can do about it. I'll get myself a berth and ship out.'

'No,' said their mother. 'A life at sea is harder than the pits in a lot of ways. You'd be away from home from one year's end to the next. You could get stuck on a ship for months at a stretch with a skipper who makes your life a misery. Some of them are real brutes.'

'Sounds like home from home,' said John.

'Well, whatever's happened here, there's certainly a lot worse things happen at sea – it's an old saying and a true one.'

'But I hate the pit, and I hate me dad, and I can't see how anything could be worse than the two o' them put together.'

'Your dad doesn't like it either, and hewing with a pick and shovel is the hardest job in the pit, you know that. Your dad's working in feet of water just now and the coal's hard getting – but he's hardly ever lost a shift, and he brings the money home. It's because of his hard work that you've never gone without, any of you.'

'Aye, and we've never gone without a good hiding either, and neither have you. "Mair kicks than ha'pennies," like our Ginny says.'

Their mother sighed. 'Ginny's got too much to say. Life was never easy for your dad, either. He was beaten black and blue by his parents.'

John's jaw was set in a line of rebellion and resentment. 'Aye, well, he's carrying on the family tradition then. So will you stop making excuses for him, Mam? There's plenty of other men round here work hard but they don't all ill-treat their families like he does. Look at her,' he nodded towards Sally, 'double pneumonia at four year old, because the old swine comes home drunk and chucks you all out into the pouring rain. And don't pretend that wasn't the cause of it, because we all know it was. If it's hard for him, he makes it a bloody sight harder for everybody that has to live with him.'

'Look, John,' pleaded their mother, 'your dad won't touch you again. It was a genuine mistake, and I know he's sorry.'

'You know more than me then. He hasn't told me he's sorry. He hasn't told our Sal, either.'

Ginny saw a change in John, they all saw it. The John of the day before yesterday had been easy, soft, pliable. Today's John was hard, unyielding and closed to argument. Their mother had no more answers for him. And it wasn't likely that their father would tell John he was sorry, they all knew that. His pride forbade it, as well as his notions of what was conducive to good discipline – plenty of physical chastisement to be administered by him and accepted without question or protest by them. He was out, taking refuge from his family at the club, and was likely to be lying low there until the events of the previous day had begun to recede from the family consciousness.

Emma looked up from where she knelt tying Lizzie's boots, a pair of battered but well polished hand-me-downs which had once been her own.

'Come on, John,' she said. 'Mam cannot help it. Get your tie on, and let's get these bairns to chapel, give her an hour's peace.'

Ginny saw a look pass between her mother and Emma. As if they understood the impossibility of deflecting John from his new purpose by argument, they changed the topic altogether.

'Go on,' said their mother. 'Get your jacket on and comb your hair. Go out for a blow while it's fine. Our Sally's not fit yet.'

'It's a bonny day. We'll maybes have a walk in the woods by the river on the way back.' Emma had Lizzie and young Arthur ready, and as soon as Ginny had re-plaited her hair and laced her boots, the five were off, muffled up against the cold.

The door of the tiny, stone-built chapel, which advertised itself proudly as 'Primitive Methodist New

Connexion', was wide open. Mr Jackson and his wife were already seated in one of the polished oak pews. Enid turned and gave them a nod, but her husband studiously failed to notice their arrival. Emma ushered the children into the pew in front of them, and John and Ginny followed.

'I wonder what the sermon's going to be?' said John. 'Thou shalt not bear false witness against thy neighbour? That might make a good one.' The contemptuous tone, intended to demean and loud enough for everybody to hear, startled Emma and made Ginny smile. Christian forbearance this was not. As she turned to face him, Ginny had the satisfaction of seeing Mr Jackson's face flush red like a beacon. Enid bit her lip, and Ginny gave her a reassuring look before glancing at John. His lips were twisted into a grimace of bitter sarcasm.

After a sermon which contained nothing to make Mr Jackson uneasy, nor anything which could give satisfaction to John, they went for a stroll by Annsdale Beck, a tributary of the River Wear, and walked towards Old Annsdale. About a dozen streets and a Norman Church, the ancient mother village was surrounded by farms and lay two or three miles from the colliery, and maybe six or seven from Durham City.

'I love this time of year, a chill in the air and the trees red and gold,' said Emma, as they dawdled along the thickly wooded beck side, kicking up fallen leaves. She stopped suddenly and turned to John. 'Don't go to sea.'

He watched Lizzie and Arthur running on in front for some moments. 'I've a good mind to. I'm sick of the way things are in our house. The way he treats us all, to begin with. It's bad enough to take a belting for something you've done, but to get one on the word of that blind old fool Jackson, without even getting the chance to go and face him with his lies is more than I can stomach.'

'But it's worse for Mam than it is for us, and she puts up with it,' Emma pleaded.

'She's got no choice. She's got bairns, no money, and no family to go to. I have got a choice, if I can get a job away from here.'

'It's a pity we've licked the Boers. You could have joined up and gone to South Africa to give them a hiding.' Ginny's eyes sparkled with the thrill of adventure.

'Yes, and maybe get killed, like the blacksmith's lad,' said Emma.

'Well, there's other places. You hear of people going to Virginia, Australia, Canada, all over the place. But you never hear tell of any of 'em coming back,' said Ginny.

'But just think about poor Mam, left behind,' urged Emma. 'She'd miss you, so would I. Especially our Sal. Look how upset she's been since yesterday. It's made her poorly. Didn't you notice?' She put her small hand on his sleeve, and looked into his face, brown eyes earnest. 'And it's not only that, John. Mam needs that bit of money you bring in. She says it makes all the difference having two men working, instead of only one.'

'Oh, well I don't know,' said John, affecting indifference, but smiling at the flattering phrase 'two men'. He paused. 'Well, maybe I won't go away. Or if I do, I'll send home as much money as I can afford.'

'If I were a man, I'd go away!' cried Ginny. 'I'd go away and make my fortune, and come back rolling in money, and lord it over everybody that ever lorded it over me. Especially that old bugger Arthur Wilde.'

Emma shook her head. 'You'd better not let the old so-and-so hear you, or you'll cop it. Think what Mam would say – "that's your father you're talking about". Don't go, John.'

'No, don't run away to sea, Johnny. If they run out of food they kill the cabin boys and eat 'em!' Ginny bared her teeth, and snapped in his direction, as if to take a lump out of him. 'So don't go to sea, Johnny. Stay here where you're safe – well, barring a regular belting, that is.'

Chapter Two

'Do you think Maria's ever going to get better, Mam?' Ginny stood by the kitchen window, the bright autumn sun hot upon her shoulders as she ironed Maria's washing, boiled, possed, dolly-blued and starched into brilliance by her mother. Maria Jude and her husband lived with Mam Smith, Maria's mother, a couple of streets away in Snowdrop Terrace.

'I don't know, pet, but they'll need their washing, anyway. Hurry up with the ironing, and we'll get it aired and take it back this afternoon. Our Em'll lend a hand if you're getting tired, or I'll take over.'

'No, I'm all right.' Ginny bent over the kitchen table, padded with a thickly folded blanket and a well-scorched old sheet, and set to again with a will, stopping occasionally to put finished items on the clotheshorse to air by the fire.

Her mother was kneeling on the clippy mat, kneading half a stone of dough in the heavy clay panchion. After giving it a final pummelling, she covered it with a tea towel, and set it to rise before the fire. 'I know one thing, though, they deserve better luck than they've got. I don't know what Martin's going to do if she dies, or her mother either, come to that. He's worshipped the ground she walks on since they were both fifteen years old.' She paused. 'When he was eighteen, he was crushed by a roof fall at the pit. I think it must have broken his back. It was six weeks before anybody knew whether he'd walk again, never mind work. But she stuck by him. She'd have married him even if they'd had to live on the parish, if he'd let her. There's not many lasses would have done that. That's for better or for worse for you. It's a miracle he was well enough to dance at their wedding, and a right bonny pair of lovebirds they were.'

'I remember that, and now she's got consumption – about the worst luck you could have, I should think.' Ginny thought for a while, then with a rare flash of insight said, 'You know, Mam, I think that's the most important thing about a man, not how clever he is, or how hard working, but what's his luck?'

'There's a lot of truth in that, Ginny,' her mother laughed. 'The secret of living a charmed life is to be born lucky. Well, I never had much luck, so I hope you may do better. Still,' she added quickly, superstitious enough not to want to tempt providence, 'there's plenty a sight worse off than us. We've a comfortable home, a good fire, and enough to eat.'

'Aye, and there's some a sight better off an' all!' exclaimed Ginny. 'And I'm all for being among 'em. What I've noticed is that it's the best people who usually have the rottenest luck – like Martin, and you, Mam!'

'Don't you start criticizing your dad again,' her mother warned so Ginny held her peace. But the notion of luck had captured her imagination, set itself into her mind as a hard, diamond-bright pole-star.

By two o'clock Ginny was packing the carefully aired and folded linen into the laundry basket. 'I think that's everything.'

'Here, I'll have a walk on with you, help you carry it,' offered John, just up and dressed after the luxury of a late sleep on his alternate Saturday off.

'Whatever you do, don't drop it in the dirt,' their mother warned. 'I don't want all that work to do again.'

'Who is it, Ma?' Ginny heard Maria call from the front room, as she and John knocked at the open kitchen door of eleven Snowdrop Terrace. A fire roared up the chimney, so that the place was warm in spite of the ventilation.

'It's Ginny back with the washing, pet,' a plump woman, with greying brown hair and a world-weary expression answered. She turned to Ginny and clucked a not entirely convincing disapproval. 'Why, bonny lass, it's all dried and ironed. I told your mam I'd do that!'

Ginny was quick to claim some credit. 'It's all right. We put them out for a good blow, so the drying wasn't much bother, and I did most of the ironing.'

'Aye, well, I hope you'll get your reward in Heaven,' she sighed, ''cause there's none down here.'

'There is,' said John, 'and Mam says she's not forgotten how many times you've helped us. So how's Maria?'

'She says she feels better, but I think she's worse if

anything,' said Martin, who was half sitting, half lying in the armchair beside the kitchen fire, with a sleeping two-year-old sprawled across his chest. 'There's no hope. There's no hope, and it's useless for us to torture ourselves by trying to hang on to any.' He spoke in a low voice, so that Maria, in the other room, could not hear what was being said.

She heard something. 'Martin? What are you talking about? Where's the bairn?'

'He's here, bonny lass, fast asleep.' Tall, fair and well proportioned, with muscles hardened by hewing coal, Martin stood up, with the child cradled in his arms. 'Come in and have five minutes with her,' he invited, 'but don't stay much longer than that. She soon gets tired.'

He led them in to her, and laid the child on the bed beside her. Her blue eyes looked unnaturally brilliant, her skin so white it seemed translucent, except for two pink spots over her cheekbones. Hair glinting in a shaft of sunlight, she pulled herself up to greet them. 'Hello, Ginny, John. How do I look today, do you think?'

'Like one of God's angels, Maria.' Ginny saw Martin stiffen and flushed, cursing her tactlessness.

Maria smiled. 'Not yet, I hope,' she answered quietly, turning to feast her eyes on the sleeping child beside her. 'Isn't he a canny bairn, Ginny? Look at his bonny hair. As old as the century. I hope he lives to be a hundred, to see it out. My golden boy. When he's asleep like this, I wish I'd half a dozen.' She looked intently at little Philip's face. His eyelids fluttered and he smiled, as if he knew what she was saying. She sighed. 'But when he's awake, he tires me out. I have to leave him to Mam and Martin. Maybe it's as well I only had the one. I don't think I'll live to see 1903, and one'll be enough for them to take care of if I'm with the angels sooner than I want to be.'

Ginny shot a glance at Martin to see his eyes fill with tears. 'Nobody's going anywhere, lass,' he said. 'You're going to get well again, and then we'll have a dozen.'

Maria smiled and the blue-veined lids began to close over her eyes. She lifted them again, and looked directly at Ginny.

'Ginny, you've to have me new shoes. I've only had them on once, and they'll not fit Mam. They'll fit you like a glove.'

'Shush,' said Martin. 'You'll get better and wear them yourself, when I take you to the races.'

'Aye, all right, Martin.' She smiled, eyelids drooping again.

Martin lifted the child and ushered them back into the kitchen. 'Come on, now. She's had enough.'

'Have you any more washing to take, Mam Smith?' asked Ginny.

'There's a couple of sheets and a few more towels want a good boil. I like to keep the poor lass sweet and clean.'

Martin had put the sleeping child down and was back in his chair, leaning forward, elbows on knees and head in his hands, a curtain of corn-coloured hair obscuring his face. Ginny had an impulse to touch it, feel the silkiness of it as she pulled it away from his eyes to speak words of consolation. Instead she stood mute, staring at him. He never looked up. John lifted the basket of bloodstained linen and they left without exchanging another word.

Mam Smith followed them across the yard. 'He's taking it bad,' she murmured.

'What other way is there to take it, like?' asked Ginny.

'It can't be easy for you either,' said John, 'she's your only daughter.'

A grimace passed over the lined face. 'Aye, well, I'm glad God gave her a good man, and a bonny bairn. She's been happy. It's a pity it's not destined to last.'

'You've about as much tact as my pit pony, our Ginny,' said John, as they got to the end of the street.

'I know, I could have bitten my tongue out as soon as I said it.'

'What do you make of it all, though?'

'It's a bad job, and I feel sorry for Martin. But it makes me feel lucky. Lucky it's not me laid in bed, gasping my last.'

'You callous little beggar. It makes me realize what we've missed. Did you see the way he was cuddling that bairn when we went in? I envy that bairn. It must be grand to have a dad like that. Philip's going to lose his mam, but he's got the best dad I ever saw.'

'He might soon have a new mam, and all. It won't be long before he gets married again, if she dies,' Ginny ventured, more to seek an opinion than to give one.

'You're wrong, Ginny. He worships her. Martin's a

good man – the best. I hope if I ever have any bairns I'll be as good a dad as him. And as good a husband.'

She grinned, unaccountably pleased to hear John's praise of Martin. Perversely, all she said was, 'Aye, and look how much good his goodness does him. Hard work and goodness don't bring Martin a ha'p'orth o' luck. The more I see, the more certain I am. Don't tell me anything else about a man. All I want to know is – what's his luck?'

John stopped short, brown eyes bright, and manner suddenly animated.

'Well, wish me luck then, Ginny. I've a feeling in my marrow. My luck's going to change from tonight on!' She stared wide-eyed and he laughed. 'It was Pay Friday yesterday, and I'm away to play cards at Jimmy Hood's.'

Ginny's jaw dropped. Jimmy's father was a notorious gambler. The family had been sold up twice because of his love of cards, dice, racing, and anything else he could throw his money away on. It was said he would place a bet on the nose of one of two flies crawling up a windowpane. Not to mention the fact that the Hoods were Catholics. Neither characteristic was likely to recommend them to her mother.

'John! Whatever would me mam say?' She shivered, as a delicious thrill coursed through her at the thought of forbidden pastimes in dangerous company, and the certainty of her mother's deepest disapproval.

'It'll be all right. If I'm not back tonight, tell Mam Mrs Hood'll give me a bed.'

'Give you a bed? I doubt they've even got a one, and

if they have you'll have bought it three times over before they've finished with you.'

'Jimmy's all right. They might not be Mam's chapel-going sort, but they're all right.'

'Aye, well, I wouldn't want to be in your shoes when you get home if you do stay out all night, that's all.'

'Never bother about me. I'm one of the big lads now. I've got ideas of my own, and if they don't always agree with Mam's ideas, well, the apron strings have got to be cut sooner or later. You'll realize that when your turn comes.'

'Oh, will I? You sound like somebody's grandfather.'

They had reached the top of their own terraced row, Pleasant View, and stood to rest for a minute. John nodded towards the River Wear. 'It's a big wide world out there, Ginny.' He thrust the basket into her arms. 'Bye,' he said.

'Bye, John,' she answered, 'see you tomorrow. Hope you'll still have your shirt.'

'Aye, me an' all.' He lingered, looking at her, then took the basket from her and dumped it in the road before throwing his arms round her to give her a suffocating squeeze. Her eyes widened with surprise as he released her.

'Why, what's up, man?'

'Nothing. Just tell Mam not to worry, and wish me luck.'

He turned and strode off, boots rattling on the cobbles, and her heart missed a beat. She called after him, 'Good luck, John, good luck!'

He raised his hand and waved a farewell, without slowing his pace to look round. She gazed after him for a minute or two, then shrugged and heaved up the basket.

'What the hell's up wi' him the day? It must be going to the Judes. It's turned him soft,' she muttered, as she carried it the last few steps home.

Chapter Three

Saturday night didn't bring John, or Sunday either. By Sunday evening, an excited and inquisitive Ginny, accompanied by her furious father, arrived on the Hoods' doorstep.

'Why aye,' Mrs Hood answered their questions. 'He came here yesterday afternoon and had a hand or two of cards with Jimmy and Tom, then the two lads said they were going for a walk for an hour. I haven't seen John since.'

'Neither have we. But I bet Jimmy knows something about it.'

A brown-haired, wiry youth appeared from behind his mother. 'You'd better come in,' he said.

They stepped into the sparsely furnished kitchen. Three jam jars half full of weak, milkless tea stood on the kitchen table. The bare stone flags were graced by a worn clippy mat upon which a couple of barefoot urchins, too young for school, sat eating bread and dripping and staring at the visitors, with their backs to a fire that roared generously up the chimney, providing the only comfort in the room. Ginny's quick eye took in the state of the place, a poor contrast with her own comfortable home. She smiled at the boys. Her father ignored them, looking pointedly at Jimmy.

'I don't know where he is exactly,' Jimmy said, his hazel eyes holding her father's stare with stunning composure, 'but I suppose he's on Newcastle docks, trying to get a ship, if he's not already got a one.'

'Cool as a bloody cucumber!' exclaimed her father, fists clenching. 'You young bugger, why didn't you come and tell us afore this time, while we could have done something to stop him?

'You couldn't have stopped him, Mr Wilde. He was set on shipping out. He had his fortnight's wages, he borrowed a shilling or two from me, and he got the train to Newcastle.'

'And what about me and his mam?' bellowed Ginny's father, face reddening and veins bulging as he towered over Jimmy. 'He's not left her a penny.'

'Well, I'm sorry about you and his mam,' replied Jimmy, a fraction less composed. 'I'm sorry for myself an' all. He was a good marrer. I'll miss him.'

'Well, hev this instead, like!' A hefty blow on Jimmy's left ear sent him reeling.

'Hey, Mr Wilde, you're not at home now, you know! This is our home, and you've gone far enough in it!' shrieked Mrs Hood, four foot ten inches of outrage. 'You'd better go now, before I get my neighbour to run and fetch the bobby!'

'Stop it, Dad, you're showing yoursel' up. Are you all right, lad?'

'I'm all right, Ginny. Never bother.'

'Come on, you,' snarled her father, storming out of the doorway. Ginny followed, stopping to mutter a few words of apology to Mrs Hood.

'Bugger that!' Her father grabbed her by her hair and dragged her out of the cottage before sticking his own head back into it. 'You want to get down to that bloody church of yours and say a few hundred Hail Marys for what you've done to my family,' he roared at Jimmy.

'Go home, Mr Wilde,' said the sixteen-year-old with some spirit, 'I've done nothing to your family. John had his mind made up long before I saw him. When he got on the train he said you'd given him the last belting he was ever going to take from you.'

'Aw, shut up, man, shut up! You're just making bloody excuses for yoursel'.' Her father didn't stay to argue further, but strode off down the street, cursing to himself. He turned and shouted to Ginny, 'Come on, you, get along home where you belong, and don't you come here again.'

Ginny gave the Hoods a broad wink and an even broader grin, then ran after her father, hugging herself with glee at Jimmy's effrontery.

Her imagination ran riot in the days that followed, weaving fantasies about John's life of adventure and excitement, of riding the ocean waves, visiting exotic ports in Africa and India, seeing new sights, smelling new smells, hearing different conversations in different accents. John, in a wide world of freedom and wonder!

There was no conversation in Annsdale except the pits, the wages, the bosses, the last strike or the next, the chapel or the club. Flights of improbable fancy about John's supposed life of variety and adventure elated her.

The rest of the household was plunged into gloom. Young Arthur protested at being in his bedroom alone and Lizzie revenged herself for all his torments by telling him that the devil was hiding under the bed, waiting to bite his toes off if he so much as stuck a foot out of the covers, an idea that none of them could dislodge. Sally cried for her favourite. Their father was more morose than ever. He earned a good wage as a first-rate hewer, but money was just that bit tighter without John's wages, less for his pocket, and less to hand over the bar for beer and conviviality. Their mother said nothing. Her face was reproach enough.

It was Emma's reaction that surprised Ginny most. She seemed almost sunk into despair. She hardly slept, and hardly ate. Eventually even their mother seemed to forget her own grief in a new worry about Emma, and Ginny lost all patience with them both.

'I don't know what's up with everybody,' she burst out, late one evening, when the younger ones were in bed. Her mother was busy preparing a bite of supper for her father's return from an evening at the club. Emma was sitting at the kitchen table, head bent over her schoolbook. Neither answered, and the remark seemed to drop into the void, until a large tear rolled down Emma's cheek, and splashed on to her exercise book. Hiding her face, she reached for a towel and carefully dabbed at the page, trying not to smudge the ink any further.

Ginny's mother sighed. 'You're a hard one, Jane. I sometimes think you've got no feelings at all.' The use of the name Jane was ominous.

'No feelings my—' Ginny almost said the word. 'He's not died. He's gone to sea. And as for the money – he'll send some, as soon as he can. He said as much, the time we were walking back from chapel, didn't he?' she appealed to Emma.

'What's this?' Their mother's cheeks coloured. 'You never told me he was planning to go.'

'He told us all he was planning to go the day after he got the belting! You saw his back yourself. He made his mind up then.'

'But you encouraged him, Ginny. You made it all sound so exciting,' Emma accused.

'I never encouraged him,' protested Ginny, aware of her mother's eyes on her. 'It was just talk. I never thought he'd really go.'

'If I were a man, I'd go away – I'd go away and make my fortune!' Emma mimicked. 'Well, that's probably just what he thinks he's doing.'

'I don't think you understand how much damage "just talk" can do, my girl. We'd all be better off now if you'd just kept quiet – John most of all.'

'No, me most of all.' Emma burst into uncontrollable weeping.

'That's not fair. It's not fair! How could I make him go? He'd already made his mind up. How could anybody blame him for going after the hiding he got?' exclaimed Ginny. 'And how can anybody blame me for making him?'

But Emma's tears went on and on, until their mother's anger at Ginny dissolved into pity for Emma. She took the weeping girl in her arms. 'Hey, hey, what's this? There's no need for it. Ginny's right, he's not dead, and knowing John he'll write as soon as he can.'

'You don't understand, Mam,' Emma gasped, between sobs.

'Well, maybe we don't – and we won't, if you won't tell us.'

Emma turned her swollen, blotchy face towards her mother and said, 'I had hopes. I was hoping to make my fortune here.'

'Hopes of what?' asked Ginny, completely mystified.

'Of staying on at school, and being a teacher.'

Their mother looked stricken. 'I understand now. You thought that with John and Ginny out at work, your dad might have let you stay on at school.'

'I know I could do it, Mam. Your dad was a teacher, and Miss Carr knew him. She says I'm clever, and I'd make a good teacher, as good as him probably, because it must run in the family. She's going to put me in for the County Council Junior Scholarship. She says I'm sure to pass, because she's been testing me with some of the old papers, and I've done well on them all. After we get the results, Mr Stringer's coming to school to see which of the pupils who get a scholarship want to go on and be a teacher. And I do, Mam, I do. I've my heart set on it. I know I can do it, if I can just get the chance.'

A teacher! Emma must think very well of herself indeed. 'So that's it! You don't care about our John at all – you only care about his wages not coming in!'

'Be quiet, Jane.' Their mother looked into Emma's bloodshot eyes. Even insensitive Ginny could see that her sister was balanced on a knife-edge between hope and despair.

'You say she's already put you in for the scholarship?' Their mother's pale face was sympathetic enough, but the eyes contained not a flicker of hope.

'No, but she will, because she's tested me with some of the old papers and she says I'm the best pupil she's ever had.'

'But you haven't passed the real scholarship yet.'

'I know I would.'

'Well, you might not, you know. We'll just wait and see what happens.' Their mother's voice was tinged with relief.

'Well, I can go and ask Lady Muck for my job back,' offered Ginny. 'I heard she's sacked Maudie, and that comes as no surprise. I'll ask her for better pay while I'm at it.'

'She's not going to give you enough to keep Emma at school.'

'I know that. But I'd be worth it. She won't get anybody that can get through as much work as me.'

'I don't dispute it, but they're not going to pay you anywhere near a putter's wage. We'll just wait and see what happens.'

★

By the time their father got home that night, Emma was in bed. After a good supper he sat down by the fire, lit his pipe, and stretched out comfortably in his chair, while Ginny helped clear the table. Her mother was pensive.

'Penny for 'em, Nance?' her father offered, using the pet name he'd given her during their courting days.

She shook her head. 'Oh, nothing. I'm probably worrying over nothing.' After a few minutes' silence, she asked, 'Everything going all right at work, Arthur?'

'That it's not. I'm in a bad stall. I can hardly bloody breathe down there, and it's as hot as hell. I'm stuck with it 'til Christmas, though, when we draw lots again. Hope for better luck next time, eh? There's not going to be much money though, lass. It's bloody hard work for nought a yard, and with our John gone . . .' He stopped, and added, 'Bairns! You work your guts out to bring 'em up, and as soon as they could start repaying you, they bugger off.' He cleared his throat and spat. A mouthful of coal-dust-blackened phlegm shot into the fire and sizzled in the flames.

'You know why he went, Arthur.' Her mother finished drying the last of the pots, and turned to face him. Ginny busied herself cleaning the sink, hoping not to be noticed and packed off to bed.

'Aye, well, I'm too tired to argue. All I know is, I got many a worse hiding than that, only I didn't bear a grudge, and I didn't desert my parents.'

'You bore a grudge, and you got away from home as fast as you could,' her mother said.

A grunt was her only reply. After a long pause, she

asked, 'Arthur, what would you say to our Emma being a teacher?'

'What's she want to be a teacher for? Give hersel' a lot of airs and graces until she ends up looking down on her mother and father. Bring no money in for years, then she'll get wed, and that'll be an end on't. Waste of time and money, and with John gone, and that one,' he nodded in Ginny's direction, 'getting hersel' the bloody sack, it's money we can't afford. Don't run away with the idea that I'm going to break my back in the pit and live from hand to mouth to keep a lot o' good-for-nothing lasses in idleness, because I'm not.'

At eight o'clock the following day Ginny, Emma and even eight-year-old Lizzie stood threading needles whilst their mother set up the quilting frame in the front room, resting one end on the windowsill, the other on the back of a chair. Sally was still asleep.

'Get as many threaded as you can, I might be able to get four or five hours in before your dad gets home while our Ginny's here to do the housework,' said their mother as she settled to the work, elbows lifted halfway to shoulder level as they rested on the frame.

Once all forty or so needles were threaded and left ready for use, Emma and Lizzie set out for school with young Arthur. Ginny cleared the kitchen table, washed pots, filled the coal scuttle, swept and polished the hearths, shook out the mats and swept the floor, before preparing vegetables for her father's dinner.

'Well, Mam, at least me being at home lets you get on

with the quilting,' she commented, as she tossed another shovelful of coal on to the front room fire.

'It does, pet, but I don't think I'm going to make a fortune quilting. There were only six of them in the quilting club to start with, and now there's only one quilt left to do after I finish this one, so we can't rely on that bit of money coming in very much longer. Your wages were more useful.'

'It's a pity there's no work at the farms at Old Annsdale just now. I wonder if any of them need any help in the house?'

'I doubt it. Why don't you go and ask the manager's wife if you can have your job back?'

'I don't want to, but I suppose I'll have to in the end. She's forever breathing down my neck, checking everything I do, and telling me how it could be done better. I wouldn't care if she were better at cleaning than I am, but she's not. She's a right sloven when she does anything herself.'

'Well, ladies don't usually make good servants.'

'I wouldn't care if she was a lady, but she's nothing but an upstart.'

'How would you know?'

There was a brief rattle on the door and Old Bob Dyer poked his grizzled head into the room. Well past working down the pit, he earned a meagre income doing odd jobs and a bit of gardening at the manager's house, as well as anything else that came in his way.

'Mrs Vine asked us to call by. To ask Ginny to go up and see her at the house this afternoon.'

'Ask? Did she say ask, or did she say tell?' demanded Ginny.

'As far as I can remember, she said ask.'

'What's up, is my replacement not up to scratch, like? Is she going to offer us me job back?' Ginny pressed.

'I think it's on the cards, but don't tell her I said so.'

'Aye, well, I might stroll along there and see what she's got to say, if I've got nothing better to do,' Ginny said, with a tilt of her chin.

'Go well before four o'clock if you're going. I think she's hevin' a tea party.'

'That woman! Who's going to the tea party?'

Bob shrugged. 'She's having her brother to stay for a bit. I don't know who else is going to be there. I'll be away then,' and he closed the door.

'You will go, won't you, Ginny?'

'Certainly. I wouldn't miss hearing what she's got to say for the world.'

The nipped-in waist and flared skirt of her black coat showed off a figure that was becoming more of an hourglass as the days went by. With black-buttoned boots brightly polished, she strutted briskly along grimy Pleasant View in the direction of the winding gear, to the tune of the railway as the engines chugged away with tubs of coal. Then along blackened Snowdrop Terrace, and away from pit and noise, through the park gates and up the hill, to cut a stretch off her journey by clambering over the park wall and on to 'Quality Row', shielded from industrial unsightliness and racket by a screen of trees. An imposing double-fronted stone-built house stood isolated from the rest. She opened the heavy wrought-iron gate and strode along the drive and up the steps to a massive crimson-painted door, noting with some satisfaction that the brass knocker was already well tarnished.

The door was answered by Mrs Vine herself, a pale-complexioned, handsome woman in her mid-thirties, whose head of flame-coloured curls was muted by the lightest sprinkling of grey. She frowned. 'What are you doing at the front door? The back's the tradesman's entrance.'

'I'm not a tradesman. And I believe I was invited.'

'Impudence. Well, now you're here, you might as well come in this way, I suppose,' and Helen Vine stood aside to allow Ginny to sweep past her.

'Every bit. Mr Dyer brought us your message.'

'Mr Dyer? Oh, you mean old Bob. I'll come straight to the point, Ginny. I'm willing to let bygones be bygones and offer you your job back, as long as you can guarantee to keep a civil tongue in your head.'

'I can guarantee I'll be civil to everybody that's civil to me. It's if they're not that I can't.'

Mrs Vine's frown deepened as Ginny looked steadily back into her disapproving pale blue eyes. She paused.

'Very well. Same terms as before. And you use the back door.' These last words were given great emphasis.

'I see Maudie wasn't a great success.' Ginny gazed pointedly round, noting the grimy and unkempt state of the house.

'She was not,' replied Mrs Vine, 'but that's not for you to comment on. Are you for coming or not?'

'I'm for coming, for an extra shilling a week.'

'What nonsense. Same terms as last time, or I'll try another girl.'

'Well, Mrs Vine, you can try every girl in the village, and you won't find a better bargain than me, even at a shilling a week extra. Still, there's nothing to stop you trying your luck. Whoever you get'll have her work cut out, cleaning up after Maudie. I don't know what you paid her, but whatever it was, you were robbed. She'd take plenty of watching, for more reasons than one, and there's others like her. The cheapest buy's not always the best bargain.'

Mrs Vine hesitated. 'All right. Get here prompt tomorrow morning, and use the back door. An extra shilling a week, and see you're worth it.'

'Aye, I am worth it, Mrs Vine, and tomorrow I'll use the back door. But just for today I'll use the front, like. You never invited me to sit down, so I'd carry your luck away if I went through the back. Good afternoon, and I hope you have a lovely tea party.'

She opened the front door again and, stretching herself to her full height with head held erect, she stepped smartly out, and bumped against a red-haired man with hand raised ready to knock. He stood back, eyes appraising her as he touched his grey bowler – eyes that were identical to Mrs Vine's, except that they held amusement, rather than disapproval.

'Pardon me.' He smiled.

'Granted,' she nodded, and smiled back, more in

triumph over her extra shilling a week and the vexation she'd given Mrs Vine than any pleasure in the sight of the dandified visitor.

'Aren't you going to introduce us?' He addressed the question to Mrs Vine, whilst keeping his eyes fixed on Ginny.

'That won't be necessary, Charlie.'

'No, it won't,' Ginny agreed. 'So long, Charlie.' She strode off swiftly in the direction of the park wall, her bearing intended to convey the idea: I'm as good as you are, if not a damned sight better!

She enjoyed her walk through the red-and-gold-leafed trees, and stopped halfway down the slope at the bandstand, empty now, and likely to be so until spring. The village was laid out before her, row after grubby monotonous row of terraced houses, with their patches of garden at the front, and yards and privies at the back, each row separated from the next by an alley just wide enough for the nightsoil men and their cart. The few which were tenanted by the deputies were slightly grander than the rest, and as their occupants descended the pit hierarchy the houses became correspondingly smaller. On her way back along Snowdrop Terrace she saw Jimmy Hood, trudging home as black as a crow.

'All right, Jimmy?'

'I can't say I am, lass. I haven't heard a thing out of this left ear since your father thumped it. I think he's bust my eardrum.'

'Get a few boxing lessons, Jimmy. When you're man enough you can bust his for him.'

'No, I think I'll call it a day while I'm in one piece. I'm not the sort to go looking for trouble. Have you heard aught from John?'

'No. I thought he'd have written by now.'

'He might not have had the chance. There's nothing to do but wait.'

'That's a poor philosophy, Jimmy. There is something to do, and I've done it. I've been and got mesel' an extra bob a week from the manager's wife.' She laughed with pleasure and self-congratulation, and walked on.

As she approached the Judes' door, she stopped, hesitant to intrude, but after a second or two, she walked down the garden path. The door was open.

'Come in, bonny lass.' His voice was deep and masculine, and her spirits lifted further at the welcome. 'Mam's gone to the shop, and taken Philip for a bit of fresh air. I'm just counting the Union dues while Maria's asleep. We'll leave the door open. It's warm enough.' The dining table was covered in piles of coppers, even a couple of ten-bob notes.

Ginny glanced towards the wraith in the bed. Maria's breathing was barely perceptible, and for a moment, Ginny thought she was dead. She suppressed a shudder, and sat at the table to watch Martin, brow furrowed as he concentrated on his task.

'I should have thought you'd more than enough to do just now without taking that job on. Cannot somebody else do it?'

'It doesn't look like it, bonny lass, and somebody better

had. We're not much more than slaves as it is. Like that song "The Real Black Slaves of our Native Land". They could do anything they liked with us if there were no Union, and they would an' all.'

'They' were the owners and managers. The word needed no explanation.

'I don't doubt that, but there's more than you to do the work that goes with it.'

He nodded. 'I suppose there is, but if we all thought like that, nothing would get done, and then there'd be no Union.'

They heard a coughing. Maria was leaning out of the bed, hand clasped over her mouth, scarlet froth oozing between her fingers. Martin was beside her in an instant, stroking her hair, soothing her.

At the sight of the blood, Ginny's heart leapt into her throat. She was up and at the door in a flash, almost out of it before she checked herself. 'Shall I fetch the doctor?'

He saw her terror. 'No, he says there's nothing he can do. You'd better get off home, Ginny, there's nothing you can do either. I'll look after her.'

He looked desolate. Despite her fear she said, 'I'll get a bowl of water and a towel.'

She went into the kitchen to collect them, and when she returned Maria lay on her pillows exhausted, blood staining her mouth, her nightdress and the sheet. Martin took the bowl from her and set it on the bedside chair. 'I'll do that. She's used to me.'

She turned her back as he washed and changed his wife, talking quietly to her all the time. Ginny tied the discarded linen into a bundle, covering the blood, while he sat by the bed, holding Maria's hand.

'I'll take this lot home, Martin.'

He seemed hardly to hear her, and made only the briefest of replies. Holding the bundle at arm's length she left, shaken and near to tears.

'What a fool,' she berated herself. She would give anything to have acted differently, not to let him see her fear. She hated the thought that he would think the less of her.

Chapter Four

Ginny was changing pillowslips in the master bedroom at the manager's house when her sharp ears picked up the mention of her own name. She crossed quietly to the open door, trying to hear the conversation through the strains of Helen Vine's party piece, laboriously practised on the new upright piano. Mr Vine was exchanging a few words with his brother-in-law as they stood by the front door.

'Oh, yes,' he chuckled softly, 'I'd like to drive a spigot into that one and let some of the uppishness out. I don't know what man wouldn't.'

'You reprehensible old dog. I don't think you should say such naughty things to me – your own wife's brother.'

Mr Vine laughed again. 'You're a man of the world, Charlie. Helen sensed it, though; it doesn't take her long to latch on to these things. So that was another good reason to get rid of her, but the substitute was so bad she's glad to get her back. She's got no cause for concern, though. I wouldn't attempt Ginny Wilde, and I wouldn't advise you to, either. Tamper with her, and you might end up floating down the Wear with a pick buried in your skull. Her father's an animal. He's raised his pick to my deputies in the mine before today. No, let well alone is my advice, if you value life and limb.'

'You make her sound more interesting than ever. Has she inherited his animal tendencies? I do hope so. I like to live dangerously.'

'You won't like living as dangerously as that. He's insubordinate, arrogant, and violent, and from what I've seen of his daughter, she's inherited two of those traits, to say the least.'

'Sounds thrilling. But why on earth do you keep either of them on?'

'I keep him on because he's not a Union agitator, and he's as strong as an ox. His father and grandfather were among the big hewers, men who used to compete with each other in the good old days, before the Union started sticking its nose in and restricting output so they could carry a lot of weaklings and old men. He can get through nearly twice the work most of the others can manage. I'd have had him sacked and evicted otherwise, and off the coalfield. She's got her job back here for the same reason – she earns her wages, and that's all she's needed to do. So you've been warned. What you do about it is your own business, but don't involve me if you come unstuck.'

'You're serious, aren't you?'

'Deadly serious. I warn you, don't bring any self-made trouble to me. On your own head be it. This is a different set-up from the one you're used to in London.'

The manager left for work, and Ginny resumed her bed-making. That pair must have thought that she was still shut in the scullery washing breakfast pots. She hardly knew whether to take what she'd heard as an insult or as a compliment, and began to laugh. Drive a spigot in, and let the uppishness out! If that really meant what she suspected it meant, who would have thought that Mr Vine could harbour such thoughts? She would never have imagined him capable of such coarseness, and she began to wonder how other men and lads she knew thought about her. To be likened to her father was an insult, but to be considered insubordinate and arrogant was rather flattering. Sacked and evicted and off the coalfield, though. It just showed what power that man wielded over her family. It was to be hoped her father kept himself fit and strong, or they'd all be homeless and destitute, and exiled from everything and everybody they knew.

So Lady Muck's blue-eyed brother had taken a fancy to her. He thought she was thrilling. She'd give him a thrill he'd never forget if he ever offered to lay a hand on her. She punched the pillows a couple of times each, and threw them into place, then turned up the cover. Her father wasn't the only one who was as strong as an ox.

After Helen and Charlie set off for a ride in the landau, Ginny gathered all the rugs and carried them into the back garden. With a scarf tied round her hair to protect it from the dust, and her apron pinned up tight, she picked up a rug and knocked it hard against the wall. Thinking herself alone she let rip with a song.

Now I'll tell ye a trick we once played on Jim
Farrins,
That one day bought a cask o' the best kippered
herrins
To eat with his coffee, his taties an' bread,
Determined a' winter to hev a cheap feed.
He took four greet big 'uns one neet doon the pit,
An' he wouldn't let us doon below taste a bit.
So a penn'orth o' jalap we put in his bottle,
And laughed fit to burst as it went doon his
throttle . . .

A fortnight's dust flew up in clouds all around her as she dashed the rugs to the rhythm. She started at Charlie's voice in her ear.

'You've a good voice, Ginny. And that's not a bad song. It might do all right in the music hall as a low comedy turn.' His pale blue eyes looked her up and down beneath the fair lashes, a half smile revealing a row of white, even teeth.

'Aye, well, it's a miners' song, and you can't get much lower comedy than that.'

'Do you mean they sing it while they're tapping at the coal face with their picks?' His voice held a mocking tone.

'I don't mean that at all. The tapping takes all the breath they've got. They wouldn't have any left over to do any singing. No, they do their singing in the club, when they're having a bit crack. They really enjoy a bit of low comedy then.'

'I think I'd have a lot in common with them.'

'I doubt it. I thought you were out, or I'd have kept quiet.'

'Oh, I just came back to collect something.'

'Well, there's nothing to collect from me, Mr Parkinson, and your sister doesn't pay us for standing here passing the time o' day. She pays us for getting the work done, so if you don't mind, I'll get on with it. There's still plenty of muck to shift after the last so-called skivvy she had.' She fixed him with an unblinking stare, and smiled.

With a quizzical lift of his eyebrows Charlie returned her smile, then something in her expression shrivelled his smile to a grimace. She stooped to pick up another rug and began dadding it against the wall. When she looked round again, Charlie was gone.

She'd done another three hours of hard labour, turning out the dining room and cleaning windows, before Mrs Vine and her brother returned.

'Thank you, Ginny. I'll give you your due, you've worked hard, and the place looks better for it. You can go now. Come at the same time tomorrow.'

'Oh, yes, you have worked hard,' echoed Charlie, 'you must be exhausted. I'll take you down to the village.'

She would have refused, but the look of deep disapproval on Mrs Vine's face was an irresistible temptation. 'That's a very kind offer, Mr Parkinson, thank you.' Eyes demurely downcast and expression deadpan she added, 'I don't think it would be manners to refuse.'

'No indeed. Collect your things. I'll wait here for you.'

Mrs Vine's face registered sheer exasperation as Ginny meekly walked in the direction of the scullery. When she returned to the hall, Charlie was holding the front door open, and she sailed through it before him, head held high.

They rode along for a minute or so before he broke the silence. 'You know, Ginny, you do have a little talent. You might do well in London. You could try your luck on the stage, and if that was no good, well, good housemaids are always in demand, at far better wages than you'll ever get in Annsdale. I suppose I shouldn't tell you that, as my own sister's so satisfied with your work, but London's exciting. I should enjoy showing you round it.'

'No thanks, Mr Parkinson. I don't know anybody in London.'

'You know me.'

At the top of Pleasant View her voice held an almost imperceptible sneer as she asked, 'Why don't you come in and meet my family, Mr Parkinson? Then we'll all know you and you'll know us, and you can find out if you really have got anything in common with the pitmen.'

He laughed, a touch uneasily. 'Perhaps I will, one day. But not today.'

She jumped down on to the cobbles. 'Cheerio, then, Mr Parkinson.'

'*Au revoir*, Ginny.'

Oh rev war? What the hell does that mean, she wondered as she watched him turn the carriage and drive away. She was disappointed he hadn't driven her to the door. She would have loved to cause a sensation among the neighbours.

Once inside the house, all thoughts of Charlie Parkinson vanished. Mam Smith was there, and both she and Emma were in tears, with her mother trying to act as comforter to both. Ginny looked at her for an explanation, knowing before she asked what it would be.

'It's Maria, pet. She passed away this morning.'

Their attempts to console Martin on the day of the funeral were futile. 'There is no God,' he said. 'It's nothing but a Jewish fairy tale.'

'We might not be able to understand God's will, but that doesn't mean He doesn't exist, Martin,' Ginny's mother protested. She was dressed in black with a scarf draped around her neck and her head held discreetly down in an attempt to hide a large black bruise under her chin, a subterfuge that seemed to Ginny to make it all the more obvious.

Martin would have none of it. 'No, there's no understanding it because it doesn't exist. That poor lass never hurt anybody in her life. Don't talk to me about any merciful God.' He met her mother's eyes. Ginny knew that he saw the bruise, and that he wouldn't humiliate her mother by making any comment. He looked towards the photograph of his blithe and bonny bride smiling down at them from her place on the mantelpiece, then at her bleach-white body lying in its open coffin supported on two dining chairs. He said again, 'There is no God.'

Mam Smith groaned. 'Oh, God help us all, he's talking blasphemy.'

The three women looked at each other. Ginny felt shocked both at the sight of Maria and at this open defiance of scripture, but murmured, 'Well, it makes you wonder, doesn't it?'

'Hush, Ginny,' her mother said. 'There might be some excuse for Martin. There's none for you.'

'I'm glad she's dead,' Martin continued, 'I was sick of seeing her suffer.' He looked up, and seeing Mam Smith's stricken face, held his peace. One of his three marrers, who, along with Ginny's father, had volunteered themselves as coffin bearers, touched him on the shoulder.

'It's time we were away, bonny lad. They've got the hearse outside.'

Martin took a last lingering look at Maria's remains. He touched her cold, white cheek, gave the blue lips a last kiss.

'I can't believe she'll never wake up again.'

'Come on, lad, bear up. It's time to go. Come by, while I get the lid on,' said another of his marrers.

As they lifted the coffin out of the house and carried it slowly down the garden and on to the hearse, a light rain began.

'For what she weighs, you wad think it was empty,' commented Ginny's father. 'We could have carried her the whole way to the chapel without feeling it.'

And save the expense of the hearse, thought Ginny, knowing that the same thought would be in everybody else's mind. After Maria's long illness money must be tight in Martin's household, but no expense was spared for this, her final journey.

The whole village was out to watch her progress to the chapel, the men bareheaded to show their respects as the cortège passed. The rain became heavier, and those who had umbrellas began to put them up. Some of the people standing in doorways joined the procession. When all had passed through the dripping porch, the chapel was packed. The stove had been lit early, and with its cream walls contrasting with the mellow wood of floor, lectern and pews, it was a warm and welcome refuge from the grey November day. The bearers set the coffin down and Martin placed a wreath of evergreens on it. The young minister gave a solemn and respectful sermon, taking as his text an excerpt from one of the epistles of St Paul, which asks, 'For what can separate us from the love of God?' Ginny doubted that Martin had heard a word of it.

The drip of the rain on black umbrellas, the shuffling of scores of feet and the muffled clip-clop of the horse's hooves on the cobbles were the only sounds to break the silence as they afterwards made slow progress towards the cemetery.

Maria could have been buried in the same grave as her father and brothers, but Martin, a man of twenty-three, had paid for a new one, talking of nothing but being buried beside her himself when the time came. As they watched the bearers lower the coffin, water dripped from the trees around them until Ginny thought that even they wept in sympathy. After the words of the burial service had been read, Martin threw the first handful of earth on to the coffin.

'Your daddy's crying with a big wide open mouth,' Sally whispered to Philip. The child wrapped his arms tightly round his father's legs but Martin seemed unaware of his son's existence. Unaware of anyone's existence, Ginny thought, with a void where her heart had once been.

Chilled almost to the marrow, the mourners began to disperse. Emma left early and took the children home, but Ginny and her parents stayed on until the family had said their private goodbyes, and returned with the funeral party.

They congregated in Mam Smith's parlour, where the now empty double bed served as a silent reminder of Maria. Wet clothes were put over the chair backs, and Mam Smith stirred up parlour and kitchen fires whilst Martin poured tots of rum for the men. The women retreated to the kitchen.

'By, it's cold,' said Mam Smith, with a shiver. 'I wish I'd thought to wrap a shawl round her. My poor bairn.' Her lip trembled as she searched her apron pocket for a handkerchief.

Ginny, who prided herself she'd never been seen to cry since her babyhood, said, 'I'll not be a minute, Mam, I just need the netty.'

She escaped thankfully into the yard, into the loneliness of the dank November afternoon. She leaned on the house wall and pushed her shoulders back against the cold bricks, sniffing and swallowing hard for several minutes to get rid of the tears. A few deep breaths restored her self-control, and, after wiping her eyes on the back of her hand, she went in.

Hot comforting tea waited. 'We'll just drink these and have a rest, and then I'll set the table,' her mother said.

'Have the men got theirs?'

'They don't want any yet, hinny. I gave them a jug of hot water to make toddies. They're all right with them.'

They sat round the fire in silence. After a few minutes Mam Smith said, 'Aye well, she had a good man. I'll always be thankful for that. God knows what he's going to do without her, though.'

'Do you remember when they danced at their wedding? Do you remember the way they looked at each other?' Ginny's mother unconsciously fingered her bruised chin. 'It did your heart good to watch them.'

'I'm not likely to forget it, bonny lass. It's a shame they couldn't dance through life as easy. Still, this is not getting the table laid. The lads must be hungry.'

Grief didn't spoil Ginny's appetite. She fell to hungrily, as did her father and the other bearers. Martin and Ginny's mother picked at the food, and Mam Smith ate nothing at all. With five pitmen sitting at the table most of the conversation was about work as usual.

'The deputy fired a shot for me yesterday. There was a blow of gas, and it took us all our bloody time to put the fire out,' said her father, 'we were lucky it didn't explode.'

'Shot-firing should be banned where naked lights are banned,' said Martin. 'What's the use of having locked safety lamps, then making a light with powder? Not to mention the fact that blasting's apt to shake the roof down. It was somebody firing a shot that nearly crippled me before I got wed.'

Ginny's father snorted. 'The use of it is that it makes quicker profits, so it's not likely to be banned.'

'You'll never make deputy, Martin. You're too fond of telling people things they'd rather not be made to know. And you're not fond enough of the bottle either,' one of his marrers joked. 'The manager was in the pit the worse for drink again yesterday. You could have got merry off his breath, man. You could smell him a mile away.'

Ginny knew Mr Vine liked a tipple, she'd smelled whisky on his breath herself from time to time, but she was surprised to hear he'd ever turned up for work after a drinking session.

'Aye, and when he drinks, the over men and deputies have to follow suit, just to stay pals, like. And we've our lives depending on them making the safety checks. It's time that Mines Inspector was round again,' said another.

Bad cavils, thin seams, roof falls, who had a near miss last week, who got fined how much for sending tubs up with the splint and stone that nobody could avoid, however careful, and the general cheating, chiselling, and contractual pilfering practised as a matter of course by owners and management – Ginny had heard it all before.

'You never hear tell o' them buggers hevin' to pull their belts in, and it doesn't matter what the market's supposed to be like,' commented her father. 'That was a good tea, Mam. You want to get more of it down you, lad, you need to keep your strength up.'

'Aye, I will, I'll have a bite later, maybe before bed. I'm not hungry just now.'

'They're not going to pay you much for the coal you'll win on what you've just eaten, and you've still got a house and family to keep going.'

Martin made no reply. Her father shrugged. 'Ah well, you know your own business best, I suppose.'

When all those with any appetite were replete with food and awash with tea, the women cleared the table and returned to the kitchen. Ginny stood at the sink washing glasses and pots, and her mother dried them, leaving Mam Smith to put everything back in its proper place. She put the best tea service and the cake stand safely away, and sighed.

'Barring Christmas, I think the last time that tea set was out was when Philip was born. I didn't think when I was putting it away after his christening that I should soon want it for his mam's funeral. I hope it's a long time before I see it again.'

'You might want it for something nice,' said Ginny.

'I can't think what that's going to be, now.'

'You've still got Philip and it'll soon be Christmas,' said Ginny's mother.

'It will. But I don't know how I'm going to face it, unless you know of any quick cures for broken hearts. I don't, and this'll take some getting over, both for me and his dad.'

'You might not think I understand you, Mam,' said

Ginny's mother, 'but I do understand a bit. I've lost my father and my brothers. My father warned me I'd never be welcome again if I married Arthur, and I've never seen any of them from that day to this. He sent me some of my mother's furniture and linen when I set up house, and that was the end of it. If you hadn't looked after me when I came here, I'd have had nobody except Arthur. I don't know what I'd have done without you.'

'Aye, it's cruel, lass, but it's not like losing one of your own bairns. I hope you may never know what that is.'

'But I do. John's gone. And I've an awful feeling I'll never see him again. It's like a premonition.'

'Well, take no notice o' them, bonny lass. I never had a premonition in my life, and there's been one tragedy after another in my family.'

There was a pause, and Ginny picked up her father's voice, full of geniality and concern, trying to ply Martin with drink.

'No, thanks, Arthur, I don't want a one.' She put a finger to her lips to signal the two women to listen.

'Go on, it'll do you good, man.'

'No really, I don't want one.'

'You do – it'll make you feel better. Drown your sorrows.'

'My sorrows are not the sort that'll drown. They'll still be there tomorrow, so I don't want a drink. What I want is my wife. Can you understand that, Arthur? I want me canny little wife, like other men have theirs. Whether they deserve them or not.'

'What? What are you getting at?'

'Some men don't deserve the wives they've got. That's what I'm getting at.'

Ginny and her mother waited on tenterhooks, fearing the inevitable violent outburst from her father. When it came, it was not as bad as expected.

'Look here, you,' said he, never a man to skirt round an issue. 'Don't you think I don't know when I'm being insulted. I'll let it pass this time, remembering what day it is. And I might let it pass for another week or two, considering your troubles. But you come it after that, sticking your nose into my business, and passing comments you've never been asked for, and you'd better be ready to settle it, man to man.' He stood up a little unsteadily, and put on his jacket.

'Mary Ann,' he called, and she appeared from the kitchen. 'I'm going on home, it's past my bedtime. I'm on the graveyard shift tomorrow. You can stop here as long as you like and look after Mam Smith. I'm all right. And a goodnight to everybody,' he said magnanimously, then, to Ginny's surprise and relief, he made a dignified exit.

Chapter Five

'There's so much more to life than pits and housework, and clever girls choose more. I can show you how much more, if you'll allow me. Come on, Ginny, don't disappoint me; I'm going away soon. Dressed up and with your hair done, you'd easily pass for eighteen.' Charlie Parkinson sat beside her at the kitchen table, offensively close.

She looked at him speculatively. Going away? Well, she wouldn't ask where to. It was none of her business, and she wouldn't give him the satisfaction of seeming to show any interest.

'No thanks, and anyway, it's not likely that my father would stand for me going to any music hall with you, even if I wanted to. You'd better take your sister. She might enjoy it.'

'But I wouldn't. Not when I'd rather be with you. Fifteen, and never been to a music hall. Never been kissed either, I shouldn't wonder.' A smile played on his lips, suggestive, quizzical. She said nothing. 'Come on,' he coaxed, 'you'd like it. You might even have enough talent to do a turn yourself, if you had the right man to introduce you to it. Your father needn't know. I'll give you a good time, and I can guarantee you'd be the best-looking girl in the place. I'll drive you there. You'll like that.'

'You might as well save all your soft soap for the other lasses, Mr Parkinson, it's wasted on me,' she replied, and returned to the task of peeling shallots for pickling. The thought of a swim in the Wear wearing a pick for headgear was obviously not enough to put Charlie off.

'What other lasses are you thinking of, Ginny – can you recommend any?'

'I can't, but maybe your sister can. You'd better ask her. I think she's on the look-out for a good catch for you. Probably a bonny farmer's daughter, who'll be like the dairy cream she makes, rich and thick.' Her eyes watered and she blinked.

'Oh, poor Ginny, you're crying at the thought of losing me!' he exclaimed in mock sympathy. 'I always have that effect on women. I can't help it. Here, take my handkerchief.'

She took the spotless white handkerchief, pressed and beautifully monogrammed, and shook it out before wiping her eyes and blowing her nose noisily into it. She thrust it back into his hand. 'It's more the thought of the poor onions losing their skins. That's what's breaking my heart.'

'And you're what's breaking mine.' Charlie inspected the slimy contents of the handkerchief, before wrapping them up and replacing the handkerchief in his pocket. 'I shall never allow this to be washed again. In future, I shall wear it pressed close to my heart, to remind me of Cruel Ginny, my black-haired beauty.'

Flattered in spite of herself, she was barely succeeding in suppressing a laugh when Helen Vine entered – so promptly that Ginny had a suspicion she'd been listening at the door.

'I don't want you distracting her, Charlie. There's too much needs to be done to get this house ready for Christmas. Ginny, go outside and sweep the leaves off the lawn. I'll finish off here,' she said sharply.

'I doubt if I'll be able to see the leaves, Mrs Vine. It's nearly dark, and it's starting to rain. Besides, Mr Dyer'll have swept up any that were left.'

Helen wavered. 'All right then, you can take a bucket of hot water with a drop of ammonia and go and wash the paintwork in the dining room. Just be careful you don't spill any of it on the polished tops. I want everything gleaming in there. I'll be doing a lot of entertaining this Christmas.'

Ginny pulled a face. Nothing like ammonia for making a mess of your hands. She went through to the scullery to gather the necessary equipment, then sallied forth into the dining room, to make shorter work of the task than Helen had anticipated. When she returned, it was her turn to overhear the tail-end of a conversation at the door.

'Don't worry, sis,' Charlie's tones were reassuring, 'the girl attracts me, I admit, but I'm not a complete fool.'

No more am I, thought Ginny grimly, before pushing open the door, and crossing the kitchen to replace the bucket. The shallots had been abandoned, and Helen was busy with a knitting needle, poking holes in the large Christmas cake and feeding it with teaspoons of spirit. The room was full of the rich aroma of fruitcake and brandy.

'I don't know if I'll have enough with one cake. I think I'd better get cook to do another to be on the safe side. What do you think, Charlie?'

'You know best.'

'Yes, I usually do. You can go now, Ginny,' she said, offhandedly, not bothering to look up to meet Ginny's eyes. 'I think it's your time.' Charlie did meet her gaze, and gave her a conspiratorial wink.

'Aye, I think so and all,' Ginny agreed, face expressionless as she went to put on her coat. No offers of any rides this time, and she would gladly have accepted one, for there was a hole in the bottom of her boot that promised to let the water in. She cut a wad of newspaper from the scullery into a thick pad the shape of the sole, and stuffed it inside the boot, before squeezing her foot into it again. Lady Muck wasn't going to have her baby brother wasting his time on a penniless hewer's daughter with holes in her boots and nothing to offer but a bonny face and a strong back. She put on her coat and slipped out of the back door. She'd been dismissed as not good enough which was all she could expect, but still it rankled.

'It's not that I mind the work, I don't,' she said later, ensconced before Mam Smith's fire having tea and a chat before walking on home. 'What I mind is having somebody like her lording it over me, pampered halfwit that she is. She wouldn't last two minutes as a pitman's wife. I'd like to see how she'd manage with the life my mam's had to face, or you. Sweep the leaves. That's to keep me out of the way of that brother of hers. He's taking too much notice of me for her liking.' She stretched her damp feet towards the warmth of the fire, hoping that the state of the soles would be noticed.

Martin frowned. 'If even half of what I hear about that feller's true, she's doing you a good turn. I hope she'll stop him taking any notice of you at all, and don't you take any notice of him. I'd pity any lass that tangled with him.'

'Would you pity me if it was me?' she asked, tilting her chin towards him.

'I would hope you've got more sense.'

'Why's that then? What have you heard?' Ginny asked, pleased at his seeming concern.

'Enough to know it's not likely he'll ever make anybody a good husband, even if he ever gets to the point of getting married, and that's all I'm prepared to say about it.'

'I suppose his wife'll hev a comfortable sitting down, though. He never seems to be short o' tin but nobody knows where he gets it from.'

'I'm told him and his sister had a tidy sum left 'em when their mother died. And he's a bit of a capitalist, among other things,' said Martin.

'What's a capitalist?' asked Ginny.

'It's somebody that's got a lot of money, enough to

buy shares in going concerns, so he can have a cut of the profits and live well off other men's labour. Like the owners of the pit, they're shareholders. If there's a fall in the price of coal, it's our wages get cut, not their profits. If there's a strike or a lock-out, they don't do so well, but even then it's other men's families that starve and get evicted. If there's an accident at the pit, it's other men and their sons who're killed or maimed, not them. They're protected from everything by their money. Nothing touches them.'

'Oh, well, it must be a grand life for that class of people.'

'It is, for people who've got no conscience. Men like me and your dad produce the wealth, and men like Charlie enjoy it. It's time there was an alteration, but I don't see it happening.' His tone was dispirited.

'You look fed up, Martin.'

'Fed up's not the word for it, bonny lass. Since Maria died, I've had a lump in my chest like a ball of lead.'

'Aye, I know that feeling well,' said Mam Smith, easing herself back into an armchair and sipping her tea.

'Why don't you go down to the club, and have a bit crack with your marrers? It might make you feel better. There's nothing to keep you in now. Or you could take me to the dancing at the Catholic Club,' Ginny said, only half in jest. 'You're a good dancer, and so am I. I should have thought you'd be glad to get out, after months of stopping in looking after Maria.'

'I wish I had her back to look after. I miss her bonny

little face and her loving ways. I miss doing for her. I haven't the heart to go out.'

'I was only joking.' She saw it was useless. Hoping for any mention of the shoes Maria'd wanted her to have was useless too; the hint wasn't going to be taken, and she couldn't bring herself to ask for them. She heaved a heavy sigh.

'Aye, well, I suppose I'd better get on home. Mam'll be wondering where I am.'

She put on her coat and stepped out into lashing rain again. Rivulets of water ran into her boots, but it wasn't Martin or the shoes she was thinking about the rest of the way home. It was the solemn way Charlie Parkinson had carefully folded his snotty hanky and pressed it to his bosom. What a clown! She began to laugh to herself, and didn't stop until she got in the door.

The following Sunday evening, Mam Smith called down with Philip to pass an hour whilst Ginny's father was out. No sooner had she stepped inside than she spotted the quilting frame lying along the staircase.

'I see you've got a one on the go, Mary Ann. Get the frame up, bonny lass, and I'll give you a bit hand with it,' she ordered their mother. 'I can't sit here and do nothing, and it's that long since I did any quilting, I'd like the practice.'

'Seeing that you're the one that taught me everything I know about it, I doubt if you need any practice, but we'll sit together for a while if you like,' their mother agreed.

So the frame went up and both women settled to the

work, with Emma threading the needles to supply them. Sally and Philip sat under the frame chattering to each other, and Ginny filled the kettle and put it to boil, then cut some slices from a stale loaf and took a seat by the fire. She raked the heart of it red hot, then impaled a slice of bread as thick as a doorstep on the brass toasting fork and held it in the fierce heat, leaning back as far as she could to keep her cheeks from burning.

'The first one ready for bed gets the first slice,' she said, looking at Lizzie and Arthur. Lizzie dashed upstairs, and was down again dressed in her nightie before Ginny had taken the bread off the fork. She handed it over, and Lizzie spread it liberally with dripping and sprinkled it with salt. Ginny began toasting the next thick slice.

'Do you want this one, Emma?' she asked, looking pointedly at Arthur, who scowled back at her, stubbornly refusing to take the hint.

'No. Let's get the bairns fed and ready for bed first. Come on, Sally and Arthur, let's have you upstairs and undressed.'

After smoothing over a lot of argument from Arthur, Emma finally managed to get the pair of them upstairs.

'By, that lad of yours is a handful, Mary Ann. But your Emma seems to be able to get him to do anything. She's good with all the bairns,' observed Mam Smith, as soon as Emma was out of earshot.

'She is. She wants to be a teacher, did you know?'

'No, but she'll make a good one. She's clever enough.'

Ginny listened intently, as her mother lowered her voice and murmured, 'Yes she is, but it won't come off.

Arthur won't let her. He says it's a waste of money.'

'Ah, no, so is the poor lass to miss the best chance she'll ever have, then?'

Their mother nodded and, her voice even lower, said with a sigh, 'She's bitterly disappointed. I feel as if I've doomed her. I feel as if I've doomed all my children. I've cut them off from every chance in life, except slaving for other people.' She sighed again. 'I've begun to think my father was right. If I'd married somebody educated, somebody more like him, there'd have been no question about it. Emma could have been a teacher if she'd wanted. And John would have had the chance of something better than the sea, or the pits.'

'If you'd married anybody like your father, you wouldn't have had a John, or an Emma, or the rest of them. They're healthy, bonny bairns, be grateful. And I suppose you married Arthur because you loved him.'

'I did, although I think now that girls the age that I was then aren't old enough to know their own minds.'

'Maria knew hers at fifteen, and she chose well enough,' Mam Smith said, and added with the faintest touch of asperity, 'but I can't deny that Martin's not very educated.'

'But he's trying to educate himself, down at the Institute. How is he?' asked their mother quickly, fearful of having given offence.

The conversation was interrupted by Emma coming down again with Sally and Arthur. Excepting Sally, the children made short work of their supper, after which the three youngest Wildes were sent up to bed.

'What a relief,' said their mother, as peace descended on the kitchen.

'You don't know when you're well off. Think yourself lucky you've still got them all round you.' Mam Smith tucked in her needle, lifted her tired grandson and sat to nurse him.

Their mother bent her head lower over the work. 'I do. I'm sorry, Mam, I'm not thinking.'

'How's Martin?' Emma poured the tea, unconsciously echoing her mother's question. Ginny put another slice of bread on the toasting fork.

'Not much better, bonny lass, no better at all, really. He swore he'd seen her the other night, bending over Philip's cot. Oh, and he looked that upset.' Mam Smith hugged the tired child tighter.

Ginny's eyes widened. 'What, you mean he saw her ghost?'

She nodded.

'That must have been terrible,' Emma said.

'No. No, it wasn't seeing her that was terrible. The terrible thing was it wasn't real.' Mam Smith turned to Ginny. 'I'm sorry about the shoes, bonny lass. I know she said they were yours. I felt that awkward the other day when you called by, and I could see the holes in your boots. But he can't bear to part with any of her things.'

No one spoke. Mam Smith sighed. 'When either of you lasses gets married, I hope you may get a man as good as Martin, except I doubt that there are any.'

'Did you get a good husband?' asked Ginny, previously

never one to waste any time wondering about what was past, but now suddenly curious.

'I did. He was a good friend of my oldest brother, and I remember him coming to our house on the Wednesday before Pay Friday, asking to take me out. I thought we would just be going for a walk, but he took me to the Co-op and bought me a cup of tea and a bun. He had five bob, and I thought, five bob on the Wednesday after Baff week! I'm having this one – he must be rich!' She chuckled at the memory, and Ginny laughed loudly with her, hoping to keep the conversation going in this more cheerful direction. 'Oh, yes, we courted a couple of years. He used to try his luck, like they all do,' she confided, and held up her left hand towards Ginny, with the thumb touching the tip of the third finger, 'but I'd say – not until I get that ring on my finger, you don't – and he didn't. That's still a good principle for any young lass. Men are all the same, have their pleasure and away like the lamplighter, and leave some poor lass holding the baby.' She glanced at Ginny. 'Have nothing to do with that sort. Look for a good honest lad. My husband wasn't rich, and he wasn't lucky either, but he was my best friend, and now he's gone, crushed in the pit along with my eldest lad.' Her jaw tightened. 'And if you'd seen how they brought them home to me, wheeled in an old handcart, and covered with a bit of filthy sacking.'

'You've got us now,' said Emma. 'We're your friends.'

'I know that, bonny lass. It's during the bad times that you get to know who your real friends are. I've learned that in life if nothing else.'

*

The contrast between a mournful evening spent with Mam Smith and the atmosphere at the manager's house was marked. Ginny knew that a tidy little inheritance had compensated the manager's wife for the death of her mother, and she had never heard a sigh of regret pass her lips, nor seen a tear escape her clear blue eyes over the loss of her. Life had dealt Mrs Vine no other blows – quite the contrary. Mrs Vine had risen in the world and made it plain that she intended to rise further.

She's still nothing but an upstart though, thought Ginny, echoing in her mind the opinion of the village. Another weighty cake had been baked and laced with brandy, pounds of mincemeat prepared, a goose, hams and pork ordered from a local farmer, as Helen Vine prepared to make her name a byword for lavish hospitality. Hospitality that would be reserved for people milady thought worth her time and effort, and none of them likely to be in need of a free meal.

'I doubt if any of this lot's going to be blessing the poor, Ginny muttered to herself as she stuffed a teaspoonful of mincemeat into her mouth to savour the rich, spicy flavour, 'there's no King Wenceslases living here.'

She knew very well that she herself was a person of utter insignificance in Mrs Vine's eyes, except in the power she had to interest Charlie. Charlie was still absent, and Ginny detected a faint and supercilious smile on her mistress's face whenever their eyes met. She burned to know what he was up to, but a consciousness of Helen's pleasure in keeping the secret from her forced her to affect complete indifference, and the consummate actress in her played the part with conviction.

Then, as she was polishing the prized piano on the afternoon before the school Christmas concert, she heard him arrive.

Chapter Six

'It's full credit to Emma, Mrs Wilde. She's really made quite a comedy of that little sketch. It seems so true to life. It gets the teetotal message across in a highly amusing way, don't you think? Will you wait to see me? I would just like a word with you.' Their mother nodded, a look of anxiety on her face.

'Oh, the sketch was my doing more than our Emma's, Miss Carr. I was the one that rehearsed Lizzie and Arthur,' Ginny whispered, determined to claim her share of the credit.

'Really, Ginny?' Miss Carr's eyebrows almost met her grey hair, and her lip curled in a sneer of disbelief. 'Just walk on with Emma and the children, dear, I won't keep your mother long.'

Ginny took Sally by the hand, and they went out with all the other concert-goers into the moonlight whilst their mother waited with Mam Smith in the schoolroom to hear what Miss Carr had to say.

'I suppose she's telling Mam what a good scholar you are. She's hardly got a civil word for me,' said Ginny. 'I don't think she's ever forgiven me for that time I found half a crown and spent it on beer and cigarettes, and sent the minister's son off home as drunk as a lord. Do you remember? I think she had some explaining to do that night about how a model child from a teetotal home could get back from school reeking of ale and tobacco smoke and hardly able to stand.' Ginny laughed at the memory, joined by Lizzie and Arthur, who loved tales of her scapegrace antics. 'But she ought to have been satisfied with the revenge she got. Mind that bruise on my hand after the caning she gave me? And he never got touched. He was just as bad as I was, only his father was the minister.'

'You're not looking for sympathy, are you?' Emma's lips were pursed in disapproval. 'Most of us would have handed that money in. A few might have spent it on sweets, but only you could have thought of spending money that didn't belong to you on drink, and then rope the minister's son into your mischief. I'll never forget how shamed Mam was, and me and all.'

'Neither will I. I was cacking mesel' thinking I was going to get a belting off old Arthur, but do you remember, he did nothing but laugh! I couldn't believe I got away with that.'

'You want to be careful. One of these days you'll go too far, and end up getting hanged.'

'Wait, wait up! They've just come out,' said Lizzie.

'I wonder what they've been saying?' said an agonized Emma.

'Emma Wilde's the best scholar on earth, and she ought to be a professor, is what they've been saying,' said

Ginny. The troubled look on her mother's face as she joined them confirmed the guess.

They walked on home in silence after parting from Mam Smith. Their father was in. He must have heard them approach, because he opened the door before they were halfway down the path. They had hardly stepped into the house before he fixed Emma with a hard stare. 'You can tell that teacher o' yours you won't be back at school in January. You're thirteen now, and old enough to be earning your keep. I've got you a job scrubbing at the Cock Inn. You start on Christmas Eve. And make sure you do the bugger clean, or you'll know about it.'

Their father was on the backshift but left his own bed early on the morning of Christmas Eve to make sure Emma got to her new job on time. 'You'd better straighten your bloody face, Madam, or I'll straighten it for you.' He lunged towards her and she flew out of the door without her coat into a dark, icy morning. He shouted after her, 'I don't want any complaints about you, either about your cleaning or about your bloody long face, so remember!'

The Cock Inn was outside the village on the Durham Road, and Emma would have a longish walk through the woods and over the beck to reach it. Ginny quietly put on her own coat and took Emma's off the peg. 'I'll take this for her before I go to work.'

'You won't,' said her father, 'you'll be lucky to get to work on time as it is. You get straight off there now, and get a move on.'

Ginny looked towards her mother, kneeling at the hearth raking out yesterday's ashes. 'It's all right, Ginny. I'll take it down later.'

'Well, you won't,' said her father, landing her mother a vicious kick on her skinny behind. Ginny saw her eyes water suddenly as she turned to look at him, saw her nose redden and the corners of her mouth droop before she turned her face back to the ashes. Ginny's jaw clenched, and her fingers curled into tight fists. Her father continued, giving emphasis to every word, 'Neither of you will, and that's the end on't. She's gone without it and she can come back without it, clever little madam that she is. She's been getting a lot too big for her bloody boots lately, with her head stuffed full of big ideas, but I'll soon cut her down to size, and I shan't be long about it.' He looked menacingly at them. 'And you won't interfere, if you know what's good for you.'

Ginny heard her mother utter a strangled sob as she left. She slammed the door as hard as she dared then hot-footed it down the path in case he came after her. She flew through streets and park with wings on her heels, teeth grinding and blood boiling as she remembered that kick and her mother's humiliation. If only she'd been born a man. Jaw still clenched, she arrived at the manager's house and threw open the back door.

Helen Vine was waiting for her, still in her dressing gown. 'You're late, and there are fires to lay and hearths to sweep and polish, so get on with it. Then set the table for three.'

The cook, an ageing coalfield widow who took

whatever work she could to make ends meet, stood by the range stirring porridge and keeping well out of the argument. As soon as Mrs Vine had turned her stately back, Ginny pulled such a gargoyle of a face at it the cook almost dropped the pan she was lifting off the stove.

'By God,' she whispered, 'it's to be hoped the wind never changes when you've got your face twisted like that. It wad scare the shite out of Old Nick.'

Ginny tied on a hessian apron, then rattled about in the cupboard for the bucket and shovel and set to with a will, thinking of her mother as she raked the ashes, the anger she felt increasing her strength and speed. She had just finished and changed her rough apron for a frilly white one when Charlie sauntered downstairs.

'What ho, Ginny!' he greeted her. 'You're quite a little hinny, all spruced up in your little frilly pinny.'

Her cheeks still flushed and her mind still fixed on her father, she gave him an unseeing stare and carried the heavy tray of crockery into the dining room, where she rapidly set the table. Charlie lounged against the door frame watching her. He caught her apron strings as she walked past him on her way back to the kitchen and held on until the bow was undone and the strings trailing. By the time she got there, the apron was hanging off her.

'I know what I'd like to do with that one!' she said to Mrs Ridley, the cook, tying it tightly again, nipping in her trim waist.

'I've an idea he knows what he'd like to do with you an' all,' was Mrs Ridley's sardonic rejoinder.

'And I know what I'd like to do with him an' all – I'd like to black both his eyes.'

The cook opened her mouth to make another jocular remark but the expression on Ginny's face as she lifted the breakfast tray strangled it in her throat. She returned five minutes later with the tray empty and her apron strings trailing.

'I don't know why that bugger's sister doesn't keep him under control,' she said. 'I would, if he were anything to do wi' me.'

'I've done you a bacon sandwich, lass,' was the only comment Mrs Ridley ventured to make.

Charlie was in the drawing room seated at the piano when she passed, playing some jaunty new tune. Helen stood by him, turning the sheet music.

'Come in here, Ginny. You like to sing. Listen to this one.' Not letting her face slip, she looked at his sister and moved towards the dining room.

'No, stop her, Helen. She's a fellow artiste. I want her to hear it.' Helen gave her a curt nod, so Ginny went in and listened.

'Perhaps I shouldn't play it, really. Perhaps it's too naughty.' Charlie wavered, giving an impression of a man torn by indecision. Finally he said, 'Never mind. I don't think it'll do any harm. It's a new song called "Dimples", and this is how it goes.' He played a couple of bars, then sang a song about a barmaid with a twinkle in her eye, ending:

There's something about that girl.
Could it be the naughty twinkle in her eye?
The bar's always full and the takings never down
Since that pert, pretty barmaid started at the
Crown.
Is it her face, or might it be her figure?
The landlord's happy, trade's getting bigger.
What a treasure he's found.
The swells come from miles around.
You can hear them say that girl's so gay,
Dimples in her cheeks, what a jolly little tease,
And some say she's got dimples in her knees.

'What's so bad about that?' asked Ginny, face dour. 'I can't see anything wrong with it.'

Charlie laughed. 'Neither can I, Ginny. Except for the singing, of course. I'm a poor singer, as you can hear. But your singing and my piano playing might do.' He smiled brightly at her, and then his face assumed a serious expression. 'But you see, in London slang, a gay woman is a prostitute.' He paused, then shrugged and added, 'Although some people might not think there's anything wrong with that either. Wouldn't you agree, Helen?'

Ginny gave him a blank, uncomprehending stare, and Helen said, 'Thank you, Ginny. You can get about your business now. There's plenty to keep you busy. And you, Charlie,' she landed him a glancing blow on his head with the flat of her fingers, 'can play something more suited to the season, and to the type of people we'll be entertaining. They'll be the local yeomanry, a different class to your low London connections.'

'Oh, very good people, very worthy, I'm sure. Very proper, and very tea-drinking.' He broke into a slow rendition of 'O Little Town of Bethlehem', and made it sound like a dirge.

'What's a prostitute?' Ginny asked, once the kitchen door was shut behind her.

The cook sat down in shock. 'It's what you'll end up as if you take much to do with yon Charlie Parkinson. You'd better ask your mother. I can't tell you.'

Helen Vine had invited a couple of prosperous farming families from Old Annsdale for the evening. Ginny and the cook spent all day preparing dishes, and all evening dispensing food and drink and clearing up the debris after the gorging and general merry-making. Ginny enjoyed the noise and bustle, and the bonhomie. She laughed to see the blunt farmer from Manor Farm cast an appraising eye over Charlie as he presented his daughter, and she caught the look of rich amusement on Charlie's face as he bowed and kissed the daughter's hand. She saw him smile as he took the hand of the daughter of the neighbouring farm. She heard the wives of the two stockmen in whispered conversation about what Charlie might be worth, and then heard Helen and Charlie casting up the farmers' accounts in conspiratorial murmurs.

'It's hard work for these buggers who've got money to think about. They can't just take any lass or lad they fancy. Those two are trading their daughters like a pair of heifers,' she remarked to the cook.

'Aye, well, they have to make sure they're getting as much as they're giving, if they can. That's business. Yon Charlie's on good form, though. He's got them all eating out of his hand by the sound of it.'

He was very entertaining. He had the party in gales of laughter from start to finish. The two daughters were immensely taken with him and their rivalry for his attention drew a wry smile from Ginny. She watched him flatter and charm them, seeming to favour the girl from the Manor at one turn, her neighbour at another. His fears of a teetotal evening were not realized. Both farmers became very well oiled as the evening progressed, and their wives weren't averse to a tipple.

Ginny hummed along to the lively music and revelled in the conversation and the intrigue, if only at second hand. As it grew late, she stood by the kitchen sink, polishing glasses that the cook was lifting out of sudsy water, when she felt another tug on her apron strings and whirled round to see Charlie, sprig of mistletoe in one hand and champagne bottle in the other. He leaned forward to kiss her and quick as lightning she sidestepped him. His lips puckered at empty air. He pulled a face and shrugged, and both he and the cook laughed.

'Next time. Well, if you won't have a kiss, have a glass of champagne, and a Merry Christmas.' His soft, gentleman's hand took hold of Ginny's housework-roughened one, still holding the glass she'd been polishing. He filled it with golden, sparkling liquid, then took another and filled it for the cook. 'If you like it, have another.' He smiled and put the half bottle down on the kitchen table, blew a kiss and, with an '*au revoir, mesdames*', returned to the drawing room.

They sniffed the liquid and sipped cautiously.

'He's a smooth one that, but you've got to laugh at him. By, this is lovely,' exclaimed the cook. 'I doubt his sister knows he's given us this. I'm fifty-odd year old, and this is the first time I've ever tasted champagne.'

'And I'm fifteen, and this is the first time I have an' all. Let's finish it off before she realizes we've got it.' Ginny quickly finished her glass, and poured herself another. 'Come on, you're lagging.'

'Steady on, lass. Have you never heard the song, "He filled her up with gin just to make her sin?" You want to be on your guard when men start giving you booze. Not that I'm complaining like. This is lovely, and I don't somehow think it's me he wants to sin with.'

'Don't be daft.' Ginny smiled, feeling happiness oozing through her stomach into her whole body. 'I'd make mincemeat of him if he tried anything with me.' She poured another glass and the pair sat down and sipped, savouring the drink on their tongues before swallowing.

'This is the life,' said the cook. 'I'd like to make a habit of this. Pity we can't have a bottle every Christmas.'

'Hear hear,' said Ginny, raising her glass with a laugh. 'I'll drink to that. I think I'd drink this to anything. The only fault with it is we should be in the drawing room with the rest of them.'

The opening bars of the barmaid song she'd heard

earlier in the day accompanied the cook's giggle. 'That'll be the day,' she said, 'when the likes of them let the likes of us into their drawing rooms.'

'The likes of them might have to wait for an invitation into mine before I've done,' said Ginny, with a tilt of her chin.

Just then, the two farmers' daughters appeared, shuffling against each other in the doorway. After a bit of nudging and giggling, the boldest one spoke up. 'Miss Jane Wilde, you're wanted in the drawing room.'

Ginny raised her eyebrows and rose to her feet. 'Hear that? And I get me full title.' Walking very steadily and chin up, she followed the two sniggering girls out of the kitchen.

Charlie was seated at the piano, hands clasped, looking solemn. 'I want you to help me to keep a promise I made to the ladies and gentlemen, Ginny. I promised them that you would sing much better than me, which is true. Then I promised them I'd get you to do it, which I hope is true.' He leaned forward and said confidentially, in a voice that could be heard by everybody, 'I'll reward you.'

'How?' She looked him straight in the eye.

'A guinea.'

'I don't know the words.'

'You can read them.'

'A whole guinea?'

'Yes.'

'All right then. But I'll have the guinea before I start.'

Charlie threw back his head and shook with laughter, joined by the rest of the company. As the mirth subsided, he reached into his pocket and tossed her a coin.

'You've got a natural there,' commented one of the farmers, wiping his eyes. Charlie nodded and handed her the sheet music. 'It's all right, you've got the tune. I'll play a couple of bars, and then you're in, got it? Ladies and gentlemen, I give you this brilliant artiste, brought to you at enormous expense – Miss Jane Wilde.'

She nodded and quickly read the words, then scanned the grinning faces of the audience. Sensing some conspiracy against her, she stared back at them, thinking that the devil may care and take them all to hell with him for all it mattered to her. She'd got the easiest guinea she'd ever earned. She wondered at her own composure as she listened to the opening bars, then launched herself into an imitation of Charlie's rendition of the song without a second thought, copying glad eye and innuendo she hardly understood. She finished with an exaggerated, leering wink that set the men and girls laughing and clapping, the mature women looking askance at each other.

'Like I said, she's a natural. She could turn professional,' repeated the farmer.

Helen gave an acid smile. 'I agree, although I'm not sure which profession you're referring to.'

'Shut up, Helen.' The manager looked at Ginny with sympathetic, bloodshot eyes.

'I don't believe we can better Ginny's turn tonight,' said Charlie, closing the piano lid, 'and so here endeth the Christmas concert, ladies and gentlemen.'

★

Much later, at home, the sight of Charlie and his sister playing a duet, their two red heads bent over the piano, and two sets of pale blue eyes glancing up from time to time to read the music stuck vividly in her mind as she put the candle down on the washstand and undressed for bed. She hummed the catchy air she'd sung at the manager's under her breath.

'Shut up, will you, I'm trying to get to sleep,' came a peevish little voice from under the covers.

'Hello, Em. Hey, Em, you're the scholar. What's a prostitute?'

Emma sat bolt upright in bed. 'A what?'

'A prostitute.'

'Ask me mam. Anyway, I'm no scholar. Thanks to me dad, I'm the skivvy at the Cock Inn and that's all I'm ever likely to be now. My life's going to be a long round of cleaning filthy spittoons, and sweeping up filthy sawdust, and cleaning filthy netties, and having to call every beery moronic bugger that walks into the pub Mister, when I could run rings round them all for brains.' Her face looked pinched and sour.

'What's happened to you? Me mam'll be washing your mouth out with soap if you go on. You never used to swear.'

'Aye, well, teachers don't swear, and skivvies do, and I'm a skivvy. So I don't care what I do or what I say now. You know, me father never drinks at the Cock because it's more deputies and overmen who go there, but he came in today apurpose to show me up. He sat at the bar and shouted right across the pub, "De the bugger clean, and mek sure you get right in the corners," and all the men were looking at me as if I was something that crawled out from under a stone. It's not enough for him to ill-use us at home, he's got to lower us when we're out as well. I'd have got some respect as a teacher, but he's not going to let that happen. I could kill him. I hope the bloody pit roof falls in and flattens him, buries him alive.'

'Steady on. I don't think even he's bad enough to deserve that. Besides, it might flatten a lot of other people an' all.'

Emma slid down in bed and turned over. 'I'm going to sleep. I want to get a few hours in before I jump out of bed to see what Father Christmas put in me stocking.'

Ginny glanced towards the end of the bed. There was no stocking. She crawled under the covers and closed her eyes, and the sights and sounds of the party whirled round inside her head – Charlie and his sister playing their duets, the lasses making eyes at him, their mothers whispering about what he might be worth, their fathers laughing and the manager sitting apart and drinking heavily, looking at her with his sad, brown, bloodshot eyes. She fell asleep as the pit roof fell in, burying them all.

Chapter Seven

Ginny rubbed away the frost on the bedroom windowpane to see the dawning of a bright chill Christmas day. A fire was crackling in the hearth when she got down to the kitchen.

'Merry Christmas, Ginny.' Her mother pushed a newspaper-wrapped parcel into her hands. A blue swelling disfigured the left side of her lip and made her smile crooked. Ginny's jaw clenched.

'How'd you get that – as if I didn't know?' Her mother shrugged. 'Aye, he's given us a grand start to Christmas. That'll be lovely for the bairns to sit and look at.'

'Open your present.'

Ginny tore the paper. Inside was a beautifully crafted piece of cream quilting about the size of a cushion. Her face relaxed as she admired the intricate pattern worked in impossibly neat little stitches.

'By, that's bonny. But what is it?'

Her mother gave a lopsided grin. 'It's a nightdress case,' she said. 'It'll look all right on your pillow. I did one for you and one for Emma. When you leave home to get married, or for a living in job, you can take it with you, to keep your nightie in. Remind you of the mother that made it.'

Ginny smiled. 'I don't think I'll be getting any living in jobs. And as for getting married, I don't know who'd have me.' She put her hand in her pocket and felt her hard, round guinea, wanting to boast 'look what I got yesterday', but something stopped her. She withdrew her hand and let her guinea lie.

'Everything's done. The vicar'll be keeping them safe until eleven o'clock at least, and I hope she comes back a better Christian than she went.' Ginny sprawled on a kitchen chair watching the cook divide hot milk between two beakers and add fragrant pitch-black liquid from the spluttering percolator.

'You're a bugger, you are. You get no better for keeping.' Mrs Ridley's rich, fat laugh matched her ruddy face and round figure.

'That smells lovely. Pass us the cake tin then.'

'I wonder you never get any fatter,' the cook commented as Ginny helped herself to a couple of sugar-encrusted pies.

'Burn it all off, with plenty of hard work,' said Ginny, cramming her mouth and stirring two teaspoons of sugar into her beaker. She put her feet up on the kitchen stool. 'This is the life. I wouldn't mind a dollop of this every day.'

'So make the most of it while you can,' advised the cook, opening the oven door to baste the meat. 'I'll just do this, then I'll put my feet up an' all. Two can play at that game.'

The Manor Farm party arrived just half an hour before the meal, and Ginny was kept hopping in and out of the dining room with glasses, sherry and beer, watching in wonderment as Charlie became utterly absorbed in farm talk and lent his ear to tales of mastitis and swine fever with as much apparent concern as if his own fortunes depended on them. The manager tried to feign an interest, but with the conversation so far adrift from his own *métier*, he looked as comfortable as a fish out of water. Helen sat sipping sherry with the farmer's wife, conversing graciously and casting occasional sharp glances at her husband, glances that Ginny supposed were intended to spur him on to greater efforts to cultivate his guests. With downcast eyes, the farmer's daughter smiled a shy response to Charlie's encouraging smiles whilst moving ever closer to her mother until she was almost sitting in her lap.

'I'll say one thing about Charlie Parkinson,' Ginny remarked to the cook on one of her numerous trips in and out of the kitchen, 'he's a master of the art of arsehole greasing.'

'Aye, well, just you remember that when he tries greasing yours,' said the cook. 'This lot's ready. You can take it to the table and go and tell her ladyship that dinner is served.'

The party did more than justice to the cook's efforts. Soup and fish courses were followed by a roast goose, a leg of pork, a sirloin of beef for those who disliked pork, every vegetable that could be procured, gravies, sauces and chutneys, and Ginny was kept busy waiting on them all.

'You'll never eat a better fowl than the ones I rear, or a better joint of pork either, but I will admit, your cook's done them justice,' the red-faced farmer bragged, paying homage to his own produce with his mouth stuffed with it.

'Yes, a good cook's indispensable. We don't go without our comforts here.' A smile of satisfaction lit up Helen's face.

'Certainly not. It's a life of luxury, and somebody's got to live it. It'd better be us. Wouldn't you agree, Clarice?' Charlie smiled conspiratorially and lifted his glass towards the farmer's daughter. She nodded in a confusion of blushes and smiles while the rest looked on with approbation.

'A good cook, a handyman, and a good clean housemaid. I suppose that's all the livestock you need to make you comfortable,' was the farmer's attempt at humour, and Helen's tinkling laugh rang out gratifyingly.

'It may be all we need, but it's not all we intend to have,' she assured him, eyes gleaming. 'Charlie's got his shares in the mine, and his business in London, of course, and a good property there. As for Robert and me, we mean to count for something. The mine's doing very well. We're set fair for real prosperity and when it materializes we'll keep a much better, larger establishment and have our servants living in, won't we,

Robert? We've already ordered one of those lovely Daimler horseless carriages they're making in Coventry, haven't we, Robert?' The manager gave a dubious nod.

'Bloody woman!' exploded Ginny, kicking the kitchen door shut after her and dumping a tray full of dirty pots on the draining board. 'Me and you – they're calling us livestock now. And when she's even richer, she's going to have a better establishment than us!'

'Ah well, never bother. If your life goes according to plan, you'll have your own drawing room and she'll have to ask for permission to come into it.'

'Sarcastic bugger,' said Ginny.

The cook laughed and struck a match. 'Mind you don't set fire to yourself with this,' she said, as she ignited the moat of brandy surrounding the Christmas pudding.

'No, I'll set her ginger wig alight instead.'

'I believe there's a race meeting tomorrow,' Charlie was saying as she got back with the pudding. 'Anybody game?'

Ginny set the flaming pudding on the table and smiled inwardly to see Helen lean away from her with a look of apprehension on her face.

'Is there? I thought you were coming to us. We're not racing people. We usually have a quiet day with family, or close friends. You will come to us tomorrow, won't you?' The farmer's wife looked anxiously at Helen. 'Only it's a bit late for us to make different arrangements now.'

'Of course,' Helen soothed, 'I'm just like you. I prefer

the company of pleasant friends to racketing round racecourses. Give me a warm and comfortable drawing room and good conversation and you can keep your shouting, vulgar racing enthusiasts. Of course you can depend on us, Hilda.'

The house was in darkness when Ginny got home. Her father lay on the bed in the front room, his thunderous expression just visible in the firelight. Ginny passed quickly through to the kitchen where her mother sat gazing vacantly into space, surrounded by the three younger children, all silent.

'What's up wi' him the day?' Ginny mouthed quietly, lifting the kettle to fill it at the sink. Her mother said nothing. Ginny set the kettle on the fire, hung up her coat, and ran upstairs to find Emma sitting up in bed reading by the light of the candle.

'What set him off?' she asked.

'How the hell do I know?' Emma shrugged. 'Have you looked outside? It's probably a full moon. He chucked his bloody Christmas dinner on the fire. I had to clean it all off the hearth.'

'Silly old bugger. Still, it must have been something.'

'She didn't look happy enough when she was putting it out, so he asked her what was wrong with her bloody clock. She told him she was worried about our John, not hearing from him. That was enough. The dinner went on the fire, and he's been in the front room and she's been in the kitchen since. She cried all through her dinner and hardly ate a thing, and me and the bairns lost our appetites an' all. I helped her clear away and wash up and then I came up here out of the way. I'm near frozen.'

'Rotten old bugger. I've been dying to get home all day, and now I'm glad I was out. Talk about Christmas Day in the workhouse – it's a treat compared to Christmas Day at the Wildes'. I'm off to Mam Smith's. It couldn't be as miserable as it is here if they'd buried half a dozen. Are you coming?'

'No. I'm not fit company for anybody, the mood I'm in. You go. I'll go down and sit with Mam after you've gone.'

'You'll not be much company for her either if you're that way out.'

Emma pushed the heavy quilt aside and swung her legs out of bed. 'Whether I am or not, I'm too cold to stay up here a minute longer.'

'Seeking sanctuary again?' Mam Smith enquired with a smile when Ginny arrived on the doorstep with Lizzie and Arthur. 'I'll put the kettle on, or maybe you need something stronger. Do you think she's old enough, Martin?'

'No, I don't. And we don't want her learning any bad habits here.' He caught the look on his mother-in-law's face. 'Sorry, I wasn't getting at you, Mam. You pour yourself a drop of brandy and enjoy it; you're old enough to know when to take it and when to leave it alone. Ginny's not very old, and she's not all that wise.'

Ginny drew herself up to her full height. 'I'm not a bairn now, you know,' she challenged.

'You're not much more, and you're not going to learn anything here that'll end up getting you into trouble. What did Father Christmas bring you, eh?' he asked the children. Lizzie held up a rag doll, and Arthur showed a can of marbles. 'By, that's clever. You must have been good to deserve them.' He smiled, but the smile soon faded, as if the effort was too great to sustain.

'Why don't you have a drink, Martin?' asked Ginny. 'It is Christmas, when all's said and done. One can't hurt you.'

'No. The way I feel, I might not stop at one.' He leaned down to play with the marbles and the boy looked up at him and laughed.

'They're good ones, aren't they, Martin?'

'The best I've ever seen.'

Ginny watched him as he examined the toys. Me mam's right, she thought, he has got a lovely head of hair. Thick, the colour of ripe corn. She had a sudden impulse to stretch out her hand and touch it, feel the silkiness of it in her fingers.

But his refusal to recognize her as an adult annoyed her. She sniffed. 'Well, as soon as I'm old enough, I never shall let a Christmas or a New Year go by without having a glass of brandy with you, Mam. Never mind what anybody else thinks. And on Boxing Day I shall always go to the races. Have you ever been to the races, Martin?'

'Aye. I don't know who hasn't. I used to like going with Maria.'

'Did you ever put much money on?'

'I might have done if there'd ever been a race with

only one horse running. It takes an optimist like Tom Hood to gamble the housekeeping money if there's more than one. You can't beat the bookies, bonny lass. The system's not set up that way. Betting's all right for people who've got a lot of money they've no use for.'

'But would you go just for a day out?'

'Aye, it's all right for a day in the fresh air. But if you can't afford to bet, you don't care which horse is first past the finishing post, so there's not a lot of interest in it. It's exciting if you've got money to splash about, you can have a grand time watching it gallop away. It would be all right for a young lass like you, that just wants to have a look at everybody's clothes, and see what her betters are wearing,' he teased.

Ginny sighed heavily, and thought she'd be glad to get back to work. Helen Vine irritated her to hell, but at least the house was buzzing with life, and Charlie knew how to make people enjoy themselves. Everybody else she knew seemed to want to wallow in misery.

'What's up, lass?' said Mam Smith, offering her a mince pie.

'I don't think I'll ever get to the races or anything else. I don't know why I talk about it. Nothing exciting's ever happened to me, or ever likely to.'

Chapter Eight

Ginny listened to the family dispute with keen interest, waiting for enough of a gap in the argument to get her message out.

'Oh, Helen, have a heart, do,' Charlie was protesting. 'Christmas Eve, and the best part of Christmas Day. I can't spend another day in such tedious company talking about swine fever and the price of cows. You go, and I'll come along at five or six. That should do for them. Hang it all, they must allow for a fellow having business of his own to attend to.'

'Business at the racecourse, Charlie? The only filly you should be concerning yourself with now is Clarice Farr. She's sweet on you. I'll swear her hand's yours for the asking, and the hand isn't empty. You're a fool if you'll risk it for a day at the races.'

'I won't risk it. I'll be along at five or six, honour bright. Better say six. And I'll be so gay and amusing I'll make a much better impression than if I'd had them depressing my spirits all day. No, I'll leave you two at the Farrs and come along later myself.'

'Charlie, you really are insufferable,' said the manager.

'Why the devil should I take more care about your courtship than you take yourself?'

'Because my sister will give you hell if you don't,' grinned Charlie, 'and because I'll reward you a hundredfold when I'm master of Manor Farm. I'll give you a full account of my winners when I get back. I'll put a bet on for you, if you like. Tell the Farrs anything you like.'

Helen stabbed a hatpin into her enormous feathered hat and gave an exasperated sigh. 'You idiot. You know from Hilda Farr's comments when you brought the subject up that they're not racing people, and if you don't come with us they're bound to know where you are. Yes, Ginny, what do you want?'

'Bob's got the horses harnessed and ready, Mrs Vine.'

She held the door open and watched them go. Back in the kitchen the cook was washing the breakfast pots.

'Come on, lass, let's hurry up and get done. If they're going to be out all day we're off home early. What her eye doesn't see, her heart won't grieve over. And if all's done, she'll never know the difference.'

'You know,' said Ginny, picking up a tea towel and swiftly drying pots, 'I never thought I'd say it, but I feel really sorry for yon Clarice Farr. She's in for a rude awakening if she thinks Charlie Parkinson's as sweet on her as she is on him. All he's sweet on is her father's property.'

'Aye, life's hard for the rich,' agreed the cook, her voice heavy with sarcasm, 'and her father's acres mean she'll never hev the pleasure of living from hand to mouth, or possing clothes in the back yard in the middle o' winter, or skivvying in somebody else's house after her man's dead and buried. It fair breaks your heart to think o' some poor bugger missing all that. Anyway, he's not got her yet, and maybe he never will. Maybe her father's not the fool they take him for.'

Ginny laughed. 'Well, somebody got out o' the wrong side o' bed today. What's up, didn't Father Christmas put anything in your stocking?'

'Well, Mrs Vine didn't. Did she put anything in yours?'

'No, but I wouldn't want it. I wouldn't want to be treated like a servant.'

The cook gave an incredulous laugh. 'Well, yer are a bloody servant, so why not?'

Put to it, Ginny couldn't explain, but being a servant and feeling like a servant seemed to her to be two different things. 'I just wouldn't want to lower meself,' she said. 'Anyway, I got an extra shilling in me wages, and I'd rather have that than any Christmas box.'

They were ready for off when they heard someone in the hall. A second or two later the kitchen door opened, and Charlie entered holding a package.

'Mrs Vine says you're to take the rest of the day off, cook,' he said, pressing it into her hands. 'Just a little Boxing Day token for the best cook in the north.' The cook gave Ginny a sidelong glance, then smiled and mumbled thanks.

'I seem to have left yours upstairs, Ginny. Bring in some coal and bank the fires while I find it.'

He disappeared, and the cook left by the back door

whilst Ginny was in the coalhouse shovelling slack. She was banking up the drawing room fire when Charlie reappeared.

'Has she gone?' he asked.

'She was away two minutes after you said. She'll be halfway home by now.'

'How'd you like a day at the races, Ginny? You seem a game sort of girl, and I'd be glad to have your company. You might even come home richer.'

She took pleasure in refusing. 'No, thanks. Racing's all right for folk who've a lot of money they've no use for. I haven't.'

She marched out by the front door, leaving Charlie to lock it, and walked on a little way under a pearl-grey sky enlivened with white streaks of cloud shot through with bolts of gold. The sun was bright on the bare trees and there was a bracing nip in the air. She breathed its fragrance and hesitated. She might never get the chance to go racing again. It would be something new, a break in the monotony, fresh air and freedom, out instead of in with her mother's misery and her father's dour face.

She turned and looked over her shoulder. 'I've changed my mind. I would like a day at the races if you still want me to come.'

Charlie walked towards her, grinning. 'That's the wonderful thing about women. You change your minds so often, but I don't mind it. I like to be kept in suspense.'

The curricle gave a smooth, comfortable ride. She sank back into the leather upholstery and listened idly to the clip-clop of the horses' hooves, the rattle of the wheels, the squeak of leather and the cawing of rooks. They passed houses bathed in golden light, fresh ploughed fields and green hills dotted with thick-fleeced sheep. A sudden sleet came down, followed just as quickly by the sun, leaving raindrops on the bare branches of lichen-clad trees glinting like diamonds. The journey was pleasure enough, and the racecourse came into view almost too soon, its track bounded by miles of white fencing.

'Do you want a bit of excitement, Ginny?' he asked, when they were through the gate.

'What sort?'

'We'll have an accumulator. If you win the first race, it makes you that bit keener when it gets to the second one, and so on. If any horse loses, you lose everything. But if you win every time, which I admit is not very likely unless you're with me, it's thrilling when it gets to the last race. Gives you something to shout about. What do you think? Will you chance your guinea?'

'I haven't got it with me,' she lied.

'I'll lend it to you.'

'I'll cheer for your horse.'

'Oh no, that won't do. It has to be your own risk or you won't feel the thrill.'

She was very reluctant. 'Well, maybe I'll just put half of it on.'

There were eight races. The prices on the first few they backed were two to one or even money. At first, Ginny was resigned to losing her ten shillings and sixpence and her eyes were as much on the fashions and the women's hats as the races, but as their horses won race after race, she began to feel a fluttering in her stomach, and her grip on the fence became tighter. At last the horses were lined up for the final race.

'Which did we bet on?' she asked.

'Fiery Jack,' grinned Charlie.

'Is he the favourite?' she begged for reassurance.

'He is not. The odds are fourteen to one.'

'What does that mean?'

'It means we've a much better chance of losing than winning. This is going to be a furious race. There are some really good horses running.'

'Well, why didn't you back one o' them then?'

He leaned back on the fence and laughed at her. 'I wanted the pleasure of stirring you up, my hinny. I shall enjoy seeing your terror if he falls back a bit, and your excitement if he gets out in front. Don't despair yet, Ginny. He may only be an old handicapper, but he knows what he's about. He was once one of the most talked about horses in jump racing. So say your prayers hard enough, and cheer loudly enough, and you can make him win.'

The horses were lined up, and a minute later they were off, with Fiery Jack trailing behind until a couple of furlongs down the field, when Ginny got him confused with other horses and lost sight of him until they hove into view again on the far side of the track.

'My God, my God,' she shrieked, 'is that him, out in front?'

Charlie seemed supremely unconcerned. 'I do believe

it is, and by about four lengths at a guess. Your prayers must have been answered, Ginny.'

She stood in front of Charlie gripping the fence, urging Fiery Jack on until she was hoarse. When they thundered up to the last fence but one he was still in the lead and putting in giant strides to get over it. She screamed him on, and then groaned as he hit the fence and stumbled over it, landing with his nose nearly touching the turf. The jockey slid down his neck and was off, she was sure. She raised her eyes to the skyline and stared at the naked trees, not daring to watch. When she looked again, the jockey was still in the saddle, but another rider had gained on Fiery Jack and was leading by a length. Fiery Jack was soon hard on his heels, with the jockey laying on the whip. Ginny shut her eyes as they took the last fence, and prayed hard. When she opened them again, the leading jockey was rolling on the ground, his horse charging on riderless and beginning to lose ground. Amid shouts and screams, Fiery Jack thundered home, first by a neck. Ginny almost fainted with relief, and then felt a surge of elation. She turned her face to Charlie with a smile that stretched from ear to ear.

'How much money do we get?'

'Bright eyes and brighter smiles. You're a typical woman, Ginny. Money makes your eyes sparkle, and your little heart beat faster.' Her back still to him he pulled her in close, placed a hand under her left breast and held it there.

'There, I can feel it, pounding away faster than Fiery Jack's hooves. It excites you, doesn't it?'

She removed his hand. 'What, the race or your paw?'

'Both. Both would excite you, given the chance.'

'Neither excites me half as much as the thought of collecting all that money.'

'Oh you women! Disgustingly mercenary creatures you are.'

'Aye, and I'm going to get mesel' a disgustingly nice pair of new boots. I suppose you're going to tell me you don't care about money, Charlie?'

'No, I like money too, but not for itself. For the things I can buy with it. Things like you, Ginny.'

'I'm not a thing. I'm a person. You can't buy people.'

'You'd be surprised.'

She took him by the hand, not wanting to prolong the conversation.

'Come on, come on. Let's get to the man and get me tin. I'll say one thing for you, Charlie; you're a lucky man. I don't care what else anybody says about you, you're a lucky, lucky man.'

They joined the crowds milling towards the bookmakers, but when Ginny caught sight of Tom and Jimmy Hood waiting in one of the queues she shrank behind Charlie, unwilling to be seen.

'Look, I'll go and wait in the carriage. There's somebody I don't want to see.'

He grinned. 'As you like. Sly puss. Do you think being seen with me might damage your reputation? You like the game, but you won't have the name. You're a girl after my own heart, Ginny.'

It was getting dark and a light snow had begun when he joined her.

'I haven't got your tin, Ginny, but you can hold your hand out for your gold.'

A pile of gold sovereigns chinked into her palm whilst she looked on, too overcome to speak.

'Of course,' he continued, 'you still owe me your ten and six stake money, and you mustn't forget that. One should always pay one's gambling debts. It's a point of honour.'

'How much did you win, Charlie?'

'A good deal more than you, my hinny, but that's between me and the bookmaker. Tuck your sovereigns in your pocket, where they'll be safe.'

Ginny obeyed, and kept her hand in her pocket around them to be doubly sure. Charlie softly brushed at the shoulders of her coat with his handkerchief, then lightly, gently, over the mounds of her breasts.

She grasped his wrist with her free hand to restrain him. He looked at her with an expression of injured innocence.

'You don't mind my brushing the snow off? I want to protect you from the damp. You might catch a chill. Sit close to me on the ride back and I'll keep you warm. There's going to be a frost tonight.'

'I'll be all right. I don't feel the cold.'

'But I do, very much. And I almost forgot, I have your Christmas box. See what I brought from London for my little hinny.'

She checked the impulse to tell him to stop calling her

hinny. The sovereigns cutting into her palm made it seem churlish to protest about such a little thing, so she watched in silence as he opened the box.

'They're jet. They'll match your eyes. It's very light, it won't hurt at all,' he said softly, running his finger lightly round her ear. 'Such pretty ears you've got, and they're already pierced. How convenient. Here, let me take these sleepers out, and put mine in. There's just enough light to see by, but I'll do it mainly by touch. I'm something of an expert.'

A hot, deep thrill in the pit of her belly surprised her as his hands caressed her ear. He handed her the sleeper and turned again to his task. She held still for him, and winced in pain as he jabbed at the lobe whilst trying to insert the long jet-and-gold drops.

'I'm sorry, little hinny, did I hurt you?' he murmured. 'Such a tiny little hole you have, but never mind, I will get it in. Ah, there. And very well it looks, I assure you.'

'That's enough of that, Mr Parkinson,' said Ginny, not really catching the innuendo, but beginning to feel out of her depth.

He drove them at a leisurely trot through the chill, clear air. As the road passed through a stretch of woodland a couple of miles distant from Annsdale Colliery, Charlie pulled the horses to a halt. The moon hung in a sky full of stars as he put an arm round Ginny's waist. His cheek almost touched hers as he pointed skyward.

'It's getting awfully cold, isn't it? See up there, the constellations? That cluster's called Orion, after the hunter in Greek mythology.'

'Is that right?' said Ginny. It was certainly getting cold, and had she been sitting next to almost anyone else she knew she would gladly have huddled in close for warmth. As it was, she removed Charlie's arm from her waist and moved away.

He gave a mocking sigh. 'Probably not, but it was a good excuse to get nearer. Oh, Ginny, after a day with you I have to go pay court to Manor Farm. It's like swapping a racer for a carthorse.'

'You can't swap what doesn't belong to you. And you don't have to go to Manor Farm if you've a mind not to.'

He shrugged. 'Perhaps I won't. You're the filly I fancy most. I think it very bad of you to have a hewer for a father instead of a landowner. What do you think of your winnings? Would you say I'd done well for you?'

'Aye, I would,' she said guardedly, her fingers tightening round the coins.

'Well, I don't ask anything for myself,' he seemed hesitant, 'but if you'd care to return the favour, I've a friend who has a deep respect for you. He sometimes stands to attention at the mere thought of you. Shall I introduce you?'

'If you like,' she said, completely taken in and consumed by curiosity.

He took her free hand and kissed it, then placed it on his trousers and closed her fingers around something very hard.

She was out of the carriage in a flash. 'I've changed my mind about your friend, Mr Parkinson. I don't want to know him after all.'

She walked briskly off the road and into the familiar woods. It was cold and hard underfoot, making clean walking, with the moon casting enough light to speed her on her way. She heard Charlie jump down after her.

'Come back, little hinny, there's no need for that. Your virtue's safe, honour bright.' He laughed, adding, 'My friend would never press himself. Perish the thought.'

She made no answer, but picked her way quickly along through trees and undergrowth. She heard him follow her for a few steps before giving up and returning to the carriage. He must have realized he had no hope of catching her, and little chance of finding his way through the woods without her. Besides, she thought, there were valuable horses and a carriage to think of, and valuable livestock at Manor Farm needing attention. She heard the click-click of his tongue as he urged the horses forward, and the rattle of hooves and wheels as he slowly drove on. After a few paces, he halted.

'Goodnight, little hinny. Dream of me, and I'll dream of you.' His voice was low and cajoling, but clear. There was a pause, then the horses trotted on at a brisker pace and were soon out of earshot.

Certain now that she couldn't be caught, the flutterings in her stomach bubbled up in her throat and escaped in laughter. She laughed until the tears ran down her cheeks, then, calmer, she wondered what she'd been afraid of. She'd outwitted Charlie. She was more than a match for him, any day.

'I know this much, though,' she promised herself as she

removed the jet earrings and slipped them into her pocket, 'next time he calls me hinny, I'll flatten him, money or no money.'

She stepped into the kitchen with cheeks flushed and eyes bright and a smile still playing at the corners of her mouth.

'By, you're looking bonny the day.' Her father was unexpectedly jovial considering his mood of the previous day, but there had never been any accounting for his tempers. He's either all sugar or all shite, Ginny thought, and if they were set fair for an all-sugar spell, so much the better. Her mother was diplomatically cheerful.

'Yes, a walk in the fresh air's put roses in your cheeks, but I thought they might have let you off a bit earlier today,' she said.

'Well, I've got a bit extra money instead, like,' said Ginny, hanging her coat up on the back of the door, with her fist still clenched around her sovereigns. 'That'll be more use, I suppose.'

'Aye, it will that,' agreed her father. 'Don't stop the workers, that's my motto. What with my bit of good luck at the cavilling, and Ginny's bit extra, you'll be all right with the housekeeping next for a while, Nance.' His use of his pet name for her mother was further proof of his good humour.

'She's always been a good little worker, Arthur.'

'Not so little now, but she's a chip off the old block all right. And we breed 'em bonny, Nance. You can't deny that.'

Ginny's eyebrows shot up in surprise at this unexpected approval. Although being compared to her father was no particular compliment, the atmosphere was so pleasant that for one mad instant she was tempted to blurt out her good luck and invite them to share it. The moment passed and she ran upstairs. Her fingers trembled as she groped in the dark for the matches on the chest of drawers. Where to hide the hoard? She struck a match and lit the candle, then with sensations of wickedness she had never felt before, she tied the sovereigns securely inside an old sock, her heart in her mouth until she had them hidden, hanging on a protruding nail under the washstand. Not the earrings though, the coins would scratch them. She'd shove them under her pillow for now.

Martin's words of defeat sprang into her mind: 'You can't beat the bookies, bonny lass.' She knew now that one person could. Charlie Parkinson could beat the bookies – he must have bankrupted one. Whatever else he was, he was the luckiest man she had ever heard of, and she'd shared his luck today. Her ten and six hadn't galloped away, but all this money had galloped towards her, thanks to Charlie. Remembering she still owed him the stake money, she took one sovereign out of the sock before secreting it away again. The last sovereign she hid in her pillowcase. She'd take that to Charlie the following day, and be out of his debt for good. Then she could start 1903 with money in her pocket, and no problems except what to spend it on.

Chapter Nine

The manager smiled at Ginny when she took in his breakfast, and asked her why she was so cheerful.

'We got a letter from John this morning, Mr Vine, so everything in the garden's lovely, as the song says.'

'Yes, I dare say that would cheer you up as well.'

Charlie had obviously told him about their excursion to the races. They must have a lovely time together gossiping like old fishwives, she thought, remembering another conversation of theirs that she'd overheard. She wondered whether the manager still had a fancy to let the uppishness out of her, but her face betrayed nothing.

'Aye, it's good to know he's safe, Mr Vine,' she said.

'Well, he was the best little putter in the north, and he took good care of the ponies. There's always a job here for him if he gets tired of life at sea.'

'I'll tell him that, Mr Vine. Thank you.'

His bleary eyes searched her face as she looked at him as if butter wouldn't melt in her mouth. If he wanted to ask her about the races he would have to come straight out with it, Ginny would give him no openings. She only hoped that Charlie hadn't told Helen as well. She would have a hard taskmistress for a few weeks to come if he had.

The manager obviously had more pressing matters to deal with. He wiped his mouth on his damask napkin, and was out of the door with hardly another word.

It was another hour before Helen and Charlie came down to breakfast. Ginny waited on them, feeling more and more certain that Helen knew nothing about the races. Charlie was his usual provoking self, pulling at her apron strings as she passed and making teasing comments at every opportunity. With Helen doing everything she could to deflect his attention from her, Ginny went about her work apparently oblivious to it all so that finally he gave up, and turned to his sister. It was then that their conversation became interesting.

'I think it's in the bag, Charlie,' said Helen, and Ginny was on the alert to know what.

He kept his voice low. 'I think so too, but you never know, Helen, a better prospect might turn up. I don't want to move too quickly.'

'There are no better prospects for you, and if you don't move, you might miss the chance. You're not the only suitor, you know.'

'But I flatter myself I'm the only suitor Clarice wants. That gives me a bit of breathing space. I'll mull it over for a while. Think of it – I'll be tied to her for the rest of my life once the step's taken. At least with Robert you've got somebody half intelligent, half presentable. Clarice doesn't pass the test either as a beauty or as a wit. I couldn't inflict her on my friends.'

'That's just it, Charlie, Clarice would be your passport to better friends, in a better class. Some of the people you knock about with are hardly fit to be seen. It's time you gave them up, Charlie. It was all fun while it lasted, but you need at least a toe in decent society.'

'I'll have you know I'm well acquainted with half of the nobility, and it's not so very long ago you were pleased enough to be among those friends of mine who're hardly fit to be seen,' he murmured with a sly smile, 'which is how you caught Robert. And you must admit, our London connections are a damned sight more entertaining.'

'But the ones who are worth cultivating will never accept you as an equal,' she frowned, and with a slight shake of her head and a quick glance in Ginny's direction, silenced him. Ginny lifted the tray of dirty dishes and headed for the kitchen. When she returned with the tea and toast, brother and sister were laughing and whispering together like a pair of conspirators.

'It's going to take a lot of thinking over, Helen. She's so attached to the mother, I shouldn't wonder if she'll want her in bed with us. It's a daunting prospect. I've always been in favour of long engagements, and I think a long one will be best in this case.' He winked appreciatively at Ginny as she set the tray down, and murmured, 'A very long engagement.'

Ginny left the room, determined to get that sovereign out of her coat pocket and be clear of her debt to Charlie once and for all, but when she felt in her pocket, it wasn't there. She searched frantically, both pockets and the whole lining of the coat, to no avail. She went over her actions before leaving the house, and concluded that she'd thought so hard about putting the sovereign in her pocket she'd imagined she'd actually done it. The letter from John had distracted her. The sovereign must still be in her pillowcase. She calmed herself with the thought that it would be safe enough there.

When she got home her worst fear was realized. Her sovereign lay on the tea table, awaiting explanation. Her father stood beside it, bathed, clean-shaven and in his best suit, gold watch chain decorating his waistcoat. His eyes travelled from the sovereign and fixed on Ginny.

'I earned it.'

'How?'

'I got it at the manager's house, for singing.'

'Singing? Who the hell gives anybody a guinea for singing?'

'Mr Parkinson.'

'Are you sure you didn't get it at the races?'

He must have heard it at the pit, probably from Tom or Jimmy Hood. She daren't risk the first-class hiding that was sure to follow being caught in a lie, so she admitted, 'Well, I did have a bit of a win at the races, as well as what I got for singing.'

'While me and your mother thought you were at work,' he said, sending her reeling with a blow to the left side of her head, 'you were showing us up having fun and games with that bloody whoremaster.'

'Arthur! Not in front of the children,' her mother protested. He ignored her, talking only to Ginny.

'Well, you go and find the rest of that bit of a win you had at the races and fetch it to me. It's going back where it came from before this day's out, lady. I'll make you sing before I've finished with you.'

Half dazed by the blow, Ginny staggered upstairs, closely followed by her father. She groped her way towards the washstand, then under it to unhook her hoard. With her back to her father, she was not too stupefied to extract a couple of coins before handing him the precious sock. He took it roughly from her and went downstairs, into the light. Ginny followed, pushing the salvaged money into her corset as she went. Back in the kitchen, he emptied the contents of the sock on to the table.

The sight of the little pile of gleaming gold in the middle of the white tablecloth made eyes pop and jaws drop.

'My God,' breathed Emma, 'that lot could make me a teacher a dozen times over.'

'Arthur, we could pay every debt we owe and keep ourselves comfortable for a year,' said their mother.

Sally took a coin and looked reverently at the king's profile. 'Doesn't it look nice? See how it shines.'

'It's not going to make you a teacher, and it's not going to pay any debts of mine,' said their father, 'and you, don't tell me you won all that on the horses. So what else have you been doing for Mr Parkinson?'

Her cheeks burned at the affront. 'Nothing,' she said,

anger overcoming fear. 'I haven't been up to anything with him or anybody else. That money belongs to me. I earned the first sovereign, and I won all the rest at the races. I backed what he told me to back, and they all won. He's lucky, that's all. Really lucky. He's the luckiest man I've ever known.'

'Aye, that bugger makes his own luck, but his luck'll run out the day he tampers with anybody belonging to me.'

'If it's Ginny's money, she should keep it,' said Emma, two bright spots of red in her cheeks as she contradicted her father for the first time in her life. 'Nobody else has any right to it.'

'You've certainly no right to it, and you won't be getting any of it either, Miss Schoolteacher. You've a right to a bit back out of your earnings at the Cock, and that's all, so settle your mind to it. And you,' he turned again to Ginny, 'don't bother to take your coat off. Get your backside out of that door. We're going to have a walk up to the manager's house, to give your fancy man his money back.'

Ginny stood her ground, chin tilted in defiance.

'Open that door, Mary Ann,' her father commanded. He took Ginny by the shoulders and turned her round bodily. A moment later his boot made contact with the small of her back, propelling her through the door and making her feel as if she'd been kicked by a mule.

Almost weeping with anger and humiliation, she stumbled along, with an occasional powerful shove from him to keep her moving. He finally strode up to the manager's front door and banged hard enough to knock the house down. When the manager opened the door, her mortification was complete.

'I've something to say to your brother-in-law, Mr Vine. I want to see him, man to man, like.'

Without a word, the manager retreated into the house. After what seemed like an eternity Charlie appeared in the doorway. Ginny heard his sister call, 'What's the matter, Charlie? What is it?'

'Nothing that concerns you, Helen.' He stepped out of the house and shut the door.

'Well?' His tone was curt, dismissive, but Ginny saw naked fear on his face when her father took hold of him by the lapels and lifted him off his feet. With his eyes about three inches from Charlie's he spoke softly, but his words were clear in the stillness of the night.

'I don't know how you carry on in London, and I don't ask, but I've heard it's a loose sort of place, full of bawdy houses and bawdy women, where everything's free and easy. That's London, but this is Annsdale. There's something you ought to know about Annsdale, and it's this: there's nothing free and easy here. The last feller that tampered with a lass he'd no intention of marrying got a good going over with a couple of pickaxe handles, and he's never been the same since. He's got a broken nose and a few teeth missing, and he's scared to go out, like. That's Annsdale. I don't want that to happen to you, so I'll tell you this: the best thing you can do while you're here is keep yourself to yourself.' He released Charlie and reached into his pocket. 'Now this is yours. It's not hers and she doesn't want it.' He turned to Ginny for confirmation. 'You don't want it, do you?'

After a moment or two she murmured a sullen, 'No.'

'Well, there yer are then, you'd better hev it back,' said her father, taking Charlie's soft hand and cramming the money into it, then holding it for a moment or two between his own calloused, sinewy ones with a grip like a vice. Charlie winced.

'So now she owes you nothing, does she?'

'No.' Charlie's voice was tremulous; the habitual mocking smile was wiped off his lips, the look of amusement in his eyes displaced by one of stark fear. He seemed completely unnerved, and Ginny looked on him with something approaching contempt. He should have stood up to her father, upheld her claim to keep the money that he had said was hers. He didn't have to live with her father. He had all the advantages over her father that money and influence could give, and yet he cowered before him. Even sixteen-year-old Jimmy Hood who had to labour down the pit for him and the other hewers had put up a better show.

'So that's it. You've got three choices. You can leave her alone, or I'll be your father-in-law, or – well, better not talk about the last choice.'

They turned and left, Ginny walking swiftly along in front, needing no encouragement to move on the return journey.

'That bugger has no mence,' her father called after her with a derisory laugh, 'he wants his mammy with him. What any lass can see in that, I don't know, it's not a man.

Don't you bring any carroty-haired chips off that block to my door. I'll drop 'em in a bucket if you do.'

She lay awake for hours that night. She'd started the day rich, happy and full of hope, and ended it poor and disillusioned, with the knowledge of John's safety her only consolation; and he'd done nothing more exciting than look at miles of ocean. Charlie, who she had thought so full of self-command and charm yesterday, today had revealed himself less of a man than wiry little Jimmy Hood. Charlie was lucky, certainly, but what else? Her father might come home filthy and spit in the fire, but at least he was a man. He had made it clear that he despised Charlie, and the more she thought of it, the more she saw Charlie through her father's eyes.

The following day at the manager's house, Charlie was nowhere to be seen, but the hint of mocking amusement usually evident on his features seemed to have transferred itself to the manager's face. He gave Ginny a sly satisfied smile before he left for work. Helen Vine's manner towards her was colder and more distant than ever. At eleven o'clock she ordered the cook to take Charlie's breakfast up to his room.

'And you, Ginny, I'll have a private word with you in the study.'

Ginny followed her into the manager's book-lined, mahogany-and-plush-furnished retreat where Helen turned on her angrily.

'You've caused a good deal of trouble here, and you

probably hope to cause more. Step out of your class and set your cap at my brother? How dare you? You think yourself so indispensable that you can't be sacked, but I'll show you. I'll send to Sweden for a living-in girl if there's any more of it, and you'll be finished here and for miles around. So, when you've scrubbed the steps and cleaned out the bins, you can walk down to the station and get a first-class ticket for the London train tomorrow morning. Mr Parkinson will be going away for a while.'

Chapter Ten

Ginny saw her mother cower back and raise her arms, defending herself from the hammer blows he began to land on her head and shoulders. He started dancing round her, looking for gaps in her defence and jabbing and punching hard when any appeared.

'You're no match for me, missus. You'll never make a champion,' he jeered. 'Go on, have a go. See if you can land a one, then.'

Eyes full of fear, her mother begged, 'Leave me alone, Arthur. Leave me alone.' She crumpled on to the floor and crouched there, shoulders hunched, protecting her face with her hands.

Her father's pit boots stood on a newspaper on the kitchen table, greased and ready for his shift, the bait tin and filled water bottle beside them. For a moment they were eclipsed by the haze of red that swam before Ginny's eyes. She snatched up the bottle and hurled it at his head with all her strength.

'Leave her alone, you bad old bugger!'

He reeled back as it hit him full in the eye. Then he turned towards Ginny, for a long moment with blank incomprehension on his face. She lifted one of his boots and sent it after the bottle with all the force she could muster. It caught him on the mouth.

'When I catch hold of you, I'll kill you,' he roared.

'Aye, why, you'll have to catch us first,' she shouted, retreating hastily into the front room and out of the door. She slammed it shut and was down the path and out of the gate before it opened again. Seeing him appear in the doorway stuffing his unbuttoned shirt into his trousers before pulling his braces up, she stooped to fill her apron with a few large stones before chasing on, loose black hair flying behind her. Like an enraged bull he charged after her in stockinged feet. Bracing himself with a hand on the gatepost he vaulted it cleanly and might have caught her, but the stony road made him step more gingerly while Ginny flew on until she had put half the length of the street between them. Enid Jackson looked up from where she knelt donkey stoning her doorstep and heaved herself to her feet.

'You rotten old bugger!' Ginny let fly with a stone that found its mark on her father's forehead.

Bolder women came to their doors, openly curious to see what the commotion was. The more timid peeped through windows.

'That's right, pelt the bugger, Ginny!' shouted one impudent wife, often treated to a hiding herself and hugely enjoying seeing the tables turned.

'Aye, give him what for, lass,' another encouraged, starting to laugh as Ginny flew on, turning now and then to lob another stone at her father, who, half-dressed and shoeless, began to hobble painfully and to slow, before stopping altogether.

'Wait 'til I get hold of you – I'll bloody murder you!' he shouted after her.

Ginny, now laughing and exhilarated and much heartened by the cheering, laughing women, threw another couple of stones from her safe distance. They whistled past his ears, the narrowest of misses.

'You've had your bit fun – and you've given 'em all something to laugh about, but you'll have to come home sometime, and then I'll give *you* something to laugh at. You'll know about it then. I'll make you wish you'd never been born,' he vowed, and turned for home, jeered at and laughed to scorn by some of the women. As he put his hand on the gatepost, he was seized by a paroxysm of coughing which bent him double, and he leaned on the gate to splutter and spit, before opening it and striding determinedly down the garden path without another glance in Ginny's direction.

She watched Mam Smith down the street, then set the two flat irons on the trivets to heat.

'Your dad hit your mammy, didn't he, Ginny?'

She looked down at Martin's young son, taken aback. 'Well aye, he did, Philip.'

'He'th not going to hit Gran, ith he?'

'No, course he's not.'

'He'th going to hit you, though, ithn't he?'

'That he's not. Not if I can help it. See that little nightshirt of yours lying on top of the basket, Philip?

Pass it here and I'll get the creases out for you. Make you look a bonny lad when you're scrubbed and ready for bed.'

He handed her the shirt and she looked into a pair of thoughtful blue eyes, wondering at his having taken so much in while seeming to notice nothing.

'Are you going to thtop here, Ginny?'

She flattened the nightshirt carefully, before reaching for the iron. 'I don't know what I'm going to do, Philip,' she answered slowly. 'I really don't know.'

She paused, deep in thought for a moment or two, then tore into the ironing, looking up now and then to see Philip migrating between the clippy mat, where he was playing with his train, and the front window, where he watched for his grandma.

'She'th a long time, Ginny.'

He no sooner had the words out than Mam Smith burst through the front door, exclaiming with relief at reaching her own safe home.

'My God, Ginny, I feel just like Daniel must have done when he got out of the lion's den – surprised to be in one piece.' She sat down suddenly without pausing to take her coat off.

Ginny reached for the old caddy, ornamented with a picture of a youthful Queen Victoria, and put the leaves in the warmed teapot before drenching them with scalding water and stirring vigorously to speed up the infusion. She poured two cups and handed one to Mam Smith, whose hand shook as she took it. Philip sat on the clippy mat between them, concentrating on his toy, running it slowly backwards and forwards over the bright shredded rags.

'"Lucky for her I've half the pit in my lungs and no bloody shoes on, or she wouldn't see tomorrow morning," is what he said to Enid before he went in the house. We went upstairs to watch for him through her back bedroom window, and we saw your mam give him a kiss before he set off to work.

'When he was well out of the way, I went into your mam's. 'What are you thinking about, Mary Ann, kissing a man who's done that to your face?' I said. 'You know what it is,' she says, 'settle your differences before they go down. They sometimes don't come back again and I wouldn't want it on my conscience.' I knew what she meant, but if you saw the mess he's made of her face!

'She didn't know whether to laugh or cry. She was crying over the good hiding, and the trouble you've got coming, but then a smile would keep breaking out at the thought of him coming in coughing and wheezing after letting a slip of a lass get the best of him, and all the women laughing. It's the first time I've ever heard her say a word against him,' Mam Smith observed, pausing to take a long drink.

'Aye, and it's the first time I've heard tell of it,' said Ginny, eyebrows raised in surprise at her mother's disloyalty.

'Well, we were sitting in the kitchen, and I heard something stir in the front room so your mam opened the door and I got the fright of my life when I saw your father standing there listening. He just smiled at me and said,

"Well, Mam, and have you seen aught of our Ginny, like?" I said no before I'd time to think. He said, "Well, she's somewhere, isn't she, and she's not at work while Mrs Vine's in London. So who's looking after Philip?" I said he was asleep in his cot and I'd just popped round to your mam's to ask for the lend of a couple of eggs. He said, "It's funny, but you've never done that before. Anyway, when you do see her, tell her to get on home. She's wanted."'

She shuddered. 'It was his voice that made my hair stand on end. Smooth as silk. He cracked on he'd forgotten his bait, and had to come back for it, though why he should come round the front with all his pit togs on when he'd gone out the back, I don't know. He'd left it by the kitchen door, so he picked it up and set off again by the back.'

'I know him like the back of my hand. That's why I didn't want to go back straight away. He'd be hoping to find me there, sly old sod. He'll have to be a lot craftier than that to take me in,' said Ginny.

'Well, I couldn't sit comfortable after he'd gone for fear he'd come back and hear us whispering about him. I felt sorry for your mam, but I came away. She wants the doctor to that face, but she wouldn't go and see him. And he intends doing worse to you if he gets the chance.'

Ginny had a sudden thought. 'Do you remember that time you came to see our Emma when she was three, when she was unconscious, and you told them to send for the doctor?'

'I'll never forget it, lass, to my dying day. I never

believed that was your doing. There were red marks on her wrists when I saw her and they came out the day after into big black bruises, just as if somebody had taken hold of her by the wrists and thrown her. It could only have been him, but you'd never have got him to admit to it.'

'I saw him do it. She wouldn't stop crying, so he picked her up by the wrists and threw her across the yard. She hit the coalhouse and just fell into a heap, with blood coming down her nose. You're the first person I've ever told. He warned me, and with everybody blaming me I really began to believe I had done it in the end.'

'Well, your mam wouldn't believe he'd done it. She didn't want to believe it, and what could she have done if she had? Three bairns and nobody to put the bread in their mouths but him. So with him insisting it was you and her believing him, what could anybody else do?'

The little boy laughed in delight as his sparkling blue eyes met a grime-encircled matching pair. Martin tossed him a couple of inches into the air and caught him in strong, coal-black hands.

'Not at work today, Ginny?' he asked, swinging Philip safely back on to his feet.

'No. Mrs Vine told us to stay away until she gets back from London next week. She reckons the cook will be there for the manager's meals, and what else there is to do will keep until she gets back.'

'You're going to lose a week's wages then?'

'I hope not. She told me to stay away – I didn't ask.'

'You'll be doing well if that comes off, a week's wages

for no work. I wish her husband would do the same for us.'

'Ginny'th going to thtop here now, Daddy,' Philip volunteered.

Martin looked enquiringly at Ginny, then at his mother-in-law. 'Is she? Nobody told me.'

'That's because we haven't had the chance, so nothing's decided yet. Listen to what the lass has to say, then make your own mind up.'

'I'm going to get a living-in job somewhere. There's always jobs for housemaids in London, or so I've been told.'

'Hold on,' said Martin, taking off his jacket and hanging it on the back door. 'Start a bit further back. There must be something I've missed. Start at the beginning.'

He crossed to the kitchen sink, to scrub his hands with yellow soap while Ginny told him the whole story. He listened without comment, and then caught hold of a rough towel to rub his hands dry.

'I'm starving, Mam. I needn't ask what's for dinner. I could smell it halfway down the street.'

Mam Smith opened the oven door and lifted the stew-pot lid, releasing a powerful mouth-watering aroma of oxtail and onion. She prodded the meat with a knife.

'Get your feet under the table, bonny lass. If I know my mother-in-law, she's made enough to feed a regiment, and she'll be offended if you don't eat your share.'

'I'm not hungry,' said Ginny, fearful of depriving them of an adequate meal.

'There's plenty for everybody, never bother,' Mam Smith assured her, ladling steaming food on to sizzling plates. 'Pull a chair up and get it down you.'

'Your mother's had another hammering then?' Martin said, when the meal was almost over.

'Aye, and this poor lass is going to be next,' Mam Smith shuddered.

They finished eating in silence, then Martin opened the kitchen door and lifted the galvanized bath off its hook on the outside wall.

'Well, this is a bit awkward, like, but I'll have to ask our new lodger to go into the front room and hide her head under the covers 'til I get my pit clothes off and get a bath,' said Martin.

'Oh, don't bother, Martin. I've seen our John in the bath before today,' she assured him.

'Aye, well, you haven't seen me in the bath, and you're not going to. Find her something to do in there, Mam, and shut the door.'

Seeing that protest would be useless, Ginny retired to the front room with a couple of pairs of socks to darn. Half an hour later Martin looked a different person, every trace of lamp oil and coal dust scrubbed from his fair hair and pale skin. She was shocked at the sight of Mam Smith sitting comfortably in the armchair, while he scooped the bathwater into an enamel pail and emptied it down the sink. That was a woman's job, and Ginny was quick to get the fact established.

'I'll do that, Martin.'

He brushed aside her offers of help and carried the bath

outside to empty the last dregs down the drain and hang the bath on its hook outside the door. Ginny's mother followed him in.

'My God!' exclaimed Ginny at the sight of the swollen, purple face.

'I know.' Her mother was hardly able to move her mouth. 'I think he's broken my cheekbone. It's so painful, and I can feel a sort of grating whenever I move it.'

'That bugger wants a horsewhipping, but don't tell him I said so,' said Mam Smith.

'I can't stay. The bairns'll be home soon. But I think he'll kill Ginny when he gets his hands on her. I don't want to bring you any trouble, but will you keep her here for a few days, leave a bit of time for his temper to cool?'

'I might cool it for him if I do come back. He might be the one that ends up stone cold. If I don't get away from here I might do for him in the end,' said Ginny, the light of battle in her eyes, 'so I think I'd better do what John did, and get a job somewhere else.'

Her mother groaned, looking really ill. 'Come on, Martin,' Mam Smith said, in alarm, 'let's get her back home. You'd better go and get the doctor and I'll put her to bed and see to the bairns 'til he gets back from the pit. He won't touch me, and if he does, I'll get him locked up.'

Chapter Eleven

It was heaven. No moods, no having to be careful what she said, no hushing Philip, or quieting their own talk when Martin was reading a paper or a book borrowed from the reading room, or dozing in the chair. It was a house of gentle mourning and mutual comfort, a shrine to the best wife, daughter and mother that ever lived, whose shoelaces few others were fit to tie. In spite of the pall of tranquil gloom, the atmosphere was one Ginny could breathe and blossom in, and express her own ideas without fear of criticism or ridicule, or being 'taken down a peg or two'. The three adults discussed the idea of a living-in job seriously together.

'I've heard of none round here, not for lasses anyway,' said Martin. 'I think there's a groom wanted up at Nobs Hall, but that's no use to you.'

'Lend me a pair of trousers. I'll chop my hair off, and crack on I'm a lad.'

He scanned her up and down, his gaze frank and open and resting for a moment or two on her swelling hips and burgeoning breasts. For a fleeting moment an ironical smile lifted the droop at the corners of his mouth. Ginny's pulse quickened. She would have given a lot to keep that smile on his lips, that light of laughter in his eyes as he looked at her.

'Aye, and you'll get away with it – if they're all blind,' he said, his face again assuming its habitual melancholy expression.

'I'd forgotten what a nice smile you've got, Martin. You used to laugh at me sometimes when I was a bairn.'

'You were enough to make a cat laugh, the pranks you got up to sometimes.'

She sighed. 'Well, if there's no jobs round here, maybe there's jobs further afield.'

He frowned. 'You're not educated enough to be a governess, and you haven't got the education or the temperament to be a nurse. There are below-stairs jobs in great houses that get you a life of drudgery and rob you of the chance of a home of your own. And you might end up a sight worse off than if you'd stayed at home.'

'Aye, it's a poor look-out for a young lass on her own. Some are just lambs to the slaughter, especially if they're good-looking,' said Mam Smith.

'Well, I can't live off you, and me father's not going to let this go on much longer without dragging me back by the hair. You see if he doesn't. I think I'll run off and join a circus, be a lion tamer. I'm qualified for that, after living with him.'

'Stay here for now, where you're safe and comfortable. He'll see sense in the end,' said Martin.

Ginny caught a look of apprehension in Mam Smith's

eyes, and returned another. Neither had much hope of that.

To see a grown man take an occasional hand with the washing-up, or take a child to bed and read him a story was something Ginny marvelled at, not that she gave Martin much chance to make himself busy with 'women's jobs'. Mam Smith's house had been clean when she arrived but was pristine whilst she stayed. Apprehension about what her father might do and how her life might have to change to escape him filled her so full of nervous energy that she couldn't keep still. The expected assault came almost as a relief.

'My God, what's that?' Mam Smith, her grey hair in Saturday-night curl papers, sat bolt upright in bed. Ginny jumped out and twitched the bedroom curtain aside. Her father looked up, caught sight of her at the window and roared at the top of his lungs, 'Come out, you. I want you back home where you ought to be, helping your mother. This lot's gone on long enough. Come out here, you clever little bugger, and I'll show you how bloody clever you are. Come out, afore I come in and fetch you.' He banged and rattled the door. Face white and heart thumping, Ginny let the curtain drop.

'Hey, you, open this door before I boot it in. Keeping a man's daughter away from her own home. Open up!'

'Don't let him in, Martin,' Ginny shrieked, flying from the bedroom in her nightgown. 'If you open the door somebody'll get murdered!' She got downstairs and wedged her foot against the front door just in time to prevent Martin from opening it.

'I'll have to face him sometime, Ginny.'

'Another day. The mood he's in now, he'll kill you. I've seen him like this before and he'll have to take it out on somebody.'

'You'd rather it was your mother or the bairns then?' asked Martin, pulling his trousers on. 'Never bother, he's not going to get in the house. I'll go out by the back and you can bolt the door after me.'

Martin was a strapping young hewer with muscles like iron, but gentle as a nursemaid and completely lacking her father's killer instinct. Still, he was fitter to stand his punishments than a downtrodden woman still recovering from the last beating.

She'd hardly slid the bolt home when she heard the sound of splintering glass and a scream from Mam Smith followed by her father's shouting. She got to the broken front window and looked out on a clear moonlit night. Martin was trying to reason with her father, keeping at arm's length from him. Her father would have none of it and finally they began trading punch for punch. Philip appeared at the bottom of the stairs, eyes wide and round.

'Back to bed, hinny,' said Mam Smith, turning him round and trying to push him back up the stairs. 'Don't come in here, you'll get your feet cut.'

'I want to thee what'th happening,' the child insisted.

'Get back up to bed, before you feel the back of my hand.' Fear and anger gave an unaccustomed sharp edge to Mam Smith's voice. Philip looked at her as if she had struck him and disappeared up the stairs without another word.

'Come by, Ginny. Let me get that lot swept up, before somebody gets cut on it.'

'Wait a bit,' said Ginny, heart in her mouth as she watched the two men exchange punches until her father lost patience with the pantomime. He closed in, took hold of a good handful of hair and in one sudden movement pulled Martin's head down and jerked his own knee up into violent contact with his face. Martin sank to the ground with a groan.

Her father bent over him and laughed. 'There you are. That's what you get for interfering in my family, and good enough for you. Think yourself lucky I'm too much of a sportsman to put the boot in while you're down or you'd get your bloody head kicked in. Send that lass of mine home tomorrow, or there's plenty more where that came from.' He looked towards the shattered window where the women stood watching, hands pressed against their mouths and shouted, 'You've caused some trouble for your kind friends tonight, so if you don't want to cause any more, you'd better get your backside home by tomorrow, and don't you forget it.' He turned and swaggered away down the road.

They ran out of the house towards the motionless figure on the ground, rolled him on to his back, and peered anxiously into his face.

'Well, thank God he's breathing,' said Mam Smith.

'Let's get him into the house,' said Ginny, heaving him to his feet. 'That's it, get his arm over your shoulder.'

Half walking and half carried, Martin finally lay on the bed in the front room. His nose and upper lip were bruised and bleeding.

'You bugger,' he said, speech slurred, 'I've heard tell o' people seeing stars, but I really did.'

'That's the first time I've heard you swear,' said Ginny.

'I think the bugger's broken my nose, and my teeth feel loose.' He rolled off the bed and staggered into the kitchen where he knelt on the floor and vomited into a pail. When the retching stopped, he stood by the sink to wash his face and rinse his mouth. 'I'll have to get to bed. I'd better lie down before I fall down.'

They helped him back to bed. He closed his eyes and lay apparently oblivious of everything around him, his face drained of colour save that caused by his injury.

'I hope he'll be all right,' Ginny whispered.

'Aye, and so do I,' said Mam Smith, in a tone which seemed to say, 'And whose fault will it be if he's not?'

'Shall I sit with you?'

Mam Smith sighed, 'No, you go up to bed and get to sleep. You can look after the bairn tomorrow while I sleep. I hope his dad'll be all right by morning.'

Upstairs, Philip was awake. 'What happened to my daddy?' he demanded.

'He'll be all right.' She got into bed beside him. An hour later she looked at him, expecting him to be asleep, but his eyes were still wide open, staring at the ceiling. She shivered and turned over. Martin, Mam Smith's one surviving substitute son, Philip's only parent, looked half dead. There'd be no peace in this house as long as she was in it. It wasn't fair to cause any more trouble for them. She couldn't stay, but how she dreaded to go back home.

'I'll brazen it out. I'll warn him I'll get the bobby on him if he touches me. He's had more than one night in the lock-up and he can go again if he starts.' The brave words belied her feelings. Her heart was pounding fit to burst her chest at the mere thought of confronting her father.

'I don't envy you, lass,' said Mam Smith, who looked weary after a night spent watching. 'I'd be terrified myself.' She paused, but didn't add the words Ginny hoped for – 'Don't go.'

Ginny laughed, to mask a pang of disappointment. 'You don't show any weakness to Arthur Wilde.'

'I'll remember that in future,' said Martin from his chair, face swollen and mottled purple and blue. 'But you're no match for him, so you stay here. He'll not catch me off guard like that again. I had a handicap last night – I didn't really want a fight. Next time I will, so it'll be more of an even contest, like.'

She knew he really meant it. Swamped by relief and elation she opened her mouth to thank him, but Philip, face twisted and near to tears, ran and hugged his father's knees. 'Don't have any more fights, Daddy.'

The sight of them together brought hope crashing to the floor. She paused and took one of Martin's calloused hands in hers, looking at the raw knuckles.

'If he comes again today it'll be no even contest with you in this state. So there's going to be nothing to fight about. I'm going to chapel this morning. That's the one place I can be sure of not bumping into him, and the minister knows a few well-off people. He might know of a job for me somewhere.'

He gave her hand a squeeze. 'You go to chapel, then mind you come back where you'll be safe.'

Her father straightened himself up from his planting and looked her slowly up and down as she walked through the gate, heart thumping, but head erect and back straight.

'By God, Lady Muck's got naught on you. You think yourself no cat shit. Has he come round yet?'

She looked him full in the face but passed on into the house without giving him a reply. Up in the bedroom, she put everything she owned into a bag, and stowed it under the bed.

Back downstairs; her mother was serving the dinner. They ate in the familiar wary silence until her father said, 'Well, I've done enough Sabbath breaking working in the garden for one Sunday, so you're safe for the time being.'

'So when can I expect the reckoning, like?' The rest of the family looked intently at their plates.

Her father eyed her as a cat might look at a mouse it had trapped to sport with later. 'Maybe tomorrow, or maybe the day after, or next week. It'll come soon enough for you, never fear.'

'And what might it entail?'

He gave her a malevolent stare, then suddenly lifted the end of the table and crashed it to the floor, clattering pots and cutlery and making everybody flinch except Ginny, who, expecting the outburst, remained outwardly unperturbed.

'I'd like to cripple you,' he said, leaning threateningly towards her, 'except it would spoil you for work. So I'll have to be satisfied with giving you a first-class belting.'

The following day, she was out with her bag while he was still in bed. She called by Mam Smith's with an address written on a piece of paper. For a moment she thought of raising her hand to knock, to ask Martin to help her, to take her in again, to protect her from her father and from her fear of the unknown she was walking into. The sight of the shattered window and the certain knowledge that she could bring him nothing but trouble checked the impulse. She scribbled a note under the address.

'This is where I'll be, if anybody wants me. I've got a job in London and I'm going. Tell Mam I'm sorry but it's for the best. I'll write as soon as I get the chance and send her some money. Tell my father I'm sorry to disappoint him. I think he was looking forward to having a bit of fun.'

She pushed it through the door before walking on to the station in a light rain, which had become a deluge by the time she arrived on the platform. Jumpy as a cat, she looked fearfully round now and then, half expecting to see her father at the back of her. A sigh of relief escaped her when the train drew in, but before the doors had opened and the few passengers alighted, she heard the sound of a man's boots rattling on the paving stones. Panic seized her and she leapt aboard, ignoring protests from the disembarking passengers.

'Ginny, wait, wait.'

The voice was not her father's. She hung out of the carriage window after all the disgruntled passengers were off, and saw Martin, hair dripping, with something in his hands.

'I saw your note. I'm glad I'm not too late. Take these. You'd better have them. Maria wanted you to.'

'I know, but you said nobody was going to wear them but her. You were going to take her to the races in them.'

'I meant it too, but I couldn't make it true. It's taken me these three months to realize that. She's past wearing them or anything else, so they'd better do you some good. You haven't got much luggage, bonny lass. The minister put you on to a job then, did he?' Martin asked, the rain running down his face.

'I've got an address, and a shilling or two to put me on. There are hundreds of jobs for housemaids in big London houses, and if I can work here for what Mrs Vine pays, I can just as well work there for more.'

He grimaced. 'From what I've heard about London, it's a rum place Ginny. I wish you wouldn't go. You're only a bairn. You're not old enough to be let out on your own.'

The train began to pull out of the station. She looked him full in his bruised and blackened face, and felt some comfort at the thought that whatever happened, she couldn't be the cause of any more injury to him. 'I'll have to grow up quick, then. Martin, you're drenched. Get away home before you get your death.'

'Oh, Ginny, if only . . .' he said, and she heard no more. She lost sight of him as the train sped round a curve in the track, and felt as though her entrails had been wrenched out.

Chapter Twelve

Ginny sat apart at a small table in a large room full of other small tables, finishing tea and toast alone in a crowd of people whose customs and manners were alien to her. People who went to bed late, and got up in the afternoon, whose accents and patterns of speech she could hardly understand, and who soon gave up trying to understand hers. She wrote three letters in the first three days to tell the people at home she was well and was sure to find a job soon, but the more she thought of home the more homesick she felt. She looked round forlornly at parties of music hall artistes, all concerned only with their own business, and thought she would die of loneliness.

It was Sunday morning in the theatrical digs Mr Vine had directed her to a couple of weeks previously. Most of the other lodgers had finished breakfast and their trunks were waiting in the hallway. Through the open door she could see the landlady, a sharp little woman with gold-rimmed spectacles balanced on a beaky nose, standing at a tiny desk, making sure all settled their accounts before they left. Ginny saw one or two of them nudge each other when they read the bill.

'A shilling for the cruet, missus? That's a bit steep, ain't it?' asked one jocular chap.

The landlady gave him a sour look over the top of her spectacles. 'I have to make a little profit, so a shilling if you please.'

'There's more than a little profit on that, missus.'

The landlady's expression soured further. 'That's the charge, and your bags don't leave this hall until your bill's paid.'

He shrugged. 'Next time I'll find different digs.'

The landlady gave him a sarcastic smile. 'You won't find any as good so convenient for the theatre, but you'll always be welcome back here, dear, as long as you're a good payer.'

There was a great bustle in the hallway as trunks were carried out and loaded on to cabs bound for the station. She heard people shouting 'cheerio' and 'see you at the Tivoli', a lot of opening and slamming of doors and the rattle of cab wheels. After the door slammed for the last time, the house was as silent as the grave.

The landlady turned to Ginny. 'Well, you only booked for two weeks, dear, you still 'ant got a job and your young man 'ant turned up either.' The beady eyes bored through her.

'He'll be here, never fear. I've got your money for this week and I'll book in for next,' said Ginny, assuming an air of confidence she was far from feeling. She hadn't banked on needing to stay for more than two weeks at the most.

'Better bring it now, dear, while I check to see whether I've got room for you next week.'

Ginny went up to her room, perturbed to think that there might be any question about being able to book in for the following week. She put on her hat and coat and counted the money left in her purse. Her heart sank. Still, no good moping. If Charlie wasn't going to turn up, she'd have to go out and find a job for herself. She looked at her new shoes and wondered what Maria would have thought to see them beat the pavements of London for hours on end. She paid the landlady on the way out, and received a curt nod. 'That's right, miss. And I'm pleased to say I can fit you in for next week. You're very lucky. It's not often I can oblige at such short notice.'

'I don't suppose you'd know where I could get a job as a housemaid?' she asked as the landlady slammed her cashbox shut and turned away.

'I'm not an employment agency, dear. Go to one of them.' She glanced again at Ginny as she turned to leave, her expression softening slightly. 'Be careful what sort you choose. They're not all reputable. You might do as well applying directly to the housekeepers as long as you can furnish good references. All the better-class districts like Hanover Square, or Hampstead, or Kensington prefer country girls to London ones.'

Ginny left the house relieved that she at least had a roof over her head for the following week, and just enough money to pay the account. She walked down Whitechapel Road, past itinerants and street traders, up Leadenhall Street and along Cornhill, gazing at banks, counting houses, jewellers and silversmiths either side; all imposing, ornate stone buildings carved with shields, cherubs and garlands. Then past famous Threadneedle Street and Lombard Street and along Watling Street to see a wedding party emerging from St Paul's – domed, massive and white under a dull white sky. Middle-aged women in enormous hats and corsages were being helped into carriages by men in Scottish kilts. She waited a while to see the bride and groom, and filled the time by taking a stub of pencil and a scrap of paper from her pocket and scribbling a list of the streets she'd passed. London looked so enormous, she'd better not count on memory to find her way back. No bride or groom came out, so she walked on with a moist breeze in her face towards a group of statues; bare-breasted women with tridents and things, not very decent in front of a Christian church, or anywhere else for that matter.

Down Ludgate Hill and more vast, carved stone buildings, some with ironwork balcony rails. She walked up a side street to look at the Old Bailey and the golden statue of Justice with her sword and scales and spiky crown standing atop the white dome. Up the hill to Fleet Street, and past Sergeants Inn Chambers, and another blindfolded justice with sword and scales, and a figure of Britannia that was on the pennies. More banks and a church, then a thin medieval building, the Old Cock Tavern, nothing like the Cock Inn at home. Then she passed a sort of fairy-tale castle, all spires and turrets and arches and leaded windows. She stopped to ask what it was and was told the Royal Courts of Justice, and thought there must be more than enough wrongdoing in London, to need so many massive courts.

Ravenous, she went into St Clements to sit down for two minutes and again note down the streets, wondering if the church were the very one that said oranges and lemons. Then along the Strand with more vast buidings and elaborate façades. At last she came upon Trafalgar Square to see the fountain and the statue of Nelson on his column guarded by four black lions, and carvings of the Battle of Trafalgar on the base. And a couple of pigeons to fill the hole in his stomach would be all right, if he could catch 'em.

More bloody columns and clocks and fancy façades, and she was fed up with it all, wondering when she would get to the sort of houses that needed servants, or servants of her sort, to be exact. Along Pall Mall and past Waterloo Place, and more columns with great British heroes on top, only now she didn't stop to look.

On, on, endlessly on, and she could imagine nothing worse than living here, with miles of streets and buildings, and not a green field in sight. Her village might consist of long terraces of blackened hovels with a skyline dominated by slag heaps and headgear, but just a ten-minute walk from home would take her into green countryside. She walked by the Queen's Chapel and past a palace flanked by a wall that must have been ten feet high, and into St James's Park.

Her mood lifted at the sight of a few trees at last, and a bit of a lake. The sound of birdsong and the quacking of the ducks cheered her. The day had brightened and she looked up to see puffy white clouds in a blue sky. She walked down the Mall towards Bukcingham Palace, smiling at the sight of people in their carriages trotting up and down. More pillars and statues, and massive wrought-iron gates everywhere, but nothing looking the least bit tarnished or in need of her skills.

She knocked on a couple of doors of the king's neighbours down Buckingham Palace Road but received curt refusals, so walked on without stopping again into Belgravia. She would certainly be out of place at any of these front doors, and felt too intimidated even to knock. It would be round the back for her, and no two ways about it. She laughed at the thought of Helen Vine giving herself such airs about her little palace at the edge of a pit village. They must need a lot of skivvies at any rate, she thought, and if Charlie's not here by tomorrow, I'll have to start knocking before I get chucked onto the streets.

Tired and discouraged, and without a soul she knew to turn to, puny little Ginny, with an even punier coin in her purse, turned back towards her lodgings, back through a city large enough to swallow Annsdale ten thousands times over, a city as hard as its stones, a city of cold and unforgiving grandeur. She'd have to learn, somehow, to survive in it.

Famished and footsore, she got back after dark, and went into dinner to see a fat, far-haired, blousy woman sitting at her table.

'Yer Ginny Wilde, ain't yer?' she asked with a friendly smile. Ginny nodded, surprised at being recognized by name by any of the outlandish population who drifted in and out of the lodgings. 'I've been asked to look out for you,' the woman continued. 'Keep a friendly eye on yer. We've got a mutual friend.'

'Charlie? When's he coming? He said he'd be here last Friday.'

'Ooh, yes, you are Ginny. Ginny the hinny, he calls yer. He says, "Daisy, you'll have to learn hinny just to understand what she says," but I can understand you all right. I've got a good ear. He said to tell yer as he begs your pardon, but he's been delayed by very important business. He's a rum one, Charlie, as I expect you know. Anyway, he's asked me to take you under my wing.'

'How? His brother-in-law said he'd be here to help me find a job.'

'He says you're going to try your luck on the halls, so I'm to take you about with me. Get your glad rags on – you can come with me this evening.'

Ginny followed her mentor through a crowded, grimy hall into a small, badly lit dressing room.

'I'll get changed now,' Daisy said. 'It saves all that pushing and shoving later.'

'My God, there's not much room, is there? And it's filthy and all.' She surveyed the tiny room, her eye taking in the stand with its tin basin half full of cold water, the tiny shelf with a couple of candles illuminating an old mirror that looked as if half the silver was off the back. Something in the corner of the room caught her attention and the corners of her mouth turned down. 'Ugh, just look at that,' she exclaimed.

Daisy cast a nonchalant eye in the direction of the full

chamber pot and shrugged. 'Probably been there since last night,' she said. 'Do me a favour, and get the stagehand to shift it.' Ginny called the man and held the door open while he carried it out.

Her companion was leaning towards the mirror, applying greasepaint. 'I'll look seventeen when I'm done,' she laughed, 'from a distance.' Ginny looked at her dubiously, thinking she looked at least as old as Mam Smith. It would take a miracle to make her look seventeen again, although there was an affectation of youth about her that Mam Smith would have despised.

'You look very nice.'

Daisy beamed at her. 'Charlie says you've a bit of talent yourself,' she said. 'You can try it out tonight. The chairman's a particular friend of mine. I know he'll let you do a turn if you like, as a favour to me.'

'I don't mind. Will I get any money for it, like?' Ginny asked, looking for a solution to the problem of the empty purse.

Daisy laughed. 'You've got all your buttons on. I'll get paid, and you might. Or you might not. It depends how you go down. You'd have to be one of the first turns, though. That means you have to warm the audience up for the acts that come after you.'

'All right,' said Ginny. 'This isn't a proper music hall though, is it? It's no better than the club me dad goes to at home.'

'It's places like this where music hall began. I've been top of the bill at some of the best ones in my time,' Daisy boasted, and gave a wistful sigh, 'but when you get a bit older and a bit fatter, they don't want to know. I started in places like these when I was about as old as you are now, then I played the best halls in the land. Now here I am again, in this old gaff. That's how it goes.'

The chairman stood at his table near the stage, portly and pompous, a thick gold watch chain stretched over his abdomen, and rings decorating his stubby fingers. He nodded towards Daisy, and looked Ginny up and down. She'd never seen a man so full of his own importance and had an urge to laugh.

'How are you these days, Miss May? We haven't seen you for a bit.'

'And you won't get a bit now you have seen me,' quipped Daisy with a giggle. Ginny joined in, wondering what the joke was, but glad of the chance to let her laughter escape.

'Quite a sense of humour she's got,' said the chairman, inclining his head towards Ginny. 'Who is she?'

Daisy introduced her, and made the request.

'All right. What are you going to sing, Miss Wilde?'

'"Johnnie Seddon's Dead",' said Ginny, giving the name of the only familiar song that she thought a Londoner would understand.

'It doesn't sound very humorous, but as it's only going to be a first turn, I expect it'll do. Might soften them up a bit for the other acts. Have you got your music?' Ginny shook her head and the chairman sighed. 'Well, go and hum a few bars in the pianist's ear, then stand by the steps and wait for me to announce you.'

She did as she was bid, then, without greasepaint or

stage clothes, got up, and was surprised to hear groans and catcalls from the audience before she even started. These people were a far cry from the polite audiences of the Methodist schoolroom or the Catholic Club at home, or even the club in which her father spent most of his evenings. A fragment of memory flashed into her mind, of her father lifting her on to the bar when she was about three years old to do a little clog dance for the men. They had all been merry and laughing, and had given her pennies. She smiled, then, undaunted and very confident of her vocal powers, she opened her mouth and sang. After the first line a wilting cabbage hit her on the knee. Hardly pausing in her song, Ginny lifted her skirts and kicked it back into the audience. She heard a few sniggers and a shout of protest, then the hubbub died down and she continued without further interruption. After some applause and a few whistles, someone shouted, 'Rubbish. Don't yer know nuffink more cheerful?'

'Yes,' she called back, enunciating carefully, thinking of a song she'd heard in the digs, 'do you like "On Southend Pier"?'

'Yes, I do.'

'All right. We'll do a duet. I'll sing it, and you go and jump off it.' Amid roars of laughter she quit the stage.

'They're not a right polite lot, are they?' she commented in stilted English when she rejoined Daisy and the chairman.

'You can't expect a very refined audience,' he said, rewarding her effort by taking her meaning the first time. 'Seats are only a bob, and that includes the price of a pint.

Anyway, you're none too polite yourself. Give as good as you get. You might go far.'

'Your song was nice, dear,' said Daisy, 'but the punters like something to make them laugh. Especially something saucy. Life's miserable enough. Most of them want to forget that when they come to the halls.

'I know a song about a barmaid,' she volunteered.

A waiter brought them drinks and they sat back to watch a couple of the acts. Daisy fidgeted. 'I can never settle properly until I've got my turn over,' she said. Ginny nodded absently, eyes intent on the stage. She watched aghast, enthralled but half disbelieving as a baritone abruptly stopped singing halfway through his aria and walked off the stage amid jeers and insults, his beautiful white shirt front plastered with rotten egg. The piano faltered to a stop, and struck up merrily again as a juggler took the stage.

'I don't know why we pay that chucker-out,' said the chairman. 'He's supposed to confiscate all that sort of muck before they come in. Daisy, you're next.'

'Rotten clientele you've got tonight,' she breathed before hurrying backstage.

'Same clientele we've always had.' The chairman took a leisurely draught of port before bringing his hammer down on the table.

'Ladies and gentlemen, at enormous expense, the management bring you Miss Daisy May. Miss May will now oblige.'

'Daisy May's an old floozy,' shouted one ruffian.

'Daisy May?' snorted another. 'I shouldn't think she'd

have to ask permission – at her age.' A roar of laughter ascended to the rafters.

'Nevertheless the lady will now oblige,' insisted the chairman.

The piano struck up and Daisy launched into a familiar number, giving it everything she had. She soon had the audience with her, joining in the chorus, and Ginny breathed a sigh of relief.

'Amazes me how she still gets away with it,' the chairman murmured. 'Her stuff's got whiskers on. She's lucky she ain't had a couple of rotten eggs lobbed her way trotting that old number out again.' He gave Ginny a speculative look. 'You can do your barmaid number later, if you like. If you don't get the bird, I'll engage you for the rest of the week.'

Ginny was silent. At least she'd had a bit of applause, and only one cabbage thrown at her. Judging by what they'd done to the act that followed hers, the audience couldn't have hated her.

'Fifteen bob,' he said, 'it's all you're worth. You've no name.'

'What about a pound?' she asked.

If I want to make many fifteen bobs I'll have to learn more of the sort of songs the audiences like, she thought. Some of the people who could teach her the ropes would be in the same house for the whole week, Daisy included. Ginny determined to make the best of her chance and learn as much from them as she could. She eavesdropped on conversations, and mimicked their speech until she managed to make herself understood without having to repeat things two or three times.

'Eddie died at the Lyceum.' The news was expressed in hushed tones. Ginny passed the gossip on to Daisy.

'Don't worry, there's no profit for the undertaker in it. It means he didn't get any applause. Feels as bad as dying, though.'

'Miss Bloggs? Voice is good but she won't get far. She don't know how to sell her stuff,' a fellow artiste remarked contemptuously over the breakfast table. Ginny nodded, and took the hint to heart.

'I wonder why we laughed so much at Dan – more than all the others?'

'Ever looked in his eyes? Saddest eyes in the whole world. If we didn't kill ourselves laughing at him, we'd cry. I think that's what real comedy is, a whisker away from tragedy.'

It was what instinct told her. You didn't need to feel like laughing yourself to be able to make others laugh, and that was just as well.

She rifled through the sheet music in the piano stool at every opportunity, hunting for the most light-hearted and amusing numbers. 'The punters like something to make them laugh. Especially something saucy,' Daisy had said. Well, if that's what they like, that's what I'll give them, she thought. Any song that looked as if it might fit the bill, she took to Daisy to make her hum the tune or pick it out on the piano keys. If Ginny liked it, she hummed it over and over again and secreted the music upstairs to copy the words into an exercise book before returning it to the piano stool. Oh, to be able to read music, to know what all those little black dots signified. She smiled. If Miss Carr could see her now, she wouldn't believe her eyes. She had never worked her brain so hard in her life.

At night, in the Trades, she worked her barmaid song wonderfully and by Thursday she could add a version of another song bursting with innuendo. She worked it with an air of round-eyed innocence, opening her arms in appeal to the audience, her disingenuous shrugs and a demure tilting of the head belied by the knowing curve of the lips and arching of the eyebrows. When she got to the last line the audience went wild. Although she was still the first turn, no missiles were thrown that night.

On Friday, the chairman put a pound in her hand.

'I'll move you up the programme. You can go on third, but work in front of the tabs like you've done up 'til now. It'll keep the audience entertained while they do a bit of scene shifting before the next act. You've got the pound you asked for; so don't forget to come tomorrow, just because you've been paid today.'

Her own earned money. It was worth braving catcalls and rotten eggs and vegetables for, but she grieved at the thought of handing the lion's share over to the landlady the following day. She chattered to Daisy about her promotion as they walked back to the digs. As they approached a street lamp, Ginny caught a melancholy expression on Daisy's face.

'You're a quick learner, Ginny. You're on the way up as long as you don't let anything distract you, and I'm coming down. I'm the fifth turn in a dive like the Trades after being in the business for thirty-odd years, and you're third after being in it for a week. I can't last much longer. I'll have to get used to a different style of living before long.'

'The audience like you, Daisy, but—' Ginny searched for the most tactful words and failed to find them.

'But what?'

'The chairman says you need some new songs.'

'Easier said than done, girl, if you haven't the money to pay for them.'

'Pay for them? What do you mean?'

Daisy laughed. 'I know you got one of yours off Charlie, and the other one out of the piano stool, but those songs don't belong to you, and some artistes will have your liver if they catch you pinching their stuff. If you tell them you didn't know, you might get away with it, for a while. That wouldn't wash for me, though.'

'How can a song belong to anybody?'

'How? How does anything belong to anybody? Because they've bought and paid for it, that's how. They've paid the songwriter what they thought the song was worth, and so no one else is entitled to sing it but them. It's their property.'

Ginny could barely grasp the notion of anyone owning a song, but when she did her face fell. She knew now that 'Johnnie Seddon' didn't fit the bill and most of the songs she'd learned at home wouldn't even be understood in London, but how could she sing songs that had been bought and paid for by somebody else?

'You'll get away with it at places like the Trades,' said Daisy, 'but if you get any further you'll have to go back to your "Johnnie Seddon"s or sing what they call free songs if you can't get your own stuff. Or,' she hesitated, 'I suppose you could try some of my old numbers until you get your own.'

The following night Daisy showed her a new way of putting her hair up, and helped her to apply greasepaint. As soon as the chairman announced her Ginny wasted no time and gave herself no airs. She hopped up on to the stage and put over her songs with punch and energy, determined to get the audience with her before they started throwing things. She succeeded, and after a couple of bows and some banter with them she was down again. She was pushing through the throng to get back to Daisy and the chairman when someone caught her by the wrist. Wrenching herself free, she spun round to come face to face with Charlie.

Chapter Thirteen

'You've made a good start, hinny. Hit 'em hard and hold 'em every time and you might go far with me to help you. Get that stuff off your face and grab your coat. I mean to show you a real music hall.'

'Where've you been, Charlie? Mr Vine sent you a telegram I was coming. He said you'd come and see me as soon as I got here.'

'I went to spend a week with Helen as soon as I heard you were on your way. Good strategy, you know; throws suspicious people off the scent. You wouldn't want anyone in Annsdale to put two and two together and come up with the right answer, would you? After that scene with your father, it might be the first conclusion they come to. Some of the baser characters might assume you've run away to join me in a life of wickedness.'

'I don't know who'd do that. I've come away to get a job. I've written to them all umpteen times.'

'You didn't tell them you'd be meeting me, did you?'

'No.'

'So you see, your own instinct warns you against

telling people you're renewing your acquaintance with naughty Charlie Parkinson, and it steers you aright, my little hinny. You needn't worry. Robert won't say anything. So as we are in the wicked metropolis together, you must let me take you out of this pothouse to a music hall worthy of the name. You can see Daisy at your digs later.'

She hesitated, remembering Mr Vine's warning against going anywhere alone with his brother-in-law.

'I don't think I'd better, Charlie.'

'My dear little hinny, you can trust me. I'm a perfect gentleman. I merely want to show you a different side of life to pits and scullery work and all that other drudgery which seems to have been your lot. You won't be much later at your lodgings than if you'd stayed here waiting for Daisy, I promise you.'

They took a cab to the Tivoli and Charlie gave the man instructions to call back in a couple of hours. Her feet sank into the thick red carpet in the foyer, and she gaped at the papered walls, the enormous marble staircase, the magnificent chandeliers, and what seemed acres of mirror and mahogany, all grand beyond belief. She caught sight of a striking black-haired girl and it was a second or two before she recognized her own reflection in a massive plate mirror, looking as handsome as anyone. The earrings Charlie'd given her after that day at the races looked exactly right, drops of jet, large and lustrous, swinging about every time she moved her head, adding to her air of vivacity and drawing the eye away from her cheap, shabby black coat. The faint blush on her cheeks deepened a shade as she saw him at the back of her, felt his breathe on her neck.

'They're almost as black as your eyes,' he murmured, 'that's why they took my fancy. I entertain great hopes of you.' He held her reflected gaze for a second longer, then put an arm round her waist and turned her in the direction of the bar. They walked towards the open doors of a saloon thick with people and cigar smoke. A well-dressed young man pressed through the crowds towards them.

'Charlie, old friend! Who's your latest?'

'Mind your own business,' laughed Charlie, 'if you've got any to mind. Your life must be damned dreary if you take such an interest in mine.'

'Not at all. I spice it up constantly. And it's not your life I'm interested in; it's your lady-friend. Introduce us,' he demanded, shamelessly ogling Ginny.

'No fear. I'll keep her to myself. Haven't you heard the song "Never Introduce your Sweetheart to a Pal"? It's good advice.'

Ginny looked at the pair of them, well fed and well dressed, with easy confident manners and soft manicured hands. Smooth, sleek, pampered strangers to hard work. Her father would have described them as a pair of idlers, and so would Martin. Seeing Charlie's acquaintance stare at her rather as the Cock Inn's mastiff might stare at the Sunday joint, she gave him a contemptuous glance and looked pointedly away. Undeterred, he laughed and addressed himself to Charlie.

'She's a spirited one – looks at me as if I'm something she's trodden in. Still, I like the proud ones. When you get tired of her, send her to me. I've no doubt she'll be properly housetrained by then.' His fat, jowly face twisted into a leering wink and he left them to elbow his way to the bar.

Ginny shuddered. 'Have you got many friends like him?'

'Sandy? He's no particular friend of mine. I see him at the races from time to time; he owns a good horse. It's funny, I'm so popular that all sorts of people like to think of themselves as my friends and I don't disillusion them. The strangest people can prove useful at times. He improves upon acquaintance.'

'He won't get the chance, as far as I'm concerned.'

'Then don't give him another thought. Have a drink before we go in. What would you like, champagne?'

She felt a twinge of apprehension. 'No, thank you, I've signed the pledge. Let's get in and see the show. That's what we've come for, isn't it?'

'You disappoint me, Ginny. I never took you for a Miss Prim. Wait here. I'm going to have one anyway. I'll bring you something suitable for a teetotaller.'

She thought she glimpsed an expression of mild annoyance on his face as he turned to follow his 'no particular friend' to the bar and wondered what she would do if they fell out. She was not physically afraid of Charlie; his cowardice during the confrontation with her father had made her despise rather than fear him, but perhaps she'd been a bloody fool to come all this way, relying on a man of his reputation, especially following her ride home with him after the races. But then, she'd enjoyed the day at the races; it had been as thrilling as he'd promised. There was a dash of adventure about Charlie that appealed to a streak of recklessness in her, and he was lucky, lucky, lucky. She'd believed his promises to be on his best behaviour because she'd needed to believe them, still needed to believe them. She crossed her fingers and held them tight. Everything would be all right. Apprehension turned again to excitement and anticipation.

He was back beside her before many minutes had passed, smiling and light-hearted, all suspicion of ill humour gone. He handed her a drink, and after a moment's hesitation she took it without protest.

'Shouldn't we go in? I don't want to miss anything.'

'Down with your drink, then. Better leave your glass here.'

Ginny lifted her glass and examined the same wonderful golden liquid she had tasted on Christmas Eve. At least it wasn't gin. Charlie smiled as she drank it down, good temper restored. They made their way up the grand staircase and through to the front row of the balcony to sit on red plush seats. She put a hand on the brass rail which topped the marble balustrade and looked around, taking in the size of the place, the hundreds of people in it, the height of the arched ceiling with its lovely gilded plasterwork, the huge pendant lamps with opaque glass bowls the size of cartwheels, the sheer opulence of it all, and the stage seeming a mile below.

'It's like being on the side of a mountain.'

'You like it?'

She nodded.

'Say "thank you for bringing me, Charlie",' he demanded.

The orchestra struck up, saving her from making any reply. One act followed another, each one better than the last. At the intermission they went down to the bar where he presented her with another large glass of champagne. He kissed her and she laughed. He laughed with her and kissed her again.

'Say "thank you, Charlie",' he insisted.

'Thank you Charlie,' she smiled. He kissed her a third time and put a hand on her breast as he led her back to her seat.

'*Pour remplir la main d'un homme honnete*,' he murmured.

'What?'

'Something the French say,' said Charlie. 'Women's breasts are most beautiful when they just fill the hand of an honest man.'

'Too big for yours then, Charlie,' quipped Ginny, not knowing quite why she said it, but laughing at her own wit. He laughed with her, the unfeigned, approving laugh of a fellow conspirator.

When the curtain came down for the last time, she was in transports at the magic of it all and her hands were sore with clapping. She sighed as Charlie ushered her out of the theatre and into the waiting cab. She felt relaxed and happy, and more elated than she could ever remember.

'Here we are,' said Charlie, as the coachman slowed to a halt. 'You enjoyed yourself tonight, Ginny?'

'Aye, I did,' she nodded, turning a flushed face towards him, eyes fired by champagne and the sights she'd seen, lips parted in a smile. The smile died when he handed her out on to the unfamiliar pavement of a Georgian terrace.

'This isn't where my lodgings are, Charlie.'

'No. This is where I live. I kept your winnings for you. From the races. I wanted to give them to you.'

'Well, I'll wait in the cab until you get them.'

He made no reply but paid the cabman, who ignored Ginny's protests and drove off. Charlie opened his front door and bowed her inside. The light from the gas mantles revealed an elegant staircase covered in a sumptuous carpet of royal blue, as thick as that at the theatre, with gilt-framed portraits hanging on the richly papered walls. Squeezing her shoulders, he bent to kiss her neck before helping her out of her coat and hanging it on the hallstand.

'Don't look so concerned. I'll give you supper, then send for a cab to take you back to your lodgings – with your money, of course.'

He ushered her into the dining room and pulled out a heavy upholstered chair. She sat down to a table beautifully set for two, awed by the sight of the finest china, silver and cut glass. He removed the silver lids from the platters.

'Mmm, game pie, a variety of meats and accompaniments and a bottle of good claret. She's opened it for us. Thinks of everything.' He gave her an encouraging smile as he filled their glasses.

'I'd rather have gone back to my lodgings.'

'You'll get a much better supper here, I assure you. Enjoy it,' he said, helping her to a slice of pie.

She was hungry and would undoubtedly get a better supper with Charlie. The food did look very appetizing. She ate for a short while in silence.

'You have very good manners for a miner's daughter, Ginny. I suppose that comes from your waiting at table at Helen's.'

She did not disguise her resentment. 'Well, you suppose wrong. I had good table manners before I started school. That comes from having a good mother. And it's just as likely in a pitman's family as anybody else's.'

'Oh, certainly, if you say so,' smiled Charlie. 'Try the claret. It's very good, especially with game pie. Breathe in the bouquet, then take a good mouthful and tell me what you think of it.'

She took a sip of the almost purple liquid. It felt astringent on her teeth, and reminded her of vinegar. 'It's not as nice as champagne.'

'It's different to champagne. Don't sip it, take a good mouthful, it tastes much better like that, and it aids digestion. Finish your glass and I'll pour you another. It's an acquired taste. The more you drink, the better you'll like it.'

'I've had enough, thank you, Charlie.'

'Nonsense, you're a woman now, not a child. Besides, this is excellent wine and we must finish it between us tonight. It won't keep.'

After the bottle was finished, he took her into the

spacious drawing room. A fire burned brightly in the large fireplace, its glow reflected in the polished furniture. She began to feel quite weak and sat down suddenly on a buttoned chaise longue.

'On second thoughts, come upstairs with me and help me find your money.'

'How do I know where you've got it? Anyway, I'm tired. You fetch it, and then take me back to my lodgings.'

'Oh, no,' said Charlie. 'I've entertained you to supper and you mustn't run off directly it's eaten. Your mother would surely disapprove of such bad manners. You owe me the pleasure of your company for at least an hour or two.' He sat down beside her.

Ginny's brow creased in puzzlement as she tried to imagine what her mother would think, and couldn't believe her mother would think she should be there at all. 'I wish I had my mother here this minute,' she said, her speech a little slurred.

'God forbid. Three's a crowd on these occasions. We are going to enjoy each other's company, Ginny.'

The lascivious expression on his face struck her as inexpressibly funny. Hearing peals of laughter, she realized that they were her own. He gave her an encouraging grin, stooped to kiss her, then knelt beside the couch. She felt his hand between her legs, and sat up, thrusting him away, shocked into near sobriety.

'Get off. You promised to be a gentleman.'

'None of that now. The most perfect gentlemen love the ladies, you know. Come on, I don't want to hurt you,' he said, determinedly grasping her by the knees and pulling her towards the edge of the seat. With equal determination she wrenched herself free, enraged at his threat.

'If it comes to that, I might hurt you an' all. Let's see who can do the most damage. I might smash a lot of the stuff in your fancy house an' all. Maybe break a few windows,' she warned, glowering at him.

Much taken aback, he became conciliatory. 'Come on, Ginny. You knew when you came here what the game was. You knew after the races, so stop playing the Puritan. With my help and guidance you might go far on the halls. I'm willing to open a lot of doors for you. Quite a few of the sort of people who could help you make your name owe me favours. You know what I want in return, and it's a fair bargain. Your alternative is to be a housemaid for the rest of your life, and stay in service to people like Helen, without a friend, in London. That's if you can get a position without a reference.'

'I can get a reference. I'm not dependent on you for that.'

'Where will you get your reference? Helen won't give you one.'

'Her husband will, and a good one an' all. He told me so before I came.'

'An employer might wonder at your having a reference from the master of a house and being unable to produce one from the mistress, you know. She might jump to quite the wrong conclusion about you and fear for her own husband,' he said. 'Unjust, I know, but that's how women's minds work. Helen might even confirm their fear. She's seen Robert eyeing you often enough and she's borne you a lot of malice since that visit from your father. She says you're an impudent young hussy determined to step out of your class. She'd probably enjoy destroying your character with every respectable employer, and where would that leave you?'

Ginny was silent, wondering where it would leave her. It was hard to think, with her head fuddled with wine, and Charlie's arguments sounded so convincing. Where was she now but in his house, without knowledge or means to get back to her lodgings? Even if she found her way, there was not one soul there to help her, and Daisy would be gone tomorrow. She probably had just enough money left for the train fare home, but what then? Back to a hiding from her father, probably the first of many, no independence, and no money. Martin would help her, but he was still full of grief for Maria and she would be the cause of no more trouble to him. There was nothing in Annsdale for her now. She had to stay in London, a tiny voice prompted, so she might as well make the very best of it. The life of the music halls was exciting. And Charlie was lucky. If she kept him on her side, a bit of that luck might rub off on her. She had no other friend.

He crossed to the window, and parted the heavy blue velvet curtains. 'We seem to have a fog coming down, and it's icy cold, you know. Makes one very glad to be safe and comfortable inside. People freeze to death on the streets quite regularly, and murders are commonplace. I hope you won't start any nonsense in my house, Ginny, because that would oblige me to call for a constable and have you thrown on to those streets. I doubt you'd find your way to your lodgings on a night like this, and a luscious young woman like you out alone in London – well, I don't care to think what the consequences might be, and I wouldn't think of it. I wouldn't make it my concern. It would be your concern, Ginny.'

'I would tell the constable what you did to me.'

'I should deny it, of course. You're completely unharmed. You could show him no evidence of my harming you in any way, unless a good supper counts as harm. Now what do you imagine a constable would think of a naughty girl who comes alone to supper at a gentleman's house? This is not Annsdale, my hinny. You would see a constable who has no personal knowledge of you and who would see no evidence other than the ruin of my house. At best, he'd put you out and send you on your way. As I've said, I don't care to think what the consequences of that might be, but you should consider it.'

'You promised to take me back.'

He shrugged and crossed over to the fire, to lean pensively against the marble mantelpiece. 'People aren't always able to keep their promises, with the best will in the world. I don't wish to go out again myself, and I ask you to remain safe and warm with me as my very welcome guest.' He stooped to lift a heavy, turned brass poker and begin idly stirring the fire. 'I don't share Helen's low opinion of you, of course. I know you're a spotless virgin, quite an orphan in the storm. You could bring out the chivalrous instinct in me, if you were more – amenable.'

'I've been told to get a ring on my finger before I let any man do what you want to do,' she said.

Charlie gave her a reassuring smile. 'You shall have a ring, and you may call yourself Mrs Parkinson. It will be just as if we are married, honour bright, and we will marry eventually. I haven't been able to get you out of my mind these past six weeks, in spite of your father, or perhaps because of him. You're a quick learner and you might pass for a duchess before long. I couldn't marry you as you are now, but I'll make you if I can, and when you're my equal, it will be a different thing.'

Even with her senses dulled by alcohol, the thought of being cast adrift friendless and penniless in those cold, unfamiliar streets was daunting. She felt resistance ebb away and he saw it. He gave her several reassuring kisses, then knelt at her feet whilst she passively allowed him to lift her skirt and pull her hips to the edge of the couch. She watched the flickering of the fire on the plaster-worked ceiling as he knelt between her knees and put his hands inside her split-leg drawers. He groaned.

'That woman's scent. Oh, Josephine.'

And the young Annsdale virgin's cheeks burned hotter than the fire as she felt his fingers and then his lips on that secret, private place between her thighs.

Chapter Fourteen

The following morning she awoke naked in his bed. He was still asleep, face suggestive of nothing but guiltless slumber. She threw on his green paisley silk dressing gown and slipped downstairs to get her own clothes. The drawing room had been cleaned and a fire lit, but her clothes were nowhere to be seen. She ran back upstairs in panic to find the bedroom curtains open, letting the sun stream in. Charlie turned towards her and threw back the bedcovers. She wrapped the dressing gown closer around her and stood for several moments rooted to the spot, watching him in shocked fascination as he caressed the erection arising from a nest of curled hair shining golden-red above his thighs.

He gave a lazy, self-satisfied laugh. 'Don't worry, no one can see in. We're too high up and too far away from the houses opposite. Come and kiss me.'

'Where are my clothes, Charlie? And where's my money?'

He fondled himself gently and sighed. 'I love these little trollops. They never forget their money, the darlings.' He gave her a smile. 'Come here. I want you to lie beside me for an hour, and then you shall have your clothes. Some clothes, at any rate. Don't worry, yours are quite safe.'

She got reluctantly into bed, noting her own dried blood on the sheets. After a moment or two he turned fully towards her and slid a hand inside the dressing gown to caress her breast. She lay rigid whilst he kissed her full on the mouth, his unshaven skin rough against hers. His mouth travelled slowly and deliberately down her neck to her breast. He covered it with kisses, and, taking the nipple between his teeth, began to bite very gently, before kissing her on the mouth again.

'You can't make matters worse now, you know,' he whispered, nibbling her ear. 'It's much, much too late, my sweet little hinny. You'll never be a virgin again. All is lost. All is lost to naughty Charlie.' He kneaded the tops of her thighs cruelly until she gasped with pain and involuntarily separated her legs.

'It's good for you, you'll see,' he coaxed, pushing his knees between her thighs. 'No, no, don't struggle, my darling.'

She heard her heartbeat pounding in her ears, and all strength suddenly deserted her. Charlie leaned heavily against her, preventing any chance of escape.

'Open your legs wide, there's a good girl, and lift your haunches. Here, here, like this. Now open them, knees well apart. Good girl, good girl.'

She felt him push his way into her, past the soreness, and start a slow, deep thrusting. 'I'm too deep in the saddle to be unseated now, even by Arthur Wilde's daughter, and I mean to ride you hard.'

She closed her eyes and winced.

'Relax. If you relax, it'll hurt less, I promise,' he said, ramming himself deliberately, rhythmically and slowly into her, with ever-increasing force. After some time, the rhythm changed and his thrusting became quicker, more urgent. Independent of her will, her hips began to rock to meet his thrusts. She moved with him. Fear and shame lost all significance and soon she cared for nothing – nothing but the sensation that consumed and threatened to explode inside her. She held on to Charlie and wrapping her legs around him, felt herself in the pit of her belly gripping him, holding him, drawing him, wanting, wanting to consume the whole of him. She was on the brink of ecstasy – then he groaned and was still.

'No, no, don't stop!'

He collapsed breathless on to the bed, red-faced. Beads of perspiration stood large on his forehead.

'Women!' he laughed, between gasps. 'First "don't start", and then "don't stop"! What a knee trembler! You're a good lay, Ginny, the best I've ever had, man or boy.' After a minute or two his breathing slowed to normal and he propped himself on one elbow to look at her.

'If I couldn't see the evidence, I wouldn't believe you were a virgin. The man was right, you're a natural. You're a natural gay lady, but you must only be gay with me for now.' He laughed softly. 'You poor thing, I haven't brought you off, and you're disappointed. I haven't the strength to rectify that just now, but give me a few hours and I promise I won't fail.'

She winced again. 'You've made me sore, Charlie.'

'It's all right,' he soothed, 'we mustn't stop now. Lovemaking is rather like claret, an acquired taste for most women, much more so than for men. You seem to be acquiring it very quickly. You'll soon like it as much as I do.'

She resisted and turned away. She felt his flaccid penis against her as he put his arms around her waist and pulled her into him.

'You remember yesterday, when you wished you had your mother here?' he said, voice hard-edged and his grip tightening painfully. 'Well, I wish I'd had your father just now. I'd have liked him to see me "tamper" with you.'

Her lip curled in scorn. If there'd been any chance of my father seeing anything you wouldn't have dared touch me, Charlie, she thought. You'd have shit yourself, you stinking coward.

'I love your solid flesh, your well-muscled thighs and haunches, your firm young breasts. What are you, Ginny, fifteen? Less than half my age, but I love the young ones. A clean, fresh provincial girl, what could be nicer? Diseased old London tarts like Daisy leave me cold. I don't know how any man can bear to touch them, but there's no accounting for taste. No, give me a fresh, full-breasted young bird like you, just the thing to warm a gentleman's bed. You shall stay here with me, so I can have the pleasure of you as often as I like. And it will save you money, you know, you must think of that.' He gave a low chuckle. 'I won't charge you for the lodging. Not in cash, anyway.'

After a warm morning bath, an undreamed-of novelty for Ginny, she tried on a lilac silk dress that Charlie said had been discarded by Helen, along with a few others, after her marriage to Robert. It was tight over the bust, and loose at the waist, but he decided that the colour suited her pale skin and black hair. The style was a little passé, but let out and taken in in the right places, and generally brought up to date, it would do very well for his hinny, she would be quite fit to be seen with him. The evening gown could be transformed into something that would do for the stage, until they found out how she performed. He knew of a good dressmaker.

Charlie waited in the cab whilst she called in at her lodgings to collect her few possessions and settle her bill. There was the usual Sunday bustle in the hall, the settling of bills, the comings and goings of artistes and the carrying out of trunks. Ginny gave the landlady her new address and asked for her letters to be sent on.

'I'll do it for a week, and that's all. There's a letter here for you now. Miss May left it – you've just missed her.' She cast a disparaging eye at the strip of silk showing under Ginny's coat. 'My, my, silk dresses are the uniform. You've obviously found a very good place.' Ginny took her letter, picked up her bag and returned swiftly to the cab, blushing to the roots of her hair.

Daisy wished her luck, and gave her permission to use the best of the songs of her youth. Ginny handed the letter to Charlie, saying she was sorry not to have seen her.

'Oh, excellent, the old girl's turned up trumps. They'll do for a start.' He said no more, but Ginny remembered Daisy's kindness with gratitude and she frowned as she recalled Charlie's earlier insulting words about her.

They road through he city to Leadenhall Street, where they alighted outside a jeweller's. She followed him down a narrow passageway to a heavy oak door. Charlie rapped loudly and impatiently with his cane. A few moments later, the door was opened by a dark-complexioned woman who showed them upstairs, into a comforable drawing room. A grey-haired man of about sixty or seventy rose to greet them.

'Mr Parkinson, as I live. And to what do I owe the honour?'

'Why, I'm to be married, Isaac; and since you're going to supply the wedding ring in payment for many recommendations I've given you, you can be the first to know.'

An ironical smile passed over the old man's face, answered by a broad grin from Charlie. 'Indeed, indeed,' he said, and led them downstairs and into the shop, where they sat down to examine trays of wedding rings.

'Are you sure these are the best you've got, you sly old son of Abraham?' Charlie demanded.

The old man assumed an expression of injured innocence. 'For a good business partner like you? Would I deceive you?'

'No more than I would you.' Charlie squeezed Ginny's hand and said, with mock solemnity, 'Choose the one you like best, my dear, you'll be wearing it for the rest of your life.' Without enthusiasm, she chose a thick, bevelled, twenty-two carat ring, and Charlie grinned triumphantly.

'My intended has the most unerring good taste,' he murmured.

'In rings, at least,' smiled Isaac, 'and I wish her joy in wearing it.'

They drove on into a park where he put the ring on her finger and kissed her. 'Now you may sign yourself Mrs Parkinson, given that you pay proper attention to your wifely duties, of course. This is your day for names, Ginny; you must have another one before it's out. You need a stage name, and one that will cut some ice, make people sit up and notice you. Think of a name that's already on everybody's lips if you can, perhaps a little aristocratic, but not obviously anyone else's name.'

'Why not Parkinson?'

'Oh, no, that won't do at all. Too prosaic, though I hate to admit it. No, a name of consequence, an English name, that'll mean something to Londoners.'

She gazed around the park, waiting for inspiration. Her gaze fell on a clump of late snowdrops, symbols of modesty and purity, but now browning and slimy. She thought fleetingly of Snowdrop Terrace and sighed.

'Where are we now?' she asked. 'Is this St James's Park?'

'It is indeed.'

'Ginny St James, then. No, just Ginny James is better.'

'By all means, let's drop the saint, my lusty little sinner. Music hall audiences do tend towards the vulgar.'

'And I think I'll sign myself that name as well. Then I won't get too confused, and if I fall down on the wifely duties, I shan't have to change it again.'

'Excellent, excellent. But you'll never tire of the sort of wifely duties I require from you, Ginny. People who take to them with such enthusiasm as you have never do. If you stop performing them for me, you'll be delighting some other lucky fellow within a fortnight. I feel jealous of him already and he isn't aware of your existence yet. Stay faithful to me as long as you can. I want to keep you to myself for a while.'

A shadow of anxiety passed over her face. 'Till death us do part, I hope, Charlie. It's not long since you were talking about a wedding.'

'Yes, I was, wasn't I?' he said, banging the head of his cane on the roof of the cab to signal the driver on. 'I fear I may have to disappoint my sister and her Manor Farm connections after all. It's too bad. Popularity is such a trial; one is always having to disappoint somebody. I can't help it; you're too irresistible. We'll fly home. The rest of our business can wait until this afternoon. My friend has a keen sense of his own importance, he won't be set aside for any consideration.'

Ginny took Maria's shoes and her quilted nightdress case into a guest bedroom and pushed them into the darkest recess of a bottom drawer, as if through them the givers might see what was to pass between her and Charlie. That done she undressed, and standing naked in front of the full-length wardrobe mirror examined the bruising on her thighs and breasts. There was evidence enough for any constable, but she would have been too ashamed to show it. She returned to Charlie's room and slipped trembling into bed, ready to render those services that Charlie demanded and Mam Smith had warned her against. The sheets were fresh, all trace of bloody conquest removed – changed by the same invisible hands that laid suppers, uncorked claret, and sent bloodstained linen out to the laundry.

He kept her waiting for what seemed an age. When he appeared, he took her unresisting into his arms and kissed her gently, rubbing his smooth, clean-shaven cheek against hers, not attempting to touch any other part of her.

'What a sweet, patient little hinny you can be,' he murmured. 'I know these things are new to you and it was all very painful and embarrassing yesterday, but girls mustn't tease, they mustn't say yes then change their minds, a man cannot tolerate it. If they do there's no alternative to rough wooing.'

Bright, silent tears filled her eyes and spilled on to her cheeks. He kissed her again, stroked her hair, and spoke in a low, gentle voice. 'I had every hope of you before you came, but now that you understand what your choices are and who the master is, I know you'll exceed all my hopes. It's in your own nature, quite apart from what I shall teach you. Don't be frightened, everything will happen quite naturally. You showed me this morning how responsive you are, so you will please me. You're the sort of girl who couldn't help it if she wanted to, my sweet, sweet little hinny. I'll devote myself to your pleasure this time and you'll see why your ridiculous village principles have no place in the lives of real, flesh and blood men and women.'

During the week that followed they did the rounds of dressmakers, songwriters, theatres, and impresarios. At Charlie's suggestion, she passed herself off as a married woman of eighteen or nineteen, and seemed to be accepted as such. He took her to a couple of shows and introduced her to his acquaintances as 'Mrs James. I have her husband's permission to squire her round London whilst he's away on business.' This announcement was usually greeted with guffaws and ribaldry, but some people actually seemed to believe it. Charlie was unperturbed whatever the reaction. She could not have said why, when they both knew to the contrary, but the thick, expensive wedding ring and the fiction of married respectability was a comfort to her.

Occasional hints about abandonment without a penny on the streets of London kept her fearful and obedient, and Charlie, now given his pleasure without reserve the instant he demanded it, became a pleasant and amusing companion. She was dismayed to find herself his eager acolyte, usually more than willing to try anything which might please him, her desire matching and sometimes even exceeding his, but when she was most eager for his attentions, it seemed to amuse him to withhold them. She thrilled to his touch in spite of herself, and was pleased by his praises. In the end she could not have told whether it was ambition, cowardice, or lust that truly held her captive. She became curious about his former lovers, but he would tell her nothing. After a particularly torrid coupling she asked him, 'You remember that first time in the drawing room, Charlie? Why did you call me Josephine?'

'Out of sympathy for the Emperor Napoleon, my hinny.'

'What?'

'When Napoleon was returning home from one of his many campaigns and looking forward to bedding his Josephine, he would send her a message, "*ne te lave pas*," or, in plain English, don't wash your parts. He liked her very ripe, you see. And on that evening you were rather well scented yourself. I found it very stimulating, and naturally I thought of Josephine.'

'That's the most disgusting thing I've ever heard.'

'Yes, I'd write a song about it if I thought it would get past the censor. It would do for the penny gaffs, though. The coarser the better for the roughs.'

When carnal appetite was utterly satiated, he would accompany her on the piano whilst she practised her songs, occasionally making corrections or suggesting improvements. He was a discerning critic, and she respected his judgement. As soon as she had Daisy's songs off, he got her a booking at one of the minor halls on a couple of pounds a week. She was a hit, and other better engagements followed. He decided she must have more songs now she had the money to pay for them, and he bought some promising new ones.

'The trick is to get the women to like you and to arouse the men. I'm sure you do that already to a degree, but we could improve on it,' he said thoughtfully one morning, resting his hands on the piano keys after taking her through a new number. 'You must study some of the experts. We'll go to the Empire Promenade after the matinee, to see the fast women.'

Ginny hung on to Charlie's arm, watching the scene intently. 'I can't believe any of these women are prostitutes, Charlie.'

'Astounding, aren't they?' He smiled, with an almost proprietorial pride. 'Utterly magnificent. But tell me, hinny, what did you think a prostitute was?'

'I don't know. Not like these, looking so well-dressed. Looking like ladies. I can't believe there's one of them a prostitute.'

'Your Methodist teachers might encourage you to imagine such women poor, shabby, degraded creatures and that may be true of those who tramp the docks and the back streets, to service sailors and other riff-raff. But think of it, Ginny. The women here attract the interest of the best men in society who can pay high prices for their services. Cultured men such as myself, who require cleanliness and beauty at the least, preferably accompanied by a degree of intelligence and refinement. How could they attract such clients if they were dirty and dishevelled?'

'They couldn't, Charlie, but they don't go near any men.'

'No. They seldom accost one and never, ever importune.' They came to an empty table. Charlie pulled out a chair for her and then sat down himself. 'But a man may take his pick. Observe them well.'

She did, and saw no trace of wretchedness. The women seemed to brim with self-confidence. Some were arrogant, if anything, and moved to and fro in a smooth, graceful fashion. There was no vulgar laughter or loud chatter, and their manners were excellent.

'See, they're very well behaved. One complaint to the management, and they're barred. All types for all tastes, from the majestic to the demure, from the bold to the modest. Human merchandise. This is the white slave trade, Ginny, that the morality mongers would love to put a stop to, but as long as the commercial value of the courtesan is at least four times that of the honest servant girl, they have little hope of success, I'm happy to say. Our gentlemen must have their pleasures.'

She felt his eyes upon her as she watched the scene, caught a glimpse of his lazy, mocking smile.

'Take note of the way they move. That's what I want you to mimic on stage, just sometimes, when it matches your song.' He was suddenly alert. 'Now look at that one over there. She looks very haughty, doesn't she? One might almost take her for a duchess. But watch.' He discreetly beckoned a tall, aloof, blonde woman. With the slow but dignified gait of a caged tigress, she approached the table. He did not invite her to sit down, but kept her standing beside him.

'Ginny the hinny, meet Charlotte the harlot,' he said, eyes twinkling and lips curving at his own wit.

Ginny flushed and felt a stab of panic. The expression on Charlotte's face reminded her of her mother after she'd received that vicious kick on Christmas Eve. She had an impulse to jump up and comfort her, but only murmured, 'For shame, Charlie.'

'Shame, hinny? Not at all,' he said softly, 'the word has little meaning either for Charlotte or for me. Wouldn't you agree, sweetheart?'

Charlotte tilted her chin and looked away, a picture of careless pride. 'If you say so, Charlie.'

He nodded his approval. 'She is magnificent, isn't she, Ginny? She'll be a duchess yet. Gentlemen occasionally marry their courtesans, and I entertain high hopes for Charlotte. With her special talents, she's well fitted to become a member of the aristocracy. How are you faring, Charlotte? I hope you're keeping enough company.'

'Enough.'

'I'm very pleased for you. I hope you don't mind our speaking to you like this. Ginny is a provincial girl. I'm trying to educate her in the ways of the world.'

'I'm glad to have been of service to you both.'

'Thank you, Charlotte. Apply yourself to your trade, my dear, and you are certain to do well from it,' said Charlie.

Thus dismissed, Charlotte walked majestically away. Deep suspicions crowded into Ginny's mind.

'Did you buy her a ring, Charlie?'

He burst out laughing. 'No, my clever little hinny, I assure you I did not. She lived in my house and we enjoyed each other's company for a time, but she saw the benefits of the trade she now plies, so it ended between us. Charlotte is a mistress of her art, and certain to give satisfaction to her many admirers. I keep a friendly eye on her. See how magnificently she's dressed. No threadbare coats or mended boots for Charlotte. She demands everything of the best, and she deserves it for the pleasure she gives.' He gave Ginny a long, speculative stare. 'I wonder which style would come most naturally to you, my hinny? Proud, merry or demure?'

'I could never do what she does, Charlie. I could never parade myself, waiting to couple with any man that wanted to give me a shilling.'

'Nonsense. You can do it with me, with enjoyment. It's very little different with others, and you could command much, much more than a shilling, I assure you.'

Her answer was swift and direct. 'I'm not doing it, Charlie. I'm never going whoring. Never. You've made me do a lot of things I never should have done, but you'll never make me do that. I would rather do away with meself than do what Charlotte does.'

He raised his eyebrows. 'Going whoring? Filthy-spoken girl, to use such disgusting language. You insult me, Ginny. I am a civilized man. I have never suggested any woman do any such thing.'

She looked him directly in his cold blue eyes, determinedly fixing his gaze. 'Aye, well, I'm glad of that, because I won't. And if you try to make me, I will do away with meself, but not before I've done away with you. And when we're both dead, the constable can do what the hell he likes about it.'

Chapter Fifteen

Ginny thought she must have misjudged him. During the following months he was the old Charlie, the clown who played the fool and made her laugh. All kindness and consideration, he seemed as keen as she to further her artistic ambitions. He attended to all the dealings with theatre managers, he arranged bookings, he negotiated her fee and her place on bills, he bought songs, paid taxes and a thousand other things that Ginny was incapable of managing. She was paid on Friday nights and she handed her money directly to Charlie. There were so many expenses associated with the performer's life, he said, that there was never any money left to speak of, and Ginny readily conceded she was only an ignorant girl and had no head for business or the keeping of accounts.

He took her to a dressmaker and had more stage clothes made. He ordered presentable afternoon and evening clothes to ensure that she would do credit to him on their outings together. He chose her underwear and night attire, and she yielded to his better taste and judgement. He would allow her to do no housework. He had servants for that, and she must remember she was no housemaid now. Her hands were soon a lady's hands, as soft and well-manicured as his. She was entirely free to concentrate on her art, and on pleasing him. Apart from a rigorous rehearsal of those barely perceptible yet instantly recognizable gestures which would enhance one or two of her songs, there was no further mention of the ladies of pleasure. He was besotted with her, he said, how could she imagine he would countenance the thought of her being with any other man?

'Marry me then, Charlie. I'm old enough now.'

'Not yet. I must bring Helen round to the idea first. That will be much easier when you're an established artiste, with a good income. These things do matter among the more well-to-do, Ginny, mercenary though that may seem to you.' He played a few bars more before continuing. 'So I'm very relieved to see that your monthlies have been regular so far. When are you due again?'

'In a week.' She said it without a blush. Charlie had taken her virginity and he knew her inside out; he had made every particle of her his own property. She almost felt she belonged to him more than she belonged to herself.

'I thought so. Be a good girl and remind me at once if they're late. A child would be a real obstacle to your career, and it would put an end to any idea of my marrying you. Luckily I know a very discreet lady who can deal with such inconveniences.' He threw himself into the jaunty tune again with enthusiasm.

'Inconveniences?'

'Late monthlies, hinny. We must take care they arrive on time, or as near as possible, then you won't be troubled with children.'

Another thing puzzled her. 'Why should me having your child stop us getting married?'

Charlie stopped playing, very patient with her naivety. 'My sweet little hinny, in the sort of society Helen and I aspire to, certain things are done, and other things are not done. Marrying a woman who has borne a child out of wedlock is certainly not done. A man would be taken for a fool. But these matters needn't trouble you. If you're overdue you'll tell me, and the matter can be resolved with very little difficulty. You will promise me that, won't you, hinny? It's for your own good, you know.' She nodded. 'That's my good little hinny. Come now, we're wasting time. You've done very well at the Athens, and Sun Palace, and the Wilkins. I was very proud of you; but the West End is quite another thing. It's the Mecca of all good artistes. We must have you rehearsed to perfection before you appear there.'

Charlie was right, as always. On her opening matinee at the Arena, the music hall profession was gathered in full force to criticize this new find. The hall was packed, the men, as usual, standing round the bar, their wives and partners seated in the stalls, ready to pick every conceivable spot off her performance. Charlie was with her in the dressing room as she made the last-minute adjustments to her dress.

The callboy rattled on her door. 'Five minutes to go, Mrs James.'

Ginny dabbed away the moisture from her top lip, then lifted her foot on to the chair and leaned forward to tie up a trailing boot lace.

'Are you nervous?' He placed his hands on her hips as she bent over.

'Terrified,' she admitted, and then felt him lift her skirt.

'Come on, my hinny, just a little tickle. Keep still for Charlie,' he insisted, holding on to her, with his foot jammed against the closed door.

'Stop it, Charlie. You must be mad,' she hissed, yet he had her well enough disciplined to make no attempt to break free from him.

'Keep still, sweet. If you struggle, it will take longer, and make enough noise to let everybody know what you're doing, and you wouldn't like that. Be very still and quiet and it will be our little secret,' he murmured.

'The chair's wobbling,' she said, in an agony of nervousness.

'Then hold on to the back and keep it still.'

She'd had her last call before he was finished with her. He pulled down her skirt and gave her a slap on her haunches to send her chasing out of the dressing room. The opening bars of her introductory music were being played for the second time before she bounded on to the stage, flushed and unfulfilled. Her performance did not suffer. She was full of zest, suggestive, saucy, laughing. Her vivacity, and something of her animal spirits transmitted itself to the audience. They sat up and took notice.

Once her act was finished she was off the stage in a trice, ignoring calls for an encore. 'Always leave them wanting a little bit more,' she whispered to herself, repeating advice given to her by many artistes, 'and that's how you've left me, Charlie.' She went directly back into the dressing room, impatient to find him and make him finish for her what he had started. Of course, he was gone. She removed the greasepaint and changed her dress, and went to the saloon. He was exactly where she had anticipated, propping up the bar with a group of other fellows.

He hailed her. 'Come and join us, Mrs James. Have a drink with some of your critics.'

She approached them, eyes sparkling and a smile on her lips, still in a state of high excitement. 'No thank you, I've another performance tonight. Was I all right?'

'Well, one of our number thinks your voice can't last, you don't use it properly, another thinks you can't dance, but the only fellow whose opinion is worth a bean is our celebrated Signor Morales here, and he, well, tell her what you think, Signor.'

'I think your detractors are all poor judges, Mrs James. Your act is a little rough, and you've a long way to go, that's evident. But you'll cover that long way pretty quickly, in my opinion. With the right material and more polish, you could have some big hits.'

'Don't you like the songs I've got, Mr Morales?'

He shrugged, pausing to remove a flake of tobacco

from his lip. 'They're well enough. But get one of the best songwriters and have some specially written for your own voice. You'll find it a good investment. You might make music hall history.'

She flushed with pleasure and beamed from ear to ear.

'Charlie, I can scarcely believe that girl's eighteen,' said another man. 'Close to, she looks quite a child.'

'Oh, I know nothing of the matter, I assure you,' said Charlie. 'How old are you, Mrs James?'

'You should never ask a lady's age, Mr Parkinson,' Ginny reproached him. 'It's simply not done.'

'You see?' shrugged Charlie, amid a chorus of laughter.

She was always nervous before going on, but the memory of Charlie's doings with her in the dressing room and the approval of Signor Morales alleviated the feelings of complete terror and carried her through the evening performance. She gave one encore, then joined Charlie to spend the rest of the evening with the audience at the bar. Most of the comments they heard about her act were complimentary, and they returned home triumphant.

'You know, I do have the most astounding good luck. I desire you and, though all seems hopeless at the time, a few weeks later, here you are, fallen into my hands as ripe as a little plum. Not only that, but a few short months afterwards I've made you a success on the halls and you're almost earning your own keep,' he observed as they lay side by side in bed that night.

'And I always said I wanted a lucky man, but I don't really feel as if I've got you, Charlie.'

'You have more of me than any woman before you. And you have a share of the luck, my hinny. I'm an excellent manager and agent. I've advanced your career further than you could have dreamed of. I've made you famous.'

'Yes, you have, and I'm grateful, Charlie, but I wish you'd marry me. I'm old enough now. I don't like living in sin like we do. It's not right.' A sudden thought struck her. 'Did you tell any o' those men at the bar what we did in the dressing room this afternoon?'

'Certainly not,' he protested, 'I fancy myself a gentleman, and gentlemen do not betray any little intimacies they may indulge in with the ladies.'

She felt reassured. 'I'm glad of that, anyway,' she said. But the thought of the dressing room would not leave her mind. She reached out to touch him, and the part she held became swollen and hard in her hand.

'You insist on an encore,' he said, 'and I'm ever your slave.'

She laughed, and without prompting sat astride him to impale herself.

'What a saucy, naughty, shameless little trollop it is.'

She saw him laughing up at her in the lamplight as she began to rise and fall upon him and something about the laugh irked her. Her slave nothing, when he denied her respectability, validity in the eyes of society, the things she wanted most from him. He was her master. She knew it, and she also knew that his corruption of and dominion over Arthur Wilde's daughter provided the best part of his pleasure with her. She laughed in return, and looking down at him thought how easy it might be to put her hands around his neck in this position and squeeze and squeeze until she had stilled that deceitful mouth and choked off that triumphant smile for ever. She said nothing for a while, then asked, 'How much money are they paying me at the Arena, Charlie?'

'At a time like this, Ginny? Women and money! Save business 'til the morning, do.'

'No, how much though? I want to send some home. Our Emma wants to be a teacher. I could send enough to make her a teacher, couldn't I?'

'You must cut yourself off from the people at home, for many reasons.'

'I can't do that, Charlie. I love them.'

'You love your father? It's the first I've heard of it.'

'I love me mam and our Emma, and the bairns,' she said, but did not add, 'and Martin, who loves his dead wife'.

He pushed her down on to the bed and rolled on top of her to begin a more urgent lovemaking.

'You love this,' he said, 'and you love the stage. But most of all, you love this.'

No, most of all I love the stage, she thought, until he brought her to a searing climax. Then she cried, 'Oh, Charlie, I love you, I love you, I love you.'

The following Friday Ginny kept money back from her pay before handing the rest to Charlie.

'I'm going to send it, Charlie. It'll make a big difference to me mam. Our Emma might even get to be a teacher,' she defied him.

'I've told you not to communicate with them, for your own good as well as to avoid any inconvenience to me. What do you imagine the situation will be when I visit Annsdale, if it gets out there that we're living as man and wife? I should be in fear of my life from that animal of a father of yours. I shudder to think what he might be capable of. And you, Ginny, what do you suppose all those good Methodist people will think about you?'

She knew he was right. To write home and tell them she was doing well on the music halls would prompt questions as to how it had all come about. They might even want to come and see her, and she shrank from the thought that anybody in Annsdale should know she was living in sin with Charlie Parkinson. Better to lie, to let them believe she'd gone into service as she'd intended in the first place. Arguments against giving Annsdale cause to despise her cut deep; but she found that she could contemplate the idea of Charlie going in fear of his life with a smile. She wavered for a moment, and then with less certainty said, 'Well, I'm going to send some, Charlie.'

'Very well,' he conceded, 'but you must send no more than a housemaid might have earned. That will cause no suspicion, and it'll be enough for them, at their station in life. It's more than they ought to expect. Morales has put me on to a first-rate songwriter, and he won't come cheap. I think you fail to understand how heavy your expenses are, Ginny. There's very little of your salary left once they've been met. Please understand that, and let me have no more nonsense about it. And don't give them your address. It won't do for then to know it.'

Ginny soon began to cover the long way spoken of by Signor Morales. On stage she developed a stillness that gave emphasis to her slightest gesture, and developed a line of banter that was always friendly unless some heckler chose to make it otherwise. Then the repartee became acid, much to the amusement of the rest of the audience. Her sense of timing was acute, and she knew how to add impact to a punchline with a variation in tempo or an understated wink or nod. She became a mistress of double entendre. Her act could never have corrupted an innocent, but no man or woman of the world could fail to grasp its meaning. They clapped and shouted approval of her slyness, and more and better offers poured in. With a couple of good songs specially written for her, she gained in confidence. Her songwriter was the best in the business.

'It's a real pleasure to rehearse a new song of mine with you, Ginny. You've a good voice, but performance and inflection matter more. You seem to grasp the meaning behind every line at first sight,' he told her after a rehearsal, while his wife sat smiling beside them, handing out tea and cakes.

'It's a pleasure for me, too,' she assured him. 'Your songs are so easy to sing.'

They were middle-aged and kindly, and Ginny felt herself really at home for the first time since her arrival in

London. The atmosphere in their house was as relaxed and comforting as that at Mam Smith's, and she began to think of them as friends. Charlie seldom accompanied her on her visits to them, and she sensed some antipathy between the two men under the veneer of politeness.

She liked most of the other artistes, and enjoyed the consciousness that she was liked in return by most of the women among them, and admired by most of the men. Some of them told her so. She gossiped enthusiastically with them in her newly acquired London accent, her black eyes dancing, her laugh ringing out at every witticism. In company she was full of life, ready for fun and anxious to be friendy, but in her private moments she was sometimes homesick, and thought often of Martin, despite feeling herself entirely Charlie's property.

'Am I earning enough money for us to be married yet?' she asked, as they rode around St James's Park one Sunday afternoon.

'Not yet, little hinny. Soon.'

She pulled a face of disappointment. 'How soon?'

He shrugged, and was silent.

'Charlie?' Still he did not answer.

'You remember what you said about my monthlies?'

The process of restoring late monthlies, spoken of in such trifling terms by Charlie, was worse than Ginny could ever have imagined. It was performed that same evening by Charlie's own housekeeper in his own bathroom, and performed cleanly and efficiently as soon as the lady had boiled the necessary equipment, scrubbed her hands, and cleansed her patient. As Charlie testified, the woman thoroughly knew her business. She had been of service to lady-friends of his on several occasions, and as long as she could set to work before the thing was too far advanced, she could guarantee a safe and satisfactory outcome. He decided to go out for the evening with friends and leave the women to their business.

After the ordeal, the housekeeper helped the weeping Ginny into bed, where she lay shocked, disgusted and quivering.

'Come, come, don't be such a baby. You'll feel better presently, now your troubles are behind you. No use crying over spilt milk. It's a price we sometimes have to pay for our pleasures. You're not the first to need my services and I daresay you won't be the last. I'll bring you a cup of tea.'

When Charlie got into bed beside her in the small hours, she turned away from him. 'How many of your lady-friends has she helped like this, Charlie?' she asked, hugging a belly now racked by cramp.

'One or two. I assure you she knows what she's about. She was a midwife once. I wouldn't have trusted my little hinny to any but the cleanest and most practised hands.'

'How many lady-friends have you had?'

'So many questions. I've never professed myself a monk, Ginny, and I'm over thirty years old. I've had a good many women, no doubt, but never one quite like you.'

She couldn't sleep, and Charlie said it was pointless for two of them to lie awake. He could do nothing to help her, and when she'd tossed and turned for half an hour he went to sleep in another room, after instructing his housekeeper to wait upon her if she needed anything. Ginny would almost rather have died than have that woman near her again. She lay hugging herself until morning, frightened and alone.

There was no matinee the following day, and when she arrived at the theatre in time for her evening performance, a kindly fellow artiste remarked on her peaky appearance.

'You need plenty of rouge on those cheeks, my dear. You're as white as a sheet.'

'I'm not feeling quite up to the mark,' Ginny admitted. 'I've a headache. I feel tired.'

'You need a restorative. Have a little brandy and soda.'

'Will it do me good, do you think?'

'My dear, have you on form in no time. There's nothing to beat it as a pick-me-up.'

She knew that feeling as she did she would never be able to deliver the goods the audience had paid for, so she took the drink and soon felt a little better. By the time she had her last call, she felt almost herself.

'How was I?' she asked anxiously, as she came off stage.

'So so. But we all have our off nights.'

'I don't want many nights as off as this one. But you're right. I was bloody awful.'

Chapter Sixteen

Ginny was relieved to prove the housekeeper right. After a week she was as well as ever, and working harder. Charlie was an assiduous agent, and started booking her at two houses a night, sending a cab to carry her between them, which sometimes put her in a fever of anxiety that she would be late for her second engagement. He rarely accompanied her now, she'd been in the business long enough not to need hand-holding, and it was 'too much for a fellow to have to see the same act ad nauseam'. He often went out alone and saw her at home later. She moved in a solitary groove of theatres, the songwriter's house, and Charlie's, almost too busy to notice the passage of time and, apart from their occasional trips to the races and their Sundays together, feeling utterly isolated. Charlie seemed hardly to notice her unless he was collecting her salary or satisfying himself with her. When her monthlies were late again, her nerves were almost at breaking point.

'I wish I'd stayed in Annsdale and taken a hiding off me father. It would have been better than this. I was warned about people like you. I was warned about you, come to that,' she shouted.

He gave a snort of derision. 'I refuse to listen to such outrageous cant. Deep down, you willed all this, my hinny. A part of you, a powerful part that your Methodist hypocrisy refuses to acknowledge, willed it all and would have it so. You worked to bring it about.'

She put her hands over her ears. 'I did not. I did not,' she screamed. 'I came to London for a living-in job because you said you'd help me to get a one, and I daren't stay at home. You tricked me into your house, and you promised to marry me, and you terrified me into letting you do as you liked with me. You raped me, Charlie.'

He took hold of her wrists and wrenched her hands away. His cheeks were flushed but his words were like ice. 'You like to delude yourself, Ginny, but think of it. You were warned about me but no warning could hold you back. Why was that? You allowed nothing to prevent you from coming to me, and the blushing virgin in you was extinguished in an hour.'

'It's not true, it's not true.' She shrieked, and sank to the floor, covering her head with her forearms as if to fend off a blow.

He knelt beside her and spoke deliberately and remorselessly. 'It is true, and now you have what you wanted more than anything else, a man who can serve you well and serve you often. I use the word serve quite accurately. I perform a service for you. It's your necessity as much as mine, more so at times, and you revel in it. It pains me to offend your Methodist sensibilities, but in plain English, Ginny, you want it, and you like it, and you could not do without it.' He attempted to push her back against the rug, but she moved away from him. He redoubled his efforts but had no more success until he had her pressed against the wall unable to move further, with his hand up her skirts and inside her split-leg drawers.

'See, Ginny, see what you wear? You came to me that night in these, as if you wanted nothing to obstruct me. My Ginny in her ever-readies. My ever-ready little hinny.'

'Liar, liar. They were all I had when I came here, and you've bought them for me ever since.'

'Wait there,' he said, tearing at his own clothing, 'and I'll show you why you've never objected to wearing them.'

'Leave me alone. I'm probably with child already.'

'No more damage to be done, then,' he reasoned. She cried softly, but ceased to struggle.

'See,' he said, 'this is what you like, and this, and this.'

She lay still and unresponsive for a while, but eventually put her arms around him and drew him to her, to begin moving with him, yielding to her own overpowering desire. At last, at last it came; that sublime eruption deep within which discharged all turmoil, made her oblivious to all care, gave her blessed, wonderful release. When she lay quiet and utterly relaxed in his arms, he gave a laugh of triumph.

'There, there, my good little hinny is quite subdued.' He laughed again and kissed her lightly on her cheek. 'My luscious little hypocrite. My Ginny. How easy and how pleasurable it is to tame you.'

*

With fear and loathing she submitted again to the skills of the housekeeper and again Charlie's unshakeable faith in his most useful servant was fully vindicated. Ginny was completely well when a few months later the time came for him to accompany her on her first tour of the provinces. Birmingham, Manchester, Leeds, Sheffield, Hull, all welcomed her with open arms.

In Newcastle, Charlie left her for the week and went to visit his sister. It was bittersweet to hear familiar accents again, and when she heard the wail of Northumberland pipes coming from a public house one night on her way to the theatre, the lump in her throat almost choked her. She longed to go to Annsdale Colliery to see them all but dared not. On the afternoon before her last performance there, she strolled down to the docks to see the late summer sun shining on ships and seagoing vessels of every description. She breathed deeply, smelling the fresh salty air, and listening to the cry of seagulls and the shouts and conversation of seamen and dockworkers.

'Ginny? Is it you?' The voice sounded uncertain.

She turned to face him. 'John!' Overwhelmed to see him, she threw herself into his arms.

'I can't believe it's you. You look like a lady.'

'And you look like a good honest lad. How long are you here for? Where've you been? Have you been home?'

He'd been to Gibraltar, Mombasa, India, lots of places, but the best of all was Cape Town, he told her, the most beautiful place on earth. She listened with rapt attention to a long account of his travels and the people he'd met, until he stopped and laughed at her round eyes and open mouth.

'Well, you look as if you're doing all right. How are the rest of them?'

The lids fell over her eyes and she turned away slightly. 'I don't know. I've been away over a year and a half. Nearly as long as you. A lot's happened since you went to sea, John. I went to live in London, and now I'm on the stage. I sing in the music halls.'

'I can't believe it. But maybe I can. You always had a taste for adventure, our Ginny. If it hadn't been for you, I might not have gone to sea. So how did you manage it?'

'I didn't. It was managed for me. I went to London looking for a job to get out of the road of me dad. Only the sort of job I got wasn't the sort I expected.' She gave him a brittle smile. 'Charlie Parkinson got me into the music halls. I live with him, John.'

'What, that brother-in-law of the manager that was the talk of the pit?'

She nodded, unable to look him in the eye.

'You live with him? You're married, then.' He glanced at her hands and took in the thick wedding ring with evident relief, but she shook her head.

'You mean you're his whore? Oh, Ginny man, you're not!'

The look of disgust in his eyes wounded her, and she moved away from him a little.

'Well, what's me mam say about it? And me father?'

'Nothing, because they don't know. They think I'm working as a housemaid. Everybody does. I daren't tell them, John. I don't know what to do. I don't know what to do except keep working the halls, and hope he'll marry me.'

'Leave him and come home with me. Let's away and see me mam.'

'I daren't. Can you imagine what me father would do? He really would kill me. And I think I'm already landed with a bairn, John, and I want to keep it but I'm afraid of what everybody will say. I can't even write to them because I've nothing good to say about myself, and the letters would be full of lies. I don't know what else to do except try to get him to marry me. It might be all right then. Don't say anything about me at home.' She burst into tears. 'Oh, John, you don't know the half. I'm so ashamed.'

'Oh, Ginny man.' He pulled her towards him and let her cry for a while. 'You look miserable even while you talk about marrying him.'

'I am. But what else can I do? Me mam'll be glad to see you, but don't tell them about me, John. Don't say anything.'

He went to see her act, watching her from the wings. 'By, our Ginny, you were always a bit of a warm 'un, but,' he laughed, 'I don't know what word I'd use to describe your turn. It's funny, though. A long way off singing pit songs, but you were funny even then.'

'Did you like it, though?'

'Aye, but I'd be careful who I took to see it.' He smiled.

She got him a room in her hotel and the rest of the evening was spent more cheerfully in laughing and talking about old times.

John threw his arms round her and gave her an affectionate squeeze before he left her the following day. He got on the Durham train just as Charlie was getting off. She let him go, feeling comforted at his acceptance of her and his concern, but wretched at the thought that it might be years before she saw him again.

'Who was that?' demanded Charlie as she watched him go.

'Somebody you'd call riff-raff, Charlie. He's my brother. He's a sailor.'

Ginny's star was in the ascendant. After her successful tour and brilliant reviews, Charlie began to demand almost exorbitant fees for her appearances, and he got them. She was well aware of his displeasure at her pregnancy but no more mention had been made of enlisting the help of his housekeeper. Charlie seemed to be handling her with kid gloves now, trying to forestall another hysterical outburst and prevent her earning a reputation among theatre managers as temperamental and unreliable. That would slow the river of money flowing his way and might even dam it up altogether, she thought. She was beginning to read him like a book.

She agreed that she must work through the early months, because no engagements would be possible during the later ones. She must work until she began to show and then she could stop work and there would be time to be married. Exhausted from twice-nightly performances, she lay in bed at night happy enough for Charlie to take his pleasure with her, but a tired and passive partner herself. When she felt her baby quicken, he left her bed, but she never felt alone. She had her living child within her, and she already loved it.

During her last performance she bled a little. A few days afterwards she fancied her child had stopped moving, and later she knew it for sure. She wanted her mother and cried. Charlie took her to see a medical man who examined her, then told her to get dressed whilst he had a few words with her husband. Charlie kissed her on the way home.

'I have to go to Annsdale on business to do with the mine, little hinny. I shall be back as soon as I can, then there'll be plenty of time to arrange a wedding. Try to eat well, and go out every day for a little fresh air. I'll give instructions to the servants about your diet. Go to bed early and have a long rest in the afternoons. I really will be back as soon as I can.'

What business to do with the mine needed his presence, she wondered. He did nothing for the mine other than to take his profits from it, but she knew better than to tax him with leaving her at such a time, and her concern was about her child, not about Charlie.

'Is everything all right with the baby, Charlie?'

'Take very good care of yourself whilst I'm away, and all will be well.'

★

Three weeks later, after a long and difficult labour, her baby girl was stillborn. The capable housekeeper wrapped the yellow, bloated little corpse with its already-peeling skin and put it in her arms. 'It's a hydrops foetalis – a golden baby. I've seen them before. They never live. None of your children by Mr Parkinson will ever live. You'll be well advised to accept my help in future.'

Ginny held her lifeless child whilst the housekeeper went to prepare her a sleeping draught. She drank it and drifted into a drugged sleep thinking it not at all odd that she'd had a golden baby to golden Charlie. Naturally the child had died. She had died to oblige her father, so that everything would be as he wanted. Charlie was so lucky. When he wanted a thing, it became so. When Ginny awoke, her baby was gone.

A few days later, whilst the housekeeper was removing a tray of food Ginny had been unable to eat, Charlie entered.

'She had the child a week ago, you say. I hope you've taken very good care of her.'

'I have indeed, sir. She's had every care, and cook has tried every delicacy to tempt her appetite, but she's not quite herself yet.'

'Poor little hinny.' He crossed over to Ginny and lifted her chin. 'I must take you out and about, blow the cobwebs away and put some roses into your cheeks.'

'Don't you want to know whether we lost a son or a daughter?'

'It makes very little difference now, surely. The important thing is to have you quite well again. *Pas de rapports pendant trois semaines*, as the French say.' He smiled and ruffled her hair fondly. 'So much more realistic than stretching the thing out to six weeks. There's no satisfactory substitute for you, little hinny.'

He threw himself into the task of restoring her to health. He lavished attention on her, took her out, had the cook prepare delicacies for her but did not mention the subject of marriage. That was well. Far from being her aim, the thought of marriage to Charlie had become her aversion. After a couple of weeks he joined her in bed.

'Please, Charlie, I'm not ready yet,' she whispered.

He sighed. 'Very well. I won't trouble you for a while yet. But in another three weeks, I expect you to be quite well again. You ought to understand something though, Ginny. I'm a very healthy man, and I must find release somewhere.'

He made no bookings for her and left her to sleep alone. She was left to her own devices, to convalesce and to mourn her child.

'Don't worry on my account, I've no interest in babies,' he told her one morning, in a consoling mood. 'Small wonder many men seek a mistress for the first time after their wives are with child. No, Ginny, babies are more than an inconvenience and we'll do much better without them. I really think everything has happened for the best.'

Chapter Seventeen

Ginny was dead inside, as dead and frayed as her baby. At night she dreamed of it silently reproaching her, seeming to ask, 'What choice had I but to die? How could I have lived?' She passed her days brooding, playing patience, or wandering alone for hours in the park. It was her second November in London, the trees were stark and rustling dead leaves covered the grass. She thought of Maria in the world of the dead and whispered to her, 'Love my child.'

'You don't look very well. All Charlie's whores look like that, sooner or later.'

She turned and recognized Charlotte sitting next to her on the park bench. A little girl of about three years old stood at her knee.

'I'm not one of his whores.'

Charlotte gave her a withering look and said no more.

'Charlie was my first. I've never known any other man.'

'No, neither had any of us before we met him. Charlie doesn't take up with whores, he makes whores of the jays he takes up with.'

The child drifted off and started to play in the dirt. Charlotte's features twisted into an expression of anger and she called a few sharp words to her. The little girl turned her face towards them, lips stretched in a smile that couldn't reach her joyless, watchful eyes. Her face was the image of Charlie's, and the apprehension in it chilled Ginny's soul.

'Charlie said you'd easily get a husband, and a rich one, too.'

'Yes, Charlie would say that, but Charlie should have been my husband. I was a respectable governess when I met him. You might find it hard to believe, but I'm a clergyman's daughter. I had a good place when I met him, and I let him gull me into his house with promises of marriage. He told me I was the most beautiful girl he'd ever seen. Who do you think her father is?'

'Charlie,' said Ginny, with absolute certainty.

'I hoped he'd marry me when she was born, but she made things worse, not better. Now I haven't got him, I've got her to remember him by and ruin my chances of getting anybody else. How do you think I'm going to get a husband with her in tow?'

'I hoped he'd marry me before my baby was born. But my baby died.' Ginny's voice sounded hollow.

Charlotte gave a sardonic smile. 'You really do have all the luck.'

'It's not luck. I wanted her to live, like yours,' said Ginny, a tear stealing down her cheek. 'It's not the child's fault. She's not to blame for anything anybody's done. What's your name, pet?'

The child did not answer but smiled on, wary, watching her mother intently. 'Her name's Jubilee,' said Charlotte. 'You're more gullible than I am. He's got you earning good money on the halls, I know. I needn't ask who's holding the purse strings. How much money of yours has he spent? You're even more stupid than I am.'

Ginny should have been shocked but was curiously flat and calm. 'I'm going to leave him.'

'No woman ever left Charlie yet, that I do know. He's too good in bed. He decides when they'll leave and then they leave to walk the streets for him. We left when he knew you were coming. He put me in a carriage with a friend of his, and when he'd finished with me I started to work the Empire. That dress you wore when I first saw you was one of mine once.'

'He told me it had belonged to his sister.' Ginny thought for a moment. 'That means you must have been living together when she came down to stay with him. Wasn't she shocked?'

Charlotte smiled the strangest smile Ginny had ever seen. 'Oh, no. She was brought up to know the world too well to be shocked, although I daresay it suits her to pretend otherwise these days. Their mother was half French, you know, with very French talents that got her admirers among our aristocracy. A certain Irish gallant did very well by her. Her daughter naturally followed in her footsteps. Mrs Vine was one of the sisterhood, and Charlie should have a brass plate on his door – Procurer to the Gentry.'

Ginny hesitated, then gave way to morbid curiosity

and hinted, 'He said something to me that day we saw you. He said it was much the same with other men as with him. He made it sound an easy way of life.'

'Yes, very easy for women who like insolence and violence and disgusting lust and putting themselves at risk of filthy disease, and having brats sired on them by men they loathe. For those who enjoy every form of degradation, the life is one long round of pleasure, and there are women like that. Unfortunately for me, I am not one of them. I detest the life. No, it's not the same with others as it is with Charlie.'

'You must hate him for what he's done to you.'

Charlotte was silent for so long that Ginny doubted she'd heard her, then, 'I have a weakness where he's concerned. If I had a thousand men to choose from, I'd still only want Charlie. No, I don't hate him. I hate you for taking him from me,' she said.

The sins of the fathers are visited on the children, Ginny thought, passing the lamplighter as she walked through darkening streets back to Charlie's house. Jubilee's apprehensive, wizened little face with its parody of a smile would not leave her mind, and she wondered despairingly if she could have been any better a mother to such a faithful copy of her flame-haired betrayer. 'Don't you bring any carroty-haired chips off that block to my door,' her father had said. Jubilee's face was replaced by Charlotte's, mouth turned down, eyes dead, expression as bitter as gall. Then came Maria's sweet face, and the face of her own baby.

'Love my bairn,' Ginny whispered.

Their faces stayed with her all the way back to Charlie's house, their voices one after the other whispering through her mind. The sins of the fathers are visited on the children. Charlotte was venting all her anger against Charlie on their innocent child. Jubilee's taut little face haunted her, smiling its ghastly smile, and Ginny felt pain at the recollection of Charlotte's sharp words to her and the question: 'How do you think I'm going to get a husband with her in tow?'

'You see? How could I live?' her own child seemed to ask, and Ginny felt too heartsick to cry.

Charlie was out when she got back. She sat in the drawing room until dinner time, when the housekeeper served a meal she could not eat. 'Mr Parkinson instructed me to tell you he won't be back. He has some business to attend to. He may be quite late.' The curt message was delivered with the faintest sneer.

'Have you anything for a headache?' Ginny asked.

'I'll bring you something directly.'

She took the medicine and went upstairs to lie down. The same faces and melancholy thoughts chased each other through her head and gave her no rest. She tried to think how to act, then came real fear as she rehearsed what she must say to him. Her headache grew worse. At two o'clock she tapped on the housekeeper's door to beg for a sleeping draught and later fell into a drugged slumber disturbed by bad, sad dreams. She woke late, jaw clenched and shoulders stiff, when the housemaid came in to tell her that Mr Parkinson wanted her to join him for breakfast.

She found him in very good spirits. 'How's my sweet little hinny today?'

She gave him a wan smile, dark circles evident under her eyes. 'I can't say I'm very well, thank you, Charlie. I waited up until two o'clock for you last night.'

'I'm very sorry to hear it, but my lateness was owing to consideration for you. Your being indisposed as you are prevents my disturbing you, and the girl I was with took more than the usual amount of coaxing. Never mind, she liked it in the end,' he smiled, 'but there will never be anyone to match my little hinny. I shall be truly glad when you're quite yourself again.'

Ginny imagined another young, green, helpless girl with no friend to protect her being coaxed by Charlie. Had she dared she might have taxed him with rape but she knew it would make no impression except to anger him, and that she did not want. She had long understood that the worse Charlie's conduct, the more elevated was the language he chose to describe it. Charlie was a gentleman. He did not abduct and rape girls who were scarcely more than children, he indulged women who really wanted his attentions with a little coaxing to help them overcome their feigned shyness and false modesty. Her head began to ache again.

'Is she going to live here?'

'Certainly not. Whatever gave you that idea? I'm very happy with you most of the time.'

'But you won't marry me.'

He shrugged. 'There's no urgency about that now, little hinny.'

'No, there isn't,' she said evenly, 'but there's an urgency for you to marry Charlotte.'

'There you have me quite mystified. Why ever should I marry Charlotte?'

'Because you've got a little girl between you.'

'I have no little girl.'

'I've seen her with my own eyes, Charlie. I saw her in the park yesterday, with Charlotte. Her name's Jubilee.'

'Very well. I have no little girl that I recognize.'

'She's the spit of you, Charlie. You can't deny her.'

'You do have some amusing colliery-village notions, Ginny. Charlotte was well paid. That account's cleared. Charlotte can live very well on the profits of her embraces. That is the path she has chosen.'

'I always thought you were heartless, Charlie, but I can't believe how heartless. It's not only that you don't love Jubilee yourself, you make her own mother hate her because of the way you treat her. Your own child. Doesn't it grieve you to think your own child's mother ill-treats her because of you? Couldn't you weep to think of it? Doesn't it make you want to run and find her, and bring her home? And Charlotte still loves you, you must know that.'

He spoke quietly and deliberately. 'Listen, Ginny. Your Methodist teachers must have told you that if a woman consents to accommodate a fellow before he's married to her, the consequences of her choice are her own. More so, if she refuses to allow him to help her out of her little difficulty. Charlotte refused the services of my excellent housekeeper. Charlotte hoped to blackmail me into marriage. She gambled and she lost. That's the end of it.'

Sensing his anger, Ginny felt a flutter of anxiety but went on with the arguments she had prepared throughout most of the night. 'What about Jubilee? What's she done to deserve being cast off by her father and hated by her mother? Charlotte punishes her because of you. She's yours and she looks like you, Charlie. All she needs is to be loved.'

'What Charlotte does with her own child is her own concern. You know, Ginny, I realize from time to time why I am still unmarried. To borrow the words of the wedding service, I'm a "for better, for richer" sort of man. Others may take "for worse" if they wish. You're being exceedingly tedious, and I beg you to stop it now.'

'You should marry Charlotte, Charlie, and look after your child.'

He sighed heavily, tossed his napkin on the table, leaned back in his chair and looked at her for several moments.

'Marry her, you say? I wouldn't even be seen with her. I wouldn't fuck her now with somebody else's prick. She's a filthy malicious whore who's obviously doing everything she can to spite me. I regret the necessity for such language, Ginny. I use it to make the matter clear enough for you.'

She blushed and hung her head, very afraid that her meddling had made things worse and not better for Charlotte and Jubilee. 'Charlotte hasn't said anything against you. But her little girl looks so miserable, it was my idea to ask you, not Charlotte's. Don't blame Charlotte. I'm sorry, Charlie.'

'Very well, but you must never mention either of them to me again.' He leaned towards her and lifted her chin. 'You do look unwell. You must drive all these matters from your mind, Ginny; they're not your concern. Concentrate on getting well. I've arranged bookings for the week after next. All this moping is doing you no good. You'll be much better working.' He drew her face towards his and kissed her lips. 'And you'll soon have your other duties to attend to, the ones we both enjoy so much.'

She nodded in submission, and suddenly looked up. 'Can I have some pocket money, Charlie?'

He gave her a quizzical look. 'May I have some pocket money, I suppose you mean. What for? I hope you're not thinking of buying drink.'

'I just want to have some money. In case I walk a long way and want to get a cab back, or I might want to call at Lyons for tea and cakes while I'm out. May I, Charlie?'

He tossed a couple of sovereigns on the table with an air of patient generosity. 'You may, little hinny. I take your renewed interest in money as a sign of improving health.'

The housemaid brought in the morning post. Unexpectedly, there was a letter for Ginny, postmarked Annsdale Colliery. It contained a postal order for the sum of every penny she had ever sent home, with a short note from her mother saying that everyone in Annsdale village and Annsdale Colliery knew she was living in sin with Charlie Parkinson. Her father had disowned her and insisted that all the money she had sent them should be returned. She was to send no more. The letter fell from her hand.

'Well, that's the end of it for me. I've got no mother and no father. I'll never dare go back home again after this. He'd kill me. I don't think I'd visit your sister for a long time if I were you.'

Charlie snatched up the letter and read it. 'How in God's name did they find out? I told you not to give them this address.'

'I didn't, and I don't know how they found out.' A thought suddenly struck her. 'If your engagement to Clarice Farr wasn't off before, it'll be off now, I should think.'

The expression on his face told it all. He was livid, and despite her own deep misery and discomfiture, she felt a small glow of satisfaction and a tiny measure of compensation in his.

'I told you no good would come of any dealings with the people in Annsdale. I'm very annoyed with you,' he said.

'I'm sorry, Charlie.' She thought that had he been like her father, he would have struck her then, but other than breaking her occasional resistance to his lovemaking, Charlie managed to control her without violence.

She took her morning bath, hating him for his treachery in maintaining his engagement with Clarice Farr, hating him for his treatment of Jubilee and

Charlotte, and for everything that had happened to her since she left Annsdale Colliery. She wallowed for an hour in the comfort of hot, scented water and thought of home. It was not her father or her mother who came to mind, but an image of Martin in the tin bath before Mam Smith's fire. She soaped herself slowly and pictured herself washing the coal dust from his hair, scrubbing his back, wrapping him in a towel when he got to his feet with the water running in rivulets off him, skin as white and muscles as hard as marble, then taking his wet, clean face in her hands and pressing her lips against his.

That could never happen now. Martin must despise her as much as everybody else did, and probably more. Charlie had ruined her, ruined her reputation, destroyed her baby; he had ruined everything. She sighed grievously as she remembered the day her father had called him a whoremaster, and wondered if there was any point in leaving him now that everybody she cared about knew she was his whore. 'Yes,' she whispered to herself, 'there is; because he'll want me again soon, and when he starts on me I'll want him, and soon I'll be with child again. The only way to avoid that is to avoid Charlie.'

She pulled out the plug and stepped out of the bath to dry herself. Once dressed, she retrieved her nightdress case and Maria's shoes. She put them in a bag with a few other items of clothing, put her two sovereigns and her postal order in her pocket, went downstairs and walked unnoticed out of the front door. She didn't stop walking until she reached the songwriter's house, then deliberately not allowing herself time for second thoughts she lifted the heavy brass knocker and rapped loudly. When his wife answered, she said, 'Will you help me? I'm ringing the curtain down on Charlie Parkinson, and I've nowhere else to go.'

Chapter Eighteen

'I mean I've left you, Charlie,' she said, stepping on to the thick blue carpet of his hallway. 'I've come to get the rest of my clothes and to ask you where you've got me booked for the week after next.'

'An end to this nonsense, my hinny,' he said, face grim. 'Now take off your hat and coat and tell me where you've been.'

'I've been at Mr and Mrs Burn's. I can tell you that without taking my things off. He's waiting in the cab for me. He'll fetch a constable if I'm not outside again in five minutes.'

'The devil he will! The impudence of the fellow! How dare he make my private affairs his business?' Charlie exclaimed, but she caught a wariness in those calculating blue eyes.

'It's my private affairs he's making his business, because I asked him to. Can I get my things, please?' she asked, her confidence increasing as she saw his diminish.

'You may. By all means.' He waved her on. She doubted he would have done that had she been alone. Dreading his following her, she ran upstairs to tear all her things out of the wardrobes and throw them into bags as hastily as she could. When she turned to heave them downstairs, he was behind her. She cried out in alarm as he took the bags from her and held her in his arms.

'No, no, hinny, this won't do. You mustn't leave,' he murmured, kissing her ear. 'You need me, and I can't do without you. You know that as well as I do.'

She wrenched herself free. 'I'm going. I felt tied to you because you're my first and you'll probably be my only one now. I'm ashamed to admit it, but you were right. I couldn't help liking what you did with me. But you're cruel, Charlie, and I would rather join a nunnery than spend another five minutes with you. If I never get another man as long as I live, I never want to be with you again. You've nearly driven me mad and I don't love you. You were right about that an' all, I never did. I'll end up in an asylum if I stay with you any longer.'

'Calm yourself, and think of the practicalities, Ginny. How long will it be before they tire of your intrusion into their household? What will you do then? And who's to look after your affairs, get your bookings, manage your accounts, pay your tax, and all the hundred other little services I've performed for you? I doubt if George is capable of it, even if he had the will.'

'I'm going, Charlie.'

'Go then, and be damned.' He shrugged, and rapidly preceded her downstairs to open the front door with a flourish. He watched her struggle down with her bags and gave her a contemptuous bow as she half dragged and half carried them out. But when he saw George sitting in the cab outside looking towards the house, Charlie's manner changed.

'Where've you got me booked?' she asked, as they stepped outside.

He hesitated for a moment, looking briefly towards George, then said, 'That information, my sweet hinny, will cost you a kiss.'

She gave him a look of contempt. 'Yes,' he persisted, 'one of your very best, longest, most loving little hinny kisses and I'll tell you where.'

The pantomime, she knew, was for George's benefit, but to save further argument she did as he asked.

'No,' Charlie murmured, 'that wasn't one of your best, but I understand what's wrong. You're still suffering the loss of our baby, but that will pass and then I shall claim a real kiss. Your engagements are at the Delphic and at Villiers. I'll see you there, but I hope you'll be home before then and I truly expect you back within the fortnight. I want you more than ever, so you see, I'm much kinder to you than you are to me. I've forgiven you already, Ginny, and I promise I won't be cross with you when you come home.'

'Can I have some of the money I earned, Charlie?'

His face assumed an expression of regret. 'I fear it's been spent on your expenses, little hinny. I'd lend you some of mine, but I'm rather short myself at the moment. I fail to see how you'll manage everything without a great deal of help, so I'll oblige you by continuing as your manager, if not your lover. Kiss me again.'

She refused. When George came forward to carry her bags and help her into the cab, Charlie pecked her on the cheek and said, '*Au revoir*, my hinny. Come home very soon.'

There followed the saddest and lowest period in Ginny's life, and she afterwards wondered at the Burns' tolerance and friendship in seeing her through it. She was depressed, often vacant. They would sometimes speak to her, and realize she was too far withdrawn into a world of her own to hear them. She became even fonder of drink. The gusto with which she had once performed her sauciest songs was gone.

'I don't know what it is,' she told them, with her own baby and Jubilee in her mind, 'I can't seem to laugh at it all any more. I think I've seen too much of the other side of the coin, and the innocent children who get hurt. I could cry at it sooner than laugh.'

When George presented her with a new number entitled 'The Wrong Chap', she read it through, then to his dismay she burst into tears and ran from the room.

There were practicalities to deal with as Charlie had warned, but they were her salvation. She wanted to be completely rid of him, wanted him to take no further interest in her or her stage career. With the help of the Burns, she hired an agent and an accountant, then discovered that Charlie had never paid any tax for her and there were over two years of arrears to be settled. She commissioned new stage clothes, tipped musicians and callboys well, and kept the goodwill of everyone she relied on. When all her expenses had been paid, the Burns took the remainder of her salary and after deducting what was reasonable for her maintenance, they banked it for her. They thought that with enough judicious saving she would soon have enough to buy a house of her own. She began to feel safe.

She appeared in pantomime over the Christmas season, steady, local work. The pantomime season ended and she was back in music hall. She sometimes saw Charlie in the audience with other pretty young women, and felt nothing but relief at having escaped him. She said as much to the Burns one Sunday.

'He's a slippery customer,' said George, 'I'm surprised he's given up so easily. But you never told us how you got involved with him in the first place.'

'I was a housemaid at his sister's. He took me to the races on Boxing Day a couple of years ago. He won, and won, and won. He put a bet on for me, and I won, and all. I thought I'd never met anybody so lucky. I thought some of it might rub off on me.'

'Mm,' mused George. 'Boxing Day races, always over the sticks. Three jockeys can throw a race – two hemming in the rest and holding them back while the third gets on to win. If the wrong one looks as if he'll win, he can contrive to fall off. They know what they're doing and some of them are willing to risk a couple of broken ribs if somebody makes it worth their while. Mr Parkinson's well known at local race meetings, but not known in the North, I think.'

Ginny's eyebrows shot up in astonishment. 'That's

exactly what happened. The leading rider fell off his horse at the last minute, and we won a fortune.'

'Of course, I don't know that that particular instance was a cheat, but such cheats are sometimes practised.'

'And I bet that was one of them, knowing Charlie.'

'Some people are very good at making their own luck,' George laughed, 'often at the expense of others.'

'You can't beat the bookies, but if you're clever enough, and dishonest enough, you can cheat the bookies,' Ginny said.

Spring came again and as the days lengthened her mood began to lift. Little by little, she felt happier and more secure. By Easter she'd bought her own small house, its little garden brightened by spring flowers. Her quilted nightdress case, the only thing she had to remind her of her mother, she put on her pillow, and Maria's shoes rested in plain view on the dressing table. She engaged a housekeeper, but, with her health and vigour returned, she often took pleasure in pinning on an apron and doing a thorough cleaning herself. She bought a hipbath, and occasionally soaked herself before the fire thinking bitter-sweet thoughts of home. She went for long walks in the clear fresh air, and in spite of her griefs the sheer joy of being alive, healthy and young began to stir within her.

When George got her to read over and rehearse another song he'd written for her, the ending was so wickedly clever that a peal of genuine laughter burst from her at the end of it.

'That's better, girl. That's more like the old Ginny,'

George approved. 'You've got your sense of fun back, and you put the song over beautifully. Here's to success.'

'But don't you think it a bit too, um—'

'Nothing of the sort,' said George with a sly smile. 'We can't help people's minds, Ginny. If some people insist on putting the worst interpretation on things, we can't help it. It's only the naughty people who'll find a naughty meaning in it.'

She began to see more of Charlie than she'd seen when she lived with him. He was at many of her performances, either with the young rakes of the town or with a lady-friend. She took care to avoid him, and engaged a stolid, middle-aged maid to be her constant companion and chaperone. She felt less compulsion to drink, and George persuaded her to limit herself to half a glass of champagne before a performance, and to avoid spirits altogether. The champagne began to taste odd after a while, and she discovered that George had persuaded her maid to add ever-increasing amounts of soda water to it. She smiled, and took it as the kindness it was intended to be. She began to command a higher salary than ever, and found she could pay all the expenses Charlie complained of plus agent's and accountant's fees, and arrears of tax and still have money to save. She felt safer, if not entirely safe, and much happier, though not entirely happy.

In summer, when quite restored to health, she performed her new song with zest and gaiety and found that well-being had brought with it stirrings of the old desires. She glimpsed Charlie standing alone in the wings, looking at her with importuning eyes. When she returned to her dressing room he was waiting for her with flowers and champagne, asking her to sup with him.

'The way I feel now, I could,' she said, the presence of her maid giving her enough confidence to make the admission. 'And I liked to be with you sometimes because you're entertaining and you're witty and full of fun, but I've seen what you're like underneath all that. You're cruel and selfish. You're evil, Charlie. I've heard about you and your sham domestic servants' agency that draws poor girls into misery. Mam Smith was right, lambs to the slaughter, and you're the Judas goat that leads them there. So go away, Charlie, I don't want to know you any more.'

He looked pained. 'Ginny, who told you this?'

'George did.'

'And has he said he knows it for a fact?' She shook her head.

'How clever of him. I should have him up for slander if he had. Let any man have a little good fortune in life, and he's sure to find himself blackguarded by the envious. My income comes from no such venture. I have some inherited money and some shares in the mines around Annsdale, which pay me well enough. I'm sometimes lucky at cards and at the racetrack. Your friend wrongs me, and so do you.'

He had such a look of injured innocence that she wavered, uncertain what to believe. He pulled her towards him and kissed her neck, murmuring, 'Haven't you missed me at all? I had hoped you would let bygones be bygones and come back to me. Surely we had some good times together? I did work hard on your account, grant me that at least.'

'I do. But you said you were paying my taxes as well, you liar.'

'I fully intended to, but you left before I had the opportunity. I miss you so much, Ginny,' he whispered, 'I miss my lusty little sinner – no other woman compares, and I know you've had no other man. I miss your soft, luscious little body, those funny little whimpering noises you make in the back of your throat when . . .'

'Oh, don't, Charlie, don't!'

'. . . when you've abandoned yourself to me. The way you move your haunches so delightfully, so sensuously when I'm deep inside you . . .'

'Oh, shush, shush!'

'The way you cry, "Oh Charlie, I love you, I love you," when I bring you to the melting point . . .'

He stopped her protests with a kiss that she returned.

'You've owed me that since the morning you left me, my sweet, cruel little hinny, and I told you then I'd come to claim it.'

The maid was watching them uncertainly throughout this interlude, waiting for instructions. Finally she moved towards the door and opened it, and then Ginny called sharply after her, 'Oh, don't leave me, don't leave me!'

She closed the door, took up a position beside Ginny and looked squarely at Charlie. With every nerve agitated and the effort costing her all her strength Ginny said, 'Oh, go, Charlie, please, please go. I'm not your little sinner any more.'

He left the flowers and champagne, and after kissing her cheek he went, with expressions of regret but no other protest. The incident unsettled her completely. The thought of him, of the things he did with her, of his touch, of his murmured approval when she did the things that pleased him, all those thoughts inflamed her, made her want to run through the streets after him to beg him to slake the fire inside her. She slept badly, racked by lust, missing intercourse with him, missing the relief it gave. Charlie had spoken the truth when he told her that it was her necessity. 'You're a natural gay lady,' he'd said. She thought of Charlotte and shivered, glad to be on the halls and not on the streets.

Agnes Burns knew what was wrong with her. 'Any woman used to regular attentions misses them, I know that from experience. I was a widow when I met George, you know. It's quite natural. Could you not marry, dear?'

She was courted by many men and would laugh and joke and return their glad eyes in public, but she was careful to keep her maid by her and never allowed herself to be alone with any of them. She felt sorely tempted to take a lover and knew that many in the profession would not have blamed her, but she feared pregnancy, disease and notoriety and dared trust none. She had offers of marriage but from no one she wanted to marry. So she resolved on a solitary life unless she met somebody like Martin, a man who was capable of loving as well as being loved. She might wait alone in perpetuity for such a one, for there was no one like Martin.

Except Martin.

Young and radiant, with that bright-eyed, glossy-haired and glowing beauty that only perfect health can bestow, full of vigour and in love with active life, she had no other outlet for her energies than her act. She threw herself wholeheartedly into it, built up a huge repertoire of songs and rehearsed them to perfection. But in spite of her enormous appetite for work she was restless. She became meticulous about her appearance, her hair and clothes. She had her maid always with her on weekdays, and on Sundays she kept company with the Burns, who treated her like a substitute daughter, and would take her out boating, or to race meetings, or any other social activity that promised enjoyment. Under their tutelage she became more and more refined until she was quite the lady. George and his wife began to hold intimate little soirées on Sunday evenings, and often happened to have some eligible bachelor among the company. Ginny was polite and sociable, but uninterested.

'Don't you like him? He's quite taken with you,' Agnes might say to her of some gentleman or another.

'Yes, he's very nice,' Ginny would reply, without enthusiasm.

'You know what I mean, more than like. Really, I don't know what you want in a man,' would be the exasperated rejoinder.

'No more do I,' Ginny would lie, thinking only of

Martin, a real man, who was acknowledged a man by the whole of Annsdale, and Annsdale was no lenient judge. All other men appeared to her untrustworthy, flabby, self-indulgent creatures by comparison. But she made no attempt to explain to Agnes and George that she prized a self-educated pitman over any fine gentleman they could produce because she knew that they could never have understood it.

She did another exhausting tour of the provinces in the autumn and returned to London to learn that John had been asking round the theatres for her and had tracked her down to the Burns'. She was upset at missing him, but glad to hear that he was well, and rejoiced that he knew she had broken with Charlie and was living a decent life.

November came, and she was haunted by memories of her baby and of Maria. Homesick, she wrote to Emma, asking her to come to stay with her in her new house over Christmas, or at least to write back with news of everybody. Although she'd had no great hopes of a reply, she was bitterly disappointed when none arrived. She sent gifts home and felt broken when they were returned. The pantomime season did something to distract her and to direct her thoughts along more cheerful channels, but when it ended, she heard that Daisy May was dead, the rumour was of drink. She knew the same fate would have awaited her had she stayed with Charlie.

She blessed the Burns for their deliverance of her and threw herself into her twice-nightly shows in and around London, using her wealth of new material.

Meanwhile, Charlie entered a new phase in his pursuit of her, one that kept her in an almost constant state of apprehension. He never lost an opportunity to accost her, whether he was with another girl or not. He would refer to her as his Galatea, and award himself full credit for the success of her career. He often sent her flowers, which she returned. He openly told her would-be suitors that he knew her in the biblical sense and was her husband in all but name, laughing at her embarrassment and the Burns' fury. She was once stung to reply that he was husband in all but name to dozens but he merely grinned and said, 'Ah, you forget that the rules of the game are rather different for men than for women, my hinny. A man is expected to pursue women and he's applauded for his success. A woman is despised. And you were such a naughty little hinny with me, quite the naughtiest I've ever had. I think it only fair to warn them.'

He proposed marriage regularly. She was never certain whether he was serious, but would not have married him now under any circumstances. She reminded her maid never to leave her alone with him.

Chapter Nineteen

It was nearing the third anniversary of her arrival in London and she pined for northern skies, a breath of northern air, the sounds of northern speech and northern music.

Daffodils bloomed in her garden, closely followed by tulips. She dreamed one night of Maria standing in bright sunlight in a garden full of flowers, holding her golden baby. They smiled at each other and Ginny had such a feeling of peace that she sighed in ecstasy, reached out to touch them and felt Maria's hand reassuringly in hers. They are happy, was her last comforting thought, a balm to her spirit as she sank into a deep and dreamless sleep.

She awoke late and while she lay with her eyes closed in that half world between sleep and wakefulness she became aware of a face barely visible through the darkness surrounding it, a face of fear staring through the gloom. Martin. She awoke with a gasp and sat bolt upright, heart racing, with a single thought in her mind. Go to him.

She talked the experience over with Agnes and George, who were no interpreters of dreams or portents and could offer no advice except that belief in such things was mere superstition. Unconvinced, Ginny insisted, 'I've got to go home. I'll fulfil tonight's engagement, but I'm cancelling the rest and I'm taking the first train home, come hell or high water. I'll send my mother a telegram to expect me.'

'Are you sure that's wise? Your father's made his feelings absolutely clear, and the signs are that your mother's given you up as well. If they blame you for shaming them in the eyes of their neighbours it might be better for all concerned if you stay away,' said Agnes.

Ginny hesitated, remembering the way her mother hid her bruises from the village for shame, then set her mouth in a determined line. 'I've got to go.'

'Then you know your own business best, and it must be so. At least matters will be resolved one way or another,' said George, 'but be warned against expecting very much. Don't build up too much hope and remember you've got friends here if they're unkind.'

Before the show she half-heard mention of a disaster somewhere, and there was talk of shareholders losing everything. Ginny tried to obliterate a sense of foreboding by concentrating her whole being on her art, on this, her last performance. On stage she was sparkling, hilarious, gaining true rapport with the audience. She dropped a deep curtsey in response to rapturous applause, then raised her head to look in wonder over row after row of laughing faces and clapping hands, feeling utterly detached, like a creature belonging to a different world a million miles away.

As she removed the greasepaint her maid told her that there had been an explosion in a mine in the north, and a lot of people stood to lose a lot of money. She hurried to join audience and fellow artistes in the bar to find out more. An impresario stopped her to congratulate her on her performance and to tempt her into his show with a small fortune. Suddenly she spotted Charlie waving at her and turned away from him to engage herself in conversation with the impresario, vainly hoping that Charlie would take the hint and go away.

'I say, Ginny, it's Annsdale, you know,' he called as soon as he was within earshot. He was waving the evening paper over his head and pushing his way through the crowds towards her. 'Scores of men trapped underground. Read it.'

He thrust the paper under her nose. She looked at it and saw only her vision of Martin's face as the floor swam up to meet her.

Dreading the discovery that Martin was either dead or buried alive, and wondering what sort of a welcome she would get in Annsdale, she lay awake all night. Before daybreak she put on the shoes he had given her, the first time she had worn them since she'd tramped the streets of London looking at the big houses, not daring to knock on any door to ask for work.

George and Agnes went with her to the station. Seeing Charlie boarding the same train in the grey dawn light, Ginny felt a stab of panic, fearing his behaviour towards her in Annsdale would be as bad as that in London, that he would make her name a byword for immorality. George nodded ominously in his direction. 'Now he's lost money on his mining investment, he'll be looking for another source of income.'

She took her seat alone in a first-class carriage, and gazed out of the window as the town sped by, comforted by the thought that London held two true friends she could return to if she found none at home. She looked for the twentieth time at the newspaper report.

> . . . a rush from the pit shaft of smoke and dust, which for a moment completely enveloped the headgear and hung like a pall over the pit and its surroundings, was a signal not to be mistaken by anyone who has experience of colliery disasters. As the boom of the explosion reverberated along the valley, men, women and children were seen rushing to the pit along roads and footways from all directions, all frantic to know the worst . . .

'Oh God, oh God.' Ginny shut her eyes for a moment, picturing them, her mother and the bairns, Mam Smith and Philip, Enid and the rest of the women of the village among them. She cursed the slowness of the train and the length of the journey, wishing herself among them right now but helpless to speed her arrival. She read on.

> Annsdale Colliery is the property of Messrs Vine, Wood, Tyas and Parkinson and Co. and is situated in a valley a few miles from Durham. Its means of communication is a line of railway connected by sidings with all the pits in the valley and thence with the whole railway network.
>
> It is to the coal trade that the area owes its present phenomenal prosperity. Instead of the few tons that were formerly sent out by different small pits in the neighbourhood, thousands of tons daily are now sent to the surface by this pit alone. From a small village Annsdale has grown to a populous and thriving district.
>
> As to the number who went down to work this morning, and the number who escaped through the Edmunds shaft, our information is uncertain. At first it was thought there were two hundred deaths, then under a hundred. Amid the excitement and grief, we have been unable to gain reliable information.

Suddenly Charlie entered her carriage and sprawled on the seat facing her, looking unusually morose.

'I wonder you dare go back to Annsdale, Charlie, with my father after you.'

He snorted. 'I have a financial interest which overrides any concerns I might have about him. A good deal of my money is sunk in that mine. An irate father pales into insignificance in the teeth of a setback like this one. In any case, what reason have I to avoid him now? See your left hand, Ginny? You still wear my ring. Your father objects to men who seduce girls they've no intention of marrying, but my dearest wish is to marry you. I'll make him my father-in-law as soon as you name the day. And if you'll excuse my saying so, you're the one who should be ashamed to go back to Annsdale, still refusing the man who has the prize of your virginity,' he looked at her and added, like a knife thrust, 'the man to whom you have borne a child. I wonder what the good people of Annsdale will think of that?'

She coloured as she took his ring off her finger, and put it into his hand. She had an impulse to beg him not to betray her, to plead with him to behave as a stranger to her when they got back, to say 'Please, Charlie, don't put me to shame,' but she knew it would only make him worse. He would apply any pressure, subject her to any humiliation, and resort to any means to get his own way. Pleas for forbearance would achieve nothing but to increase his triumph over her. Wiser by far, she thought, to give him no greater sense than he already enjoyed of his power to destroy her hopes. Charlie would act in his own interests, and she must expect it. Her feelings for Martin Jude must remain her own deep secret.

'Isn't it funny, Charlie, you wouldn't marry me when I kept asking you, and now I've made my mind up never to marry you. So why keep asking?'

'Perhaps it's the challenge, little hinny. And all my

objections to taking you for my wife have been removed. I find I quite relish the idea now. You're my equal in income. You behave and sound like a lady. I know I could safely present you anywhere. We suit each other so well in bed I haven't been able to get you out of my mind since you left me. I can give you a deeply satisfying married life. Take the ring back, Ginny.'

'No. And you can't give me a deeply satisfying married life because you can't give me love. There's no love in you. You couldn't have treated Charlotte or Jubilee as you did if there were. You wouldn't want to destroy my reputation if you loved me.'

'Exasperating girl. You drive me to it with your repeated rejection and humiliation of me, but I mean to have you, Ginny, and I will get my way in the end.'

'Do you want a pitman for a father-in-law, then? Isn't that beneath you?'

'Ah, Ginny, we live in London. Your father will remain safely tucked away deep in a mine somewhere in Annsdale, quite out of sight and out of mind. Perhaps he's among the men who are trapped, or even killed. Have you noticed something?'

'What?'

'We're quite alone in this carriage, and it will be hours before we get there.'

'Charlie, if you make one move towards me, I'll pull that communication cord. Things are a lot different now to what they were that first night in your house. I'm better known, and better dressed, and better spoken. I've got money. I've been taken for a lady, and I'd be believed. Touch me, and I'll have you thrown off the train.'

He shrugged and gave a taut smile. 'As if I would. You are too much of a lady now for that, and I'm certainly too much of a gentleman. It's very strange though, Ginny.'

'What is?'

'That you refuse me, yet you've had no other man. I take a keen enough interest in you to know for a fact that you haven't. It pleases me, because I hate a trollop, and it encourages me. But I do wonder at it. I've met none to compare with you, and I must assume you haven't met my match.'

'I wouldn't expect to meet your match in another hundred years,' she said, voice loaded with sarcasm. 'Like the song says, "I was a good little girl 'til I met you", and I went back to being a good little girl once I'd got rid of you.'

'You say such cutting things, Ginny, but I sometimes suspect there's more to it.'

To her relief, an elderly man joined them at the next station. Conversation stopped, and she sank into hideous reverie, wondering anew who might be dead, who trapped among the men and boys that she knew. Her brother Arthur must be old enough for the pit now, and her mind recoiled from the thought that he or her father or, above all, Martin, could well be one of them.

After a seemingly endless and wearying journey, they reached Annsdale and stepped off the warm train into a gust of cold wind. When she saw Emma waiting for her, Ginny's heart leapt. She went to throw her arms around her, but Emma determinedly kept her distance and her manner was cold.

'Well, here you are, and I wouldn't have recognized you. Quite the lady. We're going to have a lot more important people from London visiting us soon. I see you've brought your fancy man.' She nodded towards Charlie.

'I've got no fancy man.' Ginny marvelled at the change in Emma, who looked a grown woman. 'How bad is it?'

'Worse than you can imagine. "One woe doth tread upon another's heel, so fast they follow . . ."'

'I say, that's a quote from *Hamlet*, isn't it?' Charlie asked, a supercilious smile playing on his lips.

'What if it is?' Ginny demanded. 'What business of yours is our conversation?'

'None, none at all.' He looked at Emma, still smirking. 'Except Shakespeare translated into hinny does strike rather oddly on the ear. I mean no offence, of course.'

Even in the lamplight, Ginny saw Emma look as shamefaced as a servant girl caught stealing the spoons. Shakespeare was obviously something else Charlie thought too good for a pitman's daughter.

'Look, here's your sister in her horseless carriage, come to carry you off, Charlie. So goodbye for ever.'

'What an amusing girl you are, Ginny. Not for ever. Until I see you again, my little hinny, and so I will, very soon, when I come to ask your parents for your hand. I do hope your news is not very bad.' He took her by the waist and attempted to kiss her but she averted her face. He got into the yellow Daimler with a sigh and waved to her, but she received no acknowledgement from Helen. Without a word or a glance in Ginny's direction, she ordered her chauffeur to drive off.

'Yon's a good man to keep company with, if you can take insults as compliments,' said Emma. 'Don't bring him near me again.'

'I've not brought him, he's come on his own. And I don't want him near me.'

'He didn't seem to think so. We've not been able to hold our heads up round here since it got out about you and him. But you needn't worry about any trouble from me father, and neither need he. Not for a bit anyway, and probably never. He's trapped underground with the rest, and we don't know whether he's dead or alive. So you can come and stop with us. And I was going to tell you the worst when your fancy man interrupted us but maybe I'd better save it until you're sitting down at home.'

'He's not me fancy man,' said Ginny, 'and what was it? Tell me. Is it Martin? Is Martin dead?'

'What's Martin got to do with you? No, it's not Martin. Martin got out by the other shaft. It's the ones who were working in the dip who're still trapped.'

'I want to go and see for myself what's happened,' said Ginny. 'Will you come with me?'

'You'd better pick your bag up, then. It looks as if it cost plenty. I'll not be carrying it for you.'

'I never expected you to.'

They walked rapidly towards the pit and joined a dark fringe of people standing ankle deep in mud at the bottom of the bank, awaiting news which never seemed to come, and which all knew would be bad, come when it might. They stood patiently, illuminated by the ruddy blaze of a cresset standing at the entrance to the sawing shed. Ginny recognized a few of her former neighbours but none acknowledged her, all seeming concerned only with anxieties of their own. The policemen on duty at the mouth of the shaft clapped their gloved hands together for warmth. A couple of doctors waited, wrapped in blankets against a biting wind that swept across the dismal open space in eddying gusts. A shivering crew of reporters crowded over the pit-cabin fire.

Emma's face looked like a mask. 'We stood here all day yesterday, but there's too much wreckage in the shaft to let them get the cage down, and that's been damaged. It's all got to be shifted and mended before they can do anything. They reckon there's fires down below, and some are saying there can't be anybody left alive.'

They waited with the rest until frozen to the bone by the wind, then walked on home. Their mother was sitting at the quilting frame, looking thinner and more unkempt than Ginny could ever remember. She stopped in the doorway, suddenly nervous of going in.

Her mother didn't look up from her work. 'Well, you've come all this way, you might as well step over the threshold.'

It was the only sort of greeting Ginny felt she had any right to expect, but it was far from the one she'd hoped for. 'Hello, Mam,' she murmured.

Her mother avoided her eyes. 'Put the kettle on,

Emma. Now you're here, you'd better take your coat off, Jane.'

Ginny sat with her hands in her lap, fidgeting with the material of her dress, stealing nervous glances at her mother and clearing her throat from time to time. After a couple of minutes her mother looked her in the eye.

'I must say, you look in a better condition than the prodigal son, and a better condition than many an honest girl round here.'

Ginny's hands became still. 'Oh, don't, Mam. I haven't lived with him for over a year and if I look well, it's on money I've earned singing in the music hall, fair and square.'

'Whatever you've done, you've done enough to make sure we'll never live it down, you must know that. What makes it worse is you knew what he was before you went. Your father spelt it out for you.' Her mother's voice was harsh.

'I didn't know, not really. I was fifteen years old, how could I understand what he was like? If I could make it any different I would, but I can't.' Her lip quivered as she met her mother's stony gaze. 'I've not been with him for over a year, Mam. I never will again. Are you going to hold it against me for ever?' She averted her face to hide the tears that welled up in an instant.

'Leave her alone,' said Emma suddenly. 'She's still our Ginny.'

'How could she do it, though? I would never have thought any daughter of mine capable of it. I thought only bad girls carried on like that, ones who've never been taught right from wrong, but my own! I thought I'd given you better principles.'

'You did, and I can't explain how it happened, except I didn't seem to have any choice.'

'And you chose to make a right mess of yourself, didn't you?' her mother flashed, then added, 'Still, I suppose I'm glad you're all right, or as near to all right as you ever can be now.'

Emma poured boiling water on the tealeaves. 'She doesn't know the worst yet. When I was going to tell her, I got rudely interrupted. Then I thought it'd better keep until we got back.'

'What can be worse?' asked Ginny.

'John,' said her mother, every feature sagging and eyes dull. 'We had a message to say he's lost. Feared drowned.'

'I blamed you when we heard,' Emma admitted, handing her a cup of tea. 'I thought, if it hadn't been for our Ginny goading him on, he'd never have gone. But then the explosion happened and I thought he might just as easy have been killed in the pit. And I suppose there's a bit of hope he's still alive. Maybe he's been cast ashore somewhere, or picked up by a ship.'

'Was it John told you I was living with Charlie?'

'No. That woman who cooks for the Vines heard him and the manager rowing about you, the manager saying he ought to be ashamed of himself for breaking his word, and Charlie Parkinson telling him you'd thrown yourself at him and you were more to blame than him. Of course, she couldn't wait to blast the news all over the village. I can't think about any of this any more. I feel more dead than alive. I'll take my tea and lie in bed for a while. But I'm glad you're home, Ginny. You look after her, Em.'

After their mother had gone, Emma said softly, 'We heard about our John the day before me dad went down the pit. Of course, she blamed him, and she turned her back on him before he went, refused to give him a kiss, the first time she's ever done that since they were married. Now we'll probably never see him again. Not alive anyway, and maybe not at all. I think she's heart-broken over that, as much as everything else.'

Emma started to cut bread and cheese, whilst an exhausted Ginny rested her head on the back of her father's armchair and surveyed her old home. It looked strange yet familiar, smaller and shabbier than she remembered it, but still cosy and clean. She thought of her father trapped in pitch-blackness and shuddered. 'Poor Mam. Husband trapped in the pit and probably dead, son lost at sea, and eldest daughter a whore who's brought shame on everybody belonging to her. She must wonder what she's done to deserve it.'

'Can you keep a secret, Ginny?' Emma whispered.

'What?'

'You might not be the only one who's brought shame on everybody. I think I'm having a bairn.'

'What?' Ginny sat up straight, eyes wide open. Emma nodded.

'Jimmy Hood's sweet on me, and I'm sweet on him. He's hewing now, and earning a good wage. He asked me mam and dad if he could marry us, and they said no, because he's a Catholic and they didn't want any

Catholics in their family. Besides, they hadn't forgotten that Jimmy lent our John money to run off. We could do nothing to change their minds, so Jimmy said if I was game, he'd make them let him marry me.' She looked intently at Ginny as if willing her to understand, but fatigued from her journey and mind reeling from what she'd heard and seen so far, Ginny returned a blank stare.

'Well, I was terrified, but I said, "All right." So he set about it. He said, "They'll not be able to get us married quick enough then." Only now I think I'm pregnant, and he's trapped below ground. He's probably dead already.'

Chapter Twenty

Lizzie and Sally lay asleep as Ginny watched Emma retching into the basin early the following morning.

'I am, aren't I?' Emma asked. She described other tell-tale signs. Her breasts were engorged and so tender she could hardly bear her clothes against them. She had long missed her monthly period. She felt exhausted.

'I was like that,' Ginny commiserated. Emma looked sharply up at her and she nodded confirmation. 'Stillborn. Over a year ago.'

Downstairs, their mother was awake but drained and enervated. They took her a cup of tea and left her, saying they would keep first watch and bring her any news.

Speeding towards the pithead, Ginny saw her village in the clear light of day with a stranger's eye, taking in its dreary rows of soot-blackened cottages, its cobbled streets and unpaved alleys, the gaunt black framework at the pit mouth with the winding gear high in the air, the sombre hills of shale close by. It was rough, dirty and uncouth. Everybody she knew in London would have scorned to live there, although most might have thought it good enough for the pitmen because they too would have been despised. Outwardly as unprepossessing as the village, often blackened and smelling of lamp oil, their speech incomprehensible to outsiders, they were a race apart. It angered her to think that while their misdeeds were magnified and oft repeated, their daily heroism passed without comment, until something like this brought reporters to the scene to witness the courage and compassion of men worthy of the name. They were magnificent, and she felt a fierce pride in them.

The word on the lips of everyone they passed was that the shaft had been cleared and an exploring party had gone down, Martin among them. Ginny hurried along with Emma, determined to stay rooted to the place until he came to the surface. Beyond the boundary Ginny saw the two doctors and felt cheered, then she spotted a collection of makeshift coffins, and her heart sank. They joined the throng of other wives, parents, sweethearts, waiting as near as the police would allow. Many of their neighbours looked askance at Ginny, Enid Jackson and the Vines' cook both turning away and exchanging whispered comments behind their hands. The old Ginny would have challenged them, would have demanded openly to know what they were saying, but now, self-condemned, she shrank from them. Few people spoke to her, but one who did exchange a few words was Mrs Vine's discarded housemaid, Maudie, who was obviously with child.

'We were married last year. He went down with the

rest and I haven't seen him since. He's dead. It's not my luck for him not to be.' Maudie looked more of a sloven than ever, but the droop of her shoulders and her hollow-eyed, pasty face made Ginny wish she could take back every unkind comment she had ever made about her.

They waited for hours. At last they saw some men being brought to the bank and Martin was with them, looking aged and haggard under the dirt, but alive! Alive and on his feet. The breath Ginny had been holding escaped in one long sigh of relief and, feeling her knees buckle, she held onto Emma. She lost sight of him for a moment as reporters surrounded him and the others, full of questions, all eager for a sensational story. When the pressmen had gone and the rescuers approached, the crowd surged forward, clamouring for news. Had they seen anything of a father, a husband, a brother, a son, a sweetheart?

They had no comfort for anybody. They had passed bodies at every stride so burned and blasted by the explosion and the fire they were unrecognizable, but had brought none out because they'd been intent on finding survivors.

'We couldn't get far for the fire. In some places everything that'll burn's alight, pit props, tubs of coal, the lot. We'll hev to work in relays to put it out as far as we can,' said Martin. 'The owners are saying nobody can be alive. They're talking about blocking the pit up to cut the air off, so they can salvage as much of their property as they can.' This last news drew angry and disbelieving protests from the crowd.

'But what if some are alive?' asked Ginny, when most of the rest had dispersed. 'Don't they care about them?'

Was it contempt or pity she saw in his eyes? More like reproach. 'They care a lot more about their investment, Ginny. I would have thought you'd know that, now you're keeping company with Mr Parkinson. He's a shareholder, so you must know we're nothing to them, nothing but bloody slaves.'

'But Mr Vine's one of the owners,' Ginny said. 'I can't believe he doesn't care about any of them.'

'Aye, I admit he's a different case to the other owners. He's had to look too many of us in the eye. He's down there now, with another exploring party, but we'll see which way he jumps, when it comes to it. If his wife gets her own way, the pit'll be blocked up. She's interested in nothing but how much money can be squeezed out of it, from what I've heard. One thing's certain, he knew the pit's gassy. Everybody's known the danger but there's not many wanted to complain about it for fear of losing their jobs.'

'You'll lose yours if you're not careful. I hope you didn't say any of that to them,' Emma nodded in the direction of the retreating reporters, 'because if you did, you'll be finished. Is there any chance there's anybody left alive, Martin?'

He averted his eyes from the look of desperate, painful appeal in hers. 'There's a slim chance there might be a few alive in the remotest workings, but whether there's any chance they'll still be alive by the time we manage to get to them – not much, I wouldn't think. A couple of the lads thought they heard somebody knocking, but it's maybe wishful thinking.' He looked at Ginny's left hand. 'He's not married you yet, then?'

She flushed. 'No, because I don't want to marry him.'

He raised his eyebrows, and gave her a sharp, unreadable glance. 'I'm surprised at that, under the circumstances.'

'It's true.'

'Aye well,' he grimaced, 'time I went home, let Mam and the bairn know I'm all right, and snatch a few hours' rest before we go down again. I wish I could tell you something good about your dad and Jimmy, Emma. If we don't get them out, it won't be for want of trying. I'm glad to see you looking so well, Ginny.'

The barb found its mark, and her lip quivered at the pain and shock of it. She understood him perfectly. That she, a pitman's daughter, one of them, should consort with one of their oppressors, and not even as an honest wife but as his whore, was a betrayal of her own kind. Martin probably imagined that she was well fed and well dressed on the profits of this mine, the tomb of her father and other fathers, brothers and sons. She couldn't bear to have him think so badly of her. With a boldness born of desperation, she caught him by the sleeve as he passed her, but when he stopped to look her full in her face she couldn't hold his gaze and lowered her eyes.

'Be fair to me, Martin. It's not what you think. Not all of it anyway, and it wasn't all my fault.'

He nodded and waited for a moment or two until she released him before walking on.

'You seem to want his good opinion,' said Emma.

'I love him, Em. I don't know when I first began to realize it, but I've hardly thought about anything else for the past year and a half. I was thinking about him before then, even. Probably before I left Annsdale. I can't remember when I didn't. Now I've seen him, I'm sure. I'm going to spend the rest of my life with him, Em. I'm going to marry him.'

Emma's derisory laugh hit her like a slap in the face. 'After Charlie Parkinson? You must be insane. He didn't seem to be entertaining any thoughts of marrying you just now.'

Ginny was immovable in spite of her sister's scorn. 'It's meant to be. It's like turning a place upside down looking for something, and then realizing it's been under your nose all the time. He's the one for me, and I'm for him.'

'Well, he's certainly never been a lucky man, so he's not what you used to say you wanted. Even if he's not killed or maimed, he's likely to make himself a nuisance to a lot of powerful people. He'll be finished round here as far as getting work goes, if he's not careful.'

'Martin's his own worst enemy.'

'Maybe, but he's our best friend.'

Ginny pondered on the difference between the two men, and knew it was his ruthlessness that was Charlie's luck. Principle, honesty, loyalty, pity, any sense of decency, none presented any obstacle to Charlie, but all impeded Martin. Martin's bad luck was the result of his integrity, of his support for people who could never repay him, of his courage in demanding fair treatment for them all against the will of tyrants. The only person Martin had ever sacrificed was himself. Unless a capacity to inspire respect and love counted as luck, he was as unlucky as any man could be. But she well understood why Maria had wanted him, even while he lay in bed not knowing whether he would ever work, or even walk, again.

They went on home with the news. The three younger children were downstairs when they got back, to Ginny all grown almost beyond recognition. Thirteen-year-old Arthur, even more arrogant since starting work on the surface, turned his back on her when she walked in and refused to speak. Lizzie and Sally looked at her in awed silence until she held out her arms to them, and then they went to hug her. They ate a rough and ready meal together, and at the end of it young Arthur said, 'She wouldn't be here if me father was at home. She's a bloody disgrace.'

'Be quiet,' said his mother, 'and don't talk about things you know nothing about.'

'I'm not a bairn, and I know what she is,' he glowered, 'bloody whore.'

Ginny made no protest and was surprised when her mother did. 'You know nothing, and you say nothing outside this family about anybody in it,' she said sharply. 'There'll be plenty willing to cry her down without her own family helping them. I'm going to the pit. You'd better come with me and see if you can make yourself useful to the men. Who else will come?'

'Me,' said Emma.

'I'll fettle the kitchen and have a meal ready for you when you come back,' said Ginny.

'You won't get much ready with what's in the pantry,' said their mother.

'I've got some money. I'll send Lizzie down to the Co-op.'

'I won't be eating anything she's bought.' Young Arthur jerked his head in Ginny's direction.

'I'll get something ready for anybody that wants it,' said Ginny, 'and if you don't, Arthur, you can starve for all I care.'

She made a shopping list and despatched Sally and Lizzie to fetch groceries, then washed pots and pans, and started a thorough cleaning of the kitchen. She saw young Arthur's boots and remembered the day she would have died rather than clean them, but clean them she did, prompted by the thought that had he been a few months older, he too might be trapped. Just then she heard a knock at the front door, opened it, and found herself face to face with Martin. Her stomach tied itself in knots of apprehension.

'Me mam's out,' she said, 'they've gone back to the pit top.'

'I know that. It's you I've come to see.'

She couldn't trust herself to say anything more than 'Come in.'

He joined her in the kitchen. There was a brief pause before he looked her in the eye. 'Was that true, then? Is that the end of it between you and Parkinson?'

The long-awaited, long-dreaded ordeal was upon

her. She must undergo the torture of telling him everything, however humiliating, because Charlie would already be painting her in the blackest possible colours, would be making sure the whole village knew everything to her discredit. She must pre-empt him as far as she could. Stomach churning and heart beating so loudly she thought he must hear it, she held his gaze. 'Yes, that's the end of it. I don't know what I'll do but I'm not going back to him. I haven't lived with him for over a year.'

'How could you ever think o' getting mixed up with him in the first place, Ginny?'

She saw the hurt in his eyes and shrugged helplessly. 'You know what it was like here. You've not forgotten my father kneeing you in the face, I suppose? I wanted to stay, but how could I after that? The manager told me there were always plenty of good jobs in London for servants and he promised to give me a reference. I can see you don't believe me.'

'I do believe you. The manager told me an' all, and he was right, there always are plenty of jobs there for good servants. I've heard they can just about say what they like to their employers. They can leave one job in a morning and be in another one by the afternoon. So how did you end up living with Charlie Parkinson? How could you, Ginny? You couldn't have picked a worse man if you'd dredged through all the dross of London. It nearly killed your mother when she got to know, and your father – well, if he lives to get a hold of him there'll be a murder done, and I can't say I blame him. So how did it happen?

I know it's not my business, and I've no right to ask you but – I want to know.'

But she wanted it to be his business, as she wanted everything to do with her to be his business. She gave him the right to ask her whatever he would, and admitted that wanting to try her luck on the music halls had led her to go with Charlie to see a proper one. She told about him taking her back to his house instead of to her lodgings and owned to everything that had happened as a consequence.

'Afterwards he told me I'd gone there of my own free will because I knew he'd serve me, and I'd wanted him to, and I suppose that's what you think an' all,' she concluded, flinching at the grim set of his jaw.

Martin nodded. 'Aye, well, I can't deny that's what it looked like when we got to know.'

He sounded hard and unrelenting. Perhaps she had mistaken him, mistaken her own judgement in telling him her sordid history. Too late now. She turned away from him, cheeks as red as they'd been on that first night in Charlie's house.

'I suppose I did want to be served in the end. I wanted to be loved and cherished and all, but that never happened. I had the wrong man for that.'

He grasped her roughly by the shoulders and turned her towards him. His face was ashen. 'Ginny, there's something I've got to know. Did you go whoring for him?'

She drew breath sharply and bent almost double, hugging herself as if she'd been disembowelled.

'Did you sell yourself to other men, to make money for him? Did you?' he insisted.

'No, I didn't. No, no, no, no, no,' she cried, sinking on to a chair.

'Did you have any bairns?'

'She died,' she gasped, and began to weep.

Martin was quiet for a while, then he said, roughly, 'Aye, bad enough you did that with anybody that didn't care enough about you to put a ring on your finger, Ginny, but with him – I could be sick at the thought. You might go back to him yet, though. You might think it's your best option when some of the cats in Annsdale start digging their claws into you.'

'No, I won't,' she wept, 'never. I haven't been with him for over a year. I've got my own house and I'm never going back to him, whatever else I do or don't do.'

She cried on and on, without a word of comfort from him. Eventually he said softly, 'Are you sure you've told me everything, Ginny? Only I don't want anybody else telling me anything I don't already know.'

'Yes. I've told you everything. There were never any other men, if that's what you mean.'

'Aye, I suppose that's what I mean.'

There was a long silence. He reached out a hand as if to brush her tears away, but withdrew it.

'It's as if I've been dead along with Maria for the past three and a half years, but now I'm faced with it, I want to live. This disaster's made me realize how sweet life is. I want to see my bairn grow up. I want to do a lot o' things. Will you do something for me?'

She dabbed her eyes and whispered, 'Yes, anything.'

'If anything happens to me, be a friend to Philip and Mam Smith.'

'I will. I'll do anything you want, Martin, only be fair to me. It wasn't all my fault. It wasn't. I left him as soon as I had somewhere else to go.'

He made no answer, and when she looked up he was gone. She was left with her own thoughts, staring down at Maria's shoes, contrasting herself with their first owner. She hugged herself with distress at Martin's low opinion of her and at the pain and anger on his face when he thought of her with Charlie. But he couldn't have felt such pain if he hadn't cared for her at all. And if he'd had such a low opinion of her, he wouldn't have trusted her with Philip. Whatever the truth was, she knew now that she didn't merely love Martin. She worshipped him. And, in spite of everything, she sensed something in him that gave her hope.

Chapter Twenty-One

Jimmy Hood, her father, and all the other trapped men and boys drifted in and out of her mind, but only Martin was immovably fixed in it. He had to survive the rescue. He must. She thought of him constantly and was thinking of him when she opened the front door the following morning to Charlie, dressed immaculately in a dark suit, cravat, and bowler.

'I'm going out,' she told him, with a defiant stare.

'Very well.' He gave her an easy smile, showing his even white teeth. 'Perhaps it's as well. This is a formal call. I want a private word with your mother. I've come to atone for our past misdemeanours by making an honest woman of you. Be so good as to inform her that I'm here.'

She shut the door in his face, and went into the kitchen, followed by a prolonged and insistent knocking on the door.

'For pity's sake, Ginny, answer it,' her mother said.

'No, and don't you answer it either.'

Her mother looked nonplussed, then got up and opened the door herself. When Ginny saw Charlie enter the front room still smiling his pleasant and implacable smile she cried, 'Oh, I asked you not to,' and in a second had snatched her coat from the peg and escaped through the back door. She fled in the direction of the pit, her mind in turmoil, knowing what sort of a yarn Charlie would be spinning her mother, and thinking that the only promises he ever kept to her were the ones that resulted in her degradation. She dreaded Martin finding out about his visit and condemning her for a liar as well as a whore, then dreaded even more that he might fall a victim to the pit and never know anything more.

She stood on the bank alongside groups of others, alone in the crowd, scanning every direction, looking for him. At last he arrived with a group of other rescuers, Tom Hood among them. A father come to seek his sons; her heart went out to him. She raised an arm to wave to Martin, felt another arm encircle her waist, and turned her face into Charlie's.

'I thought I'd find you here. I'm happy to say that we have your mother's blessing.'

She broke from him and walked away, turning only to say, 'I'll never marry you, Charlie. I don't care whose blessing we've got.'

He followed her, then to her horror she saw that Martin was walking towards her, a caged canary in one hand, and his lamp in the other. She was in a fever of anxiety as Charlie drew level with them.

'You're one of the exploring party, I take it,' he said, in a superior tone. 'It's time there was an end to this folly, putting men's lives at risk for no good reason. There's nobody alive down there – anyone who knows anything about mines knows that.'

'And you're an expert on mines, I suppose?' Martin sneered.

Charlie gave him a long and disparaging look, evidently resenting a challenge from one so obviously his social inferior. 'I'm closely related to one, if a certificated manager of mines qualifies as an expert. The opinion of the manager of this mine is that rescuers are putting their lives at hazard of afterdamp, roof falls and further explosions in an attempt to find survivors that will prove utterly futile. Simply put, you risk being suffocated, crushed, burned or buried alive for nothing. Such survivors as there are have saved themselves by their own exertions. The mine should be sealed until the fires are out. By that means, the people of the village will have some employment to return to. You may not be aware that I am one of the owners.'

Such anger as she had never thought him capable of was displayed in Martin's face, and she shrank from it. He was deathly pale, his powerful shoulders hunched, his jaw clenched, his knuckles white. His eyes glittered with hatred.

'I'm well aware o' that, and I'm aware of everything else that yer are an'all. The only thing that concerns you is saving your investment, nothing else. And if the certificated manager of this mine had listened to some of us the hundred times we tried to tell him the pit was gassy and no shots should be fired, there would never have been an explosion, scores of men and boys would still be alive, and there'd be no need for anybody to risk anything. But lucky for anybody that is trapped, it's neither you nor your sister that decides when the pit gets blocked.' Martin pointed to the group of volunteers, ready for the descent. 'See them? They're men, and sons of men – people you'll never understand. They'll make their own minds up whether they want to risk their lives or not, not you, and they know the risks better than you ever could.'

Charlie flushed with anger and opened his mouth, but seeing the murderous expression in Martin's eyes he closed it again. He turned to Ginny. 'We'll discuss matters later, Ginny. I'll call and see you at home this evening,' then with a curt and uncomfortable nod in Martin's direction, he left them.

'Feather-bedded and spoon-fed all his life. It'll not matter what happens to anybody as far as that one's concerned, as long as he's all right. He'd sell his own mother for a farthing,' spat Martin, glaring contemptuously after him. 'Anyway, what matters has he got to discuss with you, if you've finished with him?'

Before she had time to say anything he turned his back on her to answer a call from the other volunteers. She watched him go down and was too upset to wait there any longer. Wringing her hands and sighing, she returned home, heartsick at his having seen her with Charlie, going over it all in her mind, wondering how she could have avoided it, what she could have done differently. She saw young Arthur and acknowledged him, but he passed her as if she were invisible; her own brother.

She wouldn't live here as a pariah. She was sick of feeling like dirt and being treated like dirt, sick of Charlie hounding her, sick of eating humble pie because of him. If she had to swallow another mouthful she would choke on it. 'If I can never live Charlie down, I may as well go back to London,' she whispered to herself, but even as she said it she knew she could never tear herself away while there was the faintest chance of winning Martin. She was fast tethered to the village by her obsession with him. To make her leave, he would have to destroy every hope, to tell her openly, brutally, that he did not want her and never would. By the time she got to the back door, her head was splitting. Lizzie and Sally had been sent out on Charlie's arrival and were still not back. She found her mother and Emma alone.

'He says he's been asking to marry you ever since before that baby was born,' her mother said, as soon as she stepped in the door.

'He does seem to think a lot about you, Ginny,' said Emma.

'He always twists things,' Ginny said. 'He didn't ask me to marry him until long after I'd left him, when I was doing all right on me own. It was me that was asking him before then. I bet he didn't tell you the rest, either, and I can't.'

She couldn't have spoken to her mother of abortion and prostitution to save her life. To all her mother's arguments, she simply kept insisting, 'It's finished between us. Finished. I would rather die than pass another five minutes with him. I've no more to say about it.'

Finally Emma said, 'Leave her alone, Mam. We cannot make her have him if she doesn't want.'

Her mother was not so easily deflected. 'He's the best chance you'll ever have. No decent man will want you now. And he said he'd see we wanted for nothing, whatever happens at the pit.'

'He always talks like that, but it never is like that. People always end up doing more for Charlie than he ever does for them. And I'll see you want for nothing, never bother about that.'

'You? How can you? You're only a girl, and I've still got two children to bring up.'

Ginny looked into her mother's gaunt face. 'I know you have, but I'm a lot better off than you think I am. I can earn a lot of money on the stage. I'd have seen you wanted for nothing before today, if you'd let me.'

'That was your father, and you know why.'

'I do, but if you only want me to marry Charlie so you'll want for nothing, you won't want for anything anyway. And if you want me to marry him because you think nobody else will have me, I don't care about that either. I'd rather never marry at all than marry Charlie.'

Her mother gave up the argument, put on her coat and left the house, saying that God willing their father would get out of the pit alive and he would see they wanted for nothing, as he always had. There would be no charity soup or parish boots for her children.

'Don't blame her. She's out of her mind with worry,' said Emma. 'I'll likely lose my job at the Cock before much longer, so she won't even have my bit. I've been doing a bit of work behind the bar an' all, whenever the landlady wants a night off. She knows she can trust me – I can pull a good pint and I always get the money right. The police turn a blind eye to me being a bit under age because there's never any trouble at the Cock, and the landlord's well in with the magistrates. But he was talking about selling up long before this lot happened. He's getting the wind up now because if the pit closes, he'll get nothing for the place.'

'She needn't worry. I can help you all, and a lot more than if I was married to Charlie, because the only person he wants to look after is himself, and maybe his sister.'

'Why did you go chasing after him in the first place, Ginny?'

'I didn't,' she said, and confided everything, including things she could never have told her mother.

'Charlie wanted the sport and he could make me want it and all, as if nothing else mattered, but he didn't want the babies it gets. Charlie liked to bed me, but he didn't want to wed me until he lost his grip on the money I earn. Love's got nothing to do with it. I know him inside out. I never really liked him at the start, but I hated him in the end, I used to think about murdering him. He nearly put me in the lunatic asylum. I'd like to forget I ever knew him, but I don't suppose I'll ever be able to do that.'

'Not with people like they are round here.'

'I know. Their eyes and ears are everywhere. I'd forgotten how much. That's one thing I do miss about London, you don't have everybody minding your business for you, pointing their fingers at you. I can't see how you and Jimmy ever got together on your own. His house is always full, and me mam's nearly always in, and anyway you say he wasn't welcome here because of helping our John and being a Catholic, and you can go nowhere else out of the way of them all.'

Emma was silent for a while, then said, 'Well, there's one place that nobody goes much when it's getting dark, and if I tell you I've probably still got "In Loving Memory" printed on me arse, you'll know where I mean.'

A burst of laughter from Ginny was answered by an uncertain little smile from Emma, but after a second or two, when she realized the import of her words, her face crumpled. Ginny held and soothed her.

'He'll get out. We've got to hope he'll get out. But no matter what happens, you'll never want for anything as long as I'm alive, never fear.' When Emma stopped crying, Ginny joked, 'By Em, it must have been a bit cold, though, this time of year.'

Emma stood up and began to wash the pots, signalling an end to that line of conversation. Ginny took the hint, and changed the subject.

'I'll do that, Em, if you'll go to the Co-op and get something to eat. I'm tired of people looking through me and whispering behind my back. I can't face them again today. Will you go?'

Emma brought the *Chronicle* back with her. She put the groceries down and sat wearily at the kitchen table, dark circles evident under her eyes. She looked exhausted but was not too tired to devour the paper whilst Ginny made a meal.

'Listen to this.' She read: '"There were at least forty members of the press at Annsdale Colliery yesterday, and not a single daily paper of any note in the Kingdom was unrepresented." I believe it and all. They're like wasps round a bloody jam pot. They get to know more about what's going on than we do, and we live here. And all these people who just come out of curiosity, to see a bit of drama, make me bilious.'

'What do they say about the rescue attempt, Em? Do they say it's hopeless?'

'It's not hopeless, no matter what they say,' said Emma, her lip trembling despite her stout denial. 'And if it was Jimmy, he'd try for any of his marrers, I know he would. So would me dad.'

Ginny returned to the task of chopping vegetables, but although she said no more she thought constantly of those dangers stressed so forcefully by Charlie, dangers Martin and the other rescuers faced that very minute and for hours to come.

'Just listen to this,' said Emma. '"Disaster Fund. It was said sixteen years ago, at the time of the Elms disaster, that the public would never be as generous again as they were on that occasion and that a permanent disaster fund should be set up. Nothing has been done in the interval, but there is enough and to spare for the present emergency without asking the public for a penny. The coal owners have made colossal fortunes drawn from the labours of the miners and the purses of consumers during the past few years, and none have been enriched more than the owners of Annsdale Colliery. They might undertake the support of all the sufferers and never feel the burden. The public sympathize deeply with the bereaved and are willing to assist them, but they are entitled to know where are the existing funds and what example is to be set by the coal owners.

'"We demand to know where is the remainder of the fund set up sixteen years ago, and why no permanent fund was established. Single accidents are continually occurring and no appeal is made to the public on behalf of the sufferers of these, yet to each individual the calamity is as great as the present one. Hence the necessity for a permanent fund on which sufferers could have a claim. Why is no permanent fund in existence? We expect the Town Clerk, who is one of the trustees, to tell us who is and who is not responsible for this piece of gross mismanagement."' Emma gave a little grunt of approval. 'I would love to know that reporter.'

'Well, who's supposed to be looking after the money, like? Where is it?' asked Ginny.

'I don't know. One of our noble lords or mine owners has it all tucked away in a bank somewhere, I suppose. That's if they haven't spent it,' said Emma, then added, 'That's something you could do if you've as much money as you reckon you've got. You could start another Disaster Fund, a Permanent Fund like he says, but let the Union look after it this time. Tell Mr Parkinson you've no money left and you're not going back to London to earn any more. If that's all he wants you for, he'll soon lose interest.'

'I wonder if I could?' mused Ginny. 'I wouldn't know where to start, or how to do it, but I suppose there's people who could help me.' She pondered for a while in silence, and two more ideas began to ferment in her mind, both breathtaking in their brilliance.

After scouring through the paper, Emma went to join her mother at the pit. Young Arthur arrived back in the middle of the afternoon, sent home by the men – filthy and so exhausted he could hardly stand. He condescended to speak to his eldest sister.

'The fires are out, as far as anybody can tell, and the ventilation's working. They've found three men alive, I don't know who. Now they've started bringing bodies out. Get me a bath ready. I'm going to bed for a bit.'

She obeyed him as unquestioningly as she would have obeyed her father, and danced willing attendance on him as long as he needed her, then put on her coat and flew against the biting wind towards the pit, there to parade frantically up and down searching fruitlessly among a crowd which seemed to number thousands for her mother and Emma.

Standing around the head gearing were the same officials and medical gentlemen, and pressmen were everywhere. The police were stopping people from crowding up the incline, and guarding the entrance to the sawing shed, an improvised dead house. Nearby, pit ambulances waited. After a while the cage began to ascend and those who were on the hill gathered round the shaft to see it bring up more of the men who had been found at the bottom, all dead.

The crowd had collected in the yard and formed an avenue through which the dead were carried to the sawing shed. People who had relatives or friends in the workings were in the front rows of one side or the other. Ginny went to join them, watching the faces of fathers and mothers, children and friends as corpse after corpse was carried past them. Some tried to lift the corner of a blanket that covered a face, others strove to catch a glimpse of shoes, or clogs, or trousers, and those who saw anything they recognized followed the body. As one corpse was carried past them, Ginny glimpsed a girl on the opposite side start and put a protective hand on her belly. Recognizing Maudie, she crossed to speak to her.

'Have you seen me mam or our Emma?'

Maudie shook her head. 'Will you come with me to the sawing shed, Ginny? I don't want to go on me own.'

'You don't think you've seen him, do you?'

'Aye. He's dead, Ginny. It's not my luck for him not to be. Will you come?'

They followed the bodies to the door of the sawing shed and stood among a group of people waiting their turn to go in. The policeman nodded in Maudie's direction as they passed him at the door. 'Make sure you look after her, she might be wanting a doctor before long,' he told Ginny.

It was hard to see on first entering the place, and the stench, a mixture burned flesh and excrement, made her feel nauseous. As her eyes became accustomed to the gloom, Ginny saw fifteen blackened and disfigured bodies lying on the floor of the shed, every one of them battered and burned beyond recognition. People were examining clothing, feeling in pockets, trying to find anything that might help them identify their own. Maudie walked down the row, face expressionless, looking intently at each numbered body until she came to one with face and hands badly charred and half his skull blasted away.

'That's him,' she said, 'that's Harry.'

'How can you be sure, Maudie?' asked Ginny, failing to see how anyone could recognize this remnant of a man, desperately hoping Maudie was mistaken, hoping her young husband was alive and whole.

'It's him, Ginny. See his socks? I knitted him his socks. I might not be much good at anything else, but I've always been a good knitter.' Ginny saw the neat, even stitches, and put her arms round Maudie's rigid, unyielding shoulders. Bleak eyed, Maudie said, 'It's awful. He was the only person in the world who ever thought anything about me. Thank God they brought him out. At least I'll know where he's buried now. He'll have a proper grave.'

Further down the row, a young girl saw a patch on a pair of trousers she identified as her own work, and sank to her knees beside another blackened corpse. 'Oh, God, have mercy, it's my brother.' Unable to bear the sight, Ginny turned to Maudie, who stood like stone, stolidly staring in front of her.

'Come on,' Ginny said, taking her by the hand, 'I'll take you home.'

They passed a policeman wiping tears from his face with the back of his hand, and walked on in silence, Ginny at a loss for words. At Maudie's door, Ginny said, 'I'll go and fetch your mam. You shouldn't be on your own.'

Maudie shrieked, 'No, I don't want her. She never had a good word for him.' She sat down on the path and began to emit howls of anguish, unlike anything Ginny had ever heard from a human being, an eerie stomach-churning noise that reminded her of a poor hare she had once heard screaming when caught in a gin trap. All attempts to comfort or to reason with her were useless, and Ginny abandoned them. She took the key and opened the door, then struggled to get Maudie on her feet and into the house. The ear-splitting wails continued as Ginny lit the lamp, then raked the ashes out of a filthy grate and lit a fire. She put the kettle on and surveyed the kitchen. Everything was in disorder, dirty and unkempt, except for a lace shawl of fine white wool still on the knitting needles.

After what seemed like hours, Maudie clutched her sides. 'The bairn's coming!' The howls began to subside.

Ginny looked at her in complete consternation. 'I'll run and fetch Mam Smith,' she said, and flew out of the cottage in the direction of Snowdrop Terrace. Half crying and half hysterical, breast heaving with exertion and emotion she burst in through Mam Smith's door.

'Maudie says the bairn's coming! She'll need soap and flannels and towels and something to wrap it in and everything. She's got nothing except a half-knitted shawl. It's awful, I've just been with her to identify her husband, it was terrible, just terrible. He was burned, and the back of his head blown off. If it hadn't been for his socks, she couldn't have recognized him. What must it be like that happens down there, if it can do that to people?' Ginny was crying, almost losing control.

Mam Smith got up from her chair before the fire and without a word began collecting everything she needed and throwing it into a bag.

Martin stood up, weary and begrimed, and held Ginny by the shoulders for a moment. 'Steady on, lass, steady on. You'll be no use to Maudie or anybody else in this state.'

She looked him in the face. 'Oh, Martin, it's the worst thing I've ever seen in me life. It's horrible, too horrible for words.'

'I know. I know what it's like,' he soothed. 'We got the first bodies out before we came away. Shush, shush now. I might have some good news for you. Have you heard about Jimmy? We got him out alive, with a couple of others.'

'Thank God, thank God. Does our Emma know?'

'Don't start thanking God too soon. He might not deserve it. He's hurt bad. I don't know whether he'll pull through. Your Emma's up at the hospital with him, with your mam and Jimmy's mam.'

'Oh, poor Emma. Oh, Martin, I'm so afraid, I'm so afraid. I wish you wouldn't go down again.' Saying it, she felt a traitor to all the men and boys still down there, to her own father and mother, to every girl with a husband or sweetheart like Jimmy, to every mother with a son, and to all those like Maudie, who, even if their loved ones were dead, wanted a body to say goodbye to and to lay in a proper grave. But it was true. If she could, she would have given the owners their wish to seal the pit. She would have done anything to prevent him going down again.

He gave her a look of wonderment. 'You've got to be where your sympathies are, lass, whatever the cost.'

'Come on,' said Mam Smith abruptly, her coat on and bag packed. 'Let's be off.'

A good fire was blazing when they reached Maudie's cottage, and the kettle was boiling. They hadn't long to wait. Maudie soon gave birth to a small, sickly looking infant, and Mam Smith guessed she had been only about seven months gone. They tried him at the breast, but he wouldn't suck so they wrapped him and laid him at the foot of the bed whilst they washed Maudie, dressed her in a clean nightgown and remade the bed with Mam Smith's own clean bedding.

'I don't think we'll wash the bairn. He looks that feeble, I think a bath might kill him,' murmured Mam Smith as she picked the child up and put him in his mother's arms. She cast an expert eye over Maudie, lying passively in bed with her eyes half closed. 'His mother doesn't look any too well, either.'

'I'll go and fetch her some brandy,' said Ginny, remembering its qualities as a pick-me-up. Mam Smith looked at her as if she'd gone mad.

'You'll do no such thing. She's got a bairn now. She needs to be in her senses to look after him. If you want to make yourself useful, the best thing you can do is go and fetch her mother, or one of her sisters. She shouldn't be left on her own tonight. I can't do any more for her, and I'm needed at home.'

Ginny felt foolish and humiliated. 'But she said not to bring her mam. She didn't want her.'

'Try one of her sisters, then,' Mam Smith shrugged, and without more ado she put on her coat and hat, picked up her bag, and on her way out gave Ginny a cold, wounding nod.

Reluctant to leave Maudie to go in search of anyone, she put the kettle on again. The baby was awake, so they tried him at the breast just as Mam Smith had done. He sucked a little.

'What are you going to call him, Maudie?'

'Harry,' said the girl, as if stating the obvious, as if there were only one name in the world. 'Thanks for helping me, Ginny. Don't you want to get on home?'

'I won't leave you on your own. I'll stop for a while.'

While Maudie dozed in bed with her baby, Ginny washed the tea things and all the other dirty crockery she found laid about, banked up the fire, then put out the lamp and collapsed exhausted into an armchair.

She sat by the warmth of the coal fire, wondering which man's labours had won it from the earth and whether he was sitting so comfortably just now. An image of her far-off, fêted, waited-upon life in London drifted fleetingly into her thoughts, reminding her that she must write to Agnes and George Burns. Bone-tired, she lay back in the chair and closed her eyes, unable to sleep for the wind bellowing and roaring round the house. It put her in mind of some great black beast in pain, venting its almighty groans of despair, sounding both terrified and terrifying.

Chapter Twenty-Two

A weak, pathetic wailing woke her from an uneasy sleep just before dawn. She stretched her back and rubbed her aching shoulders, wondering what the matter was, then got up and lit the lamp to see Maudie sitting up in bed, trying to soothe the baby.

'What's wrong with him?' She stared helplessly at Ginny, and for a moment or two, Ginny stared just as helplessly back. Then, suddenly inspired, she said with authority, 'Nothing that a feed won't cure. Try putting him to the breast. And you'll have to feed yourself, or your milk won't come in properly.'

The fire still burned and the cottage was warm and comfortable. Ginny made tea and breakfast for Maudie, then washed her baby with warm water from the range. It was light before she left, to walk through streets already alive with people making their way to the pit.

At home, the air was heavy with expectation, her mother and Emma facing each other over the kitchen table. Ginny's walking in seemed to serve as a distraction from the business in hand. After demanding the reason for her being out all night, her mother said, 'Mr

Parkinson was round looking for you. He said you'd arranged for him to come. You were expecting him.'

'I didn't ask him. That was his idea. And he knows very well I'd rather he'd stopped away.'

'And I suppose you know what's wrong with Emma?' Her mother looked at her sharply. Ginny nodded. Her mother turned to Emma and said, with uncharacteristic bitterness, 'I wondered when you were going to let me in on your secret. You must think I'm deaf and blind. I've heard you retching every morning for weeks and I get a whiff of sickness every time I go upstairs. Not to mention the washing we haven't done for you lately, and seeing you looking done in. You might have thought I had enough to do, without you bringing trouble home. I suppose this is because your father said no to the wedding.'

'We love each other,' was all Emma had to say.

'Well, I'm glad you do, because neither of you seems to have much thought for anybody else. I suppose there's not much choice now, so the sooner you are married the better, and I hope you don't live to regret it.'

'I won't.'

'I wish I could be as certain. He's Catholic, in case you've forgotten, so he'll do nothing to stop any more babies coming. You might end up having one every year, and a man who can't work to keep them. I don't know how you'll keep yourself out of the poorhouse then, because I shan't be able to help you.'

'It's all right. I'll help them,' said Ginny.

'It sounds as if you're going to work miracles,' her mother said, without conviction.

★

The two disgraced daughters were soon walking together towards the hospital, both glad to escape the house, Emma in agonies to know how Jimmy was and Ginny as desperate for news of Martin. Passing the pit on their way, they stopped to watch still more bodies being brought to the surface. The sawing shed could hold no more, and the processions of corpses and their followers were now making a track to the pay office. That place was almost full, and someone said that the cart shed was being fitted up as the next morgue. When they heard that Martin had gone down again, Ginny choked back a rising panic and could barely tear herself away from the scene to go on with Emma.

'He's got a compound fracture of his right shin and he's lost a lot of blood from it. There are three or four cuts on his head, he's got a lot of bruises and his left ear's burned, but at least he's conscious now. You can see him for a minute or two, but don't stay longer,' the ward sister told them.

They were shocked at the sight of him, propped on pillows in the hospital bed, the pallor of his skin almost matching the starched sheets, only relieved by the purple and blue of the bruises and the black burn of his ear. He gave them a tired smile.

'I never thought I'd see you again, bonny lass,' he told Emma. 'I never thought I'd see the light of day again.'

Emma took his hand and held it fast. 'Oh, Jimmy man,

when they told me you were alive! I can't tell you.' Her grip tightened.

'Aye, you can squeeze all you like. I think it's the only bit of me that's not sore.'

'What happened, Jimmy?'

'I was working in one of the banks a long way from the shaft when I heard such an almighty crack, I thought it had burst my eardrums. I knew it must be a gas explosion and I'd visions of the roof coming in, so I ran for the main way to try and get out.' His hazel eyes widened, the irises darting from right to left, as if he were watching the scene right then. 'When I got nearly there I saw the fire, just like a flood, just like a river of flames, roaring down the main way, filling the whole passage. Another minute and I'd have been right in its path. I was helpless. It just lifted me off my feet and dashed me back into the side road. I ended up flat on my back. I couldn't move for the pain in my leg, and I thought I'd broken my back and all. I must have passed out after that.' His face relaxed and he sighed heavily. 'But at least I don't need the last rites yet, not like that poor lad down there.'

They followed his glance towards a man down the ward whose arms, hands and face were badly burned. He seemed delirious and kept calling out pitifully in a language they'd never heard before. The priest, an emaciated middle-aged man dressed in a shabby black suit almost green with age, stood mumbling prayers in Latin by his bed.

'Who is he?'

'He's a Hungarian, I don't know what his name is. He came with a couple more and they got work at the pit about three months ago. They've lived in the pit yard ever since. The other two are still trapped,' said Jimmy. The mere effort of speaking seemed to exhaust him.

'Has the priest been to see you? Have you asked him about getting married yet?' asked Ginny. Emma shook her head at her, a warning look in her eyes.

'Aye, he's been to see me, but I haven't done much talking.'

The priest had finished his ritual and was packing his things away. He gave the man a final blessing, then walked down the ward towards them. After nodding an acknowledgement to Ginny and Emma, he said, 'I'll look in and see how you are tomorrow, Jimmy.' Jimmy nodded, and the priest passed on to leave the ward.

Ginny stood up. 'I'll leave you two alone. See you outside, Em.'

'Father!' The word felt strange in her mouth. He turned and waited for her at the hospital door. 'Will you marry them? Will you marry Emma and Jimmy?'

'Emma's the girl with Jimmy now, is she?'

Ginny nodded.

'Have they said they want to get married?'

'They've got to get married.'

'I see,' said the priest, his lined face grave. There followed scores of gentle questions. Did her parents know, did they agree to it? Did his parents know? There were many difficulties. Emma wasn't a Catholic, would she agree to bring her children up in the faith? The bishop would have to agree to it. There were many, many difficulties.

'But can't you ask Mr and Mrs Hood?' Ginny asked. The priest hesitated.

'They have one son still trapped in the mine, their youngest. They have another almost at death's door here. How can I give them any more to contend with?'

'But what if Jimmy is at death's door? What if he dies? What about his bairn and our Emma? At least if they're married, the baby'll have a name and it won't be so bad for them. Will you ask them? Will you try to get them to say yes? They'll listen to you.'

He sighed. 'It's a hard thing you're asking. I don't think you realize how hard. But yes, I'll see Jimmy and your sister now, and if they want me to, I'll speak to his parents.'

She didn't follow him back to the ward, but waited for Emma outside, an excess of nervous energy driving her to pace continuously backwards and forwards. Suddenly a low, thunderous rumbling shook the very ground under her feet, stopping her in her tracks, then an almighty boom stopped the breath in her throat. She picked up her skirts and ran.

Huge volumes of smoke were bellowing from the pit mouth and the crowd on the bank was increasing rapidly. Her mother stood with Mam Smith and Philip. Ginny threaded her way swiftly through the throng towards them, but they knew no more than she. The officials were trying to lower the cage but someone said that the pit bottom was too full of debris to get it down completely, and nobody could tell what was happening down below.

Charlie and Helen arrived. The chauffeur drove their open Daimler towards the police cordon, forcing the crowd to make way for them and stopping only when the wheels began to sink in the mud. Helen remained in her seat, her pale complexion and luxuriant red curls contrasting strikingly with the fashionably cut black outfit she was wearing. Her demeanour was one of haughty disdain rather than grief, putting Ginny suddenly in mind of the ladies of the Empire Promenade. Charlie jumped down and walked up the hill with the authority of an owner, unchallenged and unhindered by the police. He spent some time conversing with the officials, then scanned the bank and saw Ginny. As he pushed his way through the crowd towards her, she sensed the hostility of many of those nearby. But if Charlie felt it, he disregarded it as he came to stand close beside her.

'It's worse than they thought. The headgear's seriously damaged and the signalling apparatus from the mouth to the bottom's broken. One of the cages is smashed to atoms, and as you can see, the enginemen are trying to secure the wire rope to those rails and beams that extend across the mouth of the shaft; no easy feat considering it weighs several tons. They'll have the devil's own job to lower the cage from there. The balance is against them. So it's going to be some time before we know any more. Robert's down there, probably having sacrificed his life on a fool's errand. And for whom are you waiting, Ginny? You look as distressed as I've ever seen you.'

'My father's trapped down there, in case you'd

forgotten. I'm waiting for news of him, and everybody else.'

He looked at her sharply. 'Oh, my duplicitous little hinny. That look on your face is not there on your father's account. I've a notion it's there for that brute who was so insulting to me the other day.'

She gave him no answer. He lifted her hand and kissed it, holding it for a moment or two while he examined the chaffed skin and broken nails. 'You're beginning to look like a collier's wife, drab and old before your time. If I'm right and that man is your object, I warn you, Ginny, it's hopeless. Think again. He can never give you what you need. He won't transplant to London, and you'll never settle here now you've had a taste of the metropolis, and the adulation of the crowd. You've shown far too much promise to throw yourself away on someone who can only hinder you. Forget him, Ginny.'

She snatched her hand away and turned her face from him. He sighed. 'Still, the question is probably academic. It's unlikely the poor fellow has survived, although one couldn't wish him dead, of course. We'll talk later. I'm taking Helen home. This is no place for her, and I doubt if there'll be any news for hours. It's pointless to stand here.'

She looked at him, and the smile he gave her as he turned to go froze the blood in her veins. She'd seen the same smile when he'd given her comfort and reassurance after their baby's death. She stood motionless, overcome once more by the feeling that the baby had died because Charlie had willed it so.

Emma joined her as the Daimler was reversing out of the mud. 'Did you tell him you're staying here?' she whispered. Ginny, face taut with apprehension, shook her head. Emma began to tell her what the priest had said. Ginny was too preoccupied to take it in, but the mention of Martin's name behind her made every nerve quicken, and she strained to hear Mam Smith's voice.

'Before he went down he said, "Pray for me." That's him that reckoned there was no God after Maria died. I said, "I pray for you every day of my life, son, and I always will."'

Massive volumes of black smoke still issued from the pit mouth, bearing silent witness to the force of the explosion. Ginny sank to her knees and held her face in her hands, praying to God to remove the curse of Charlie from her life, praying to God not to let him win this time. She would go away, she bartered frantically, if only He would keep Martin safe. She would go away and never see him again.

After what seemed an eternity of watching, they saw the enginemen carefully lower the cage, and, after a long agony of suspense, winch it slowly up again. Ginny held on to Emma when she saw Tom Hood and Martin supporting Mr Vine between them. The doctors examined the half-suffocated manager and one of them got into the ambulance with him. The only man without a relative awaiting him was driven away.

Martin and Tom stopped to exchange a few words with officials and press. As soon as they were released, relatives and friends surged forward to greet them. To all enquiries they shook their heads – Martin grey-faced under the coal dust, Tom Hood grief-stricken, with white tracks down his face where his tears had washed away the grime.

Emma and Ginny huddled round their mother as if to shield her from the knowledge that her husband was lost. Martin clasped his son and then his mother-in-law in long, fierce embraces, looking all the while at Ginny. He called to her mother, 'I'll hev to come and see you, Mary Ann. There's a lot I've got to tell you, but not here.'

'I'm glad to see you looking so well, Martin,' Ginny called to him, almost sobbing with relief.

When the Government Inspector of Mines declared the pit too dangerous to allow any more exploring parties down and ordered the shafts to be sealed with her man still below and maybe alive, Ginny's mother tried to run up the incline to the pit mouth, and it was as much as two burly policemen could do to restrain her. Mrs Hood, knowing her son was lost to her for ever, became delirious. Friends carried her home unconscious, with Tom following in a state of near collapse himself. Martin hardly knew which party to help, but in the end went with Tom, half carrying him, leaving Mam Smith to help Emma and Ginny with their mother.

They couldn't move her. She walked up and down the length of the cordon like a creature demented, with a policeman tracking her to prevent her breaking through again. Ginny and Emma tried to take hold of her to drag her away but she thrust them off with the strength of a madwoman. Finally, fearing that she had lost her reason, they waited for her to wear herself out with raving and pacing so that they could take her home. They were surrounded by other mothers, fathers, brothers, sisters and children, weeping and crying out in as much distress.

It was almost dark before they saw Martin again, and by that time most of the watchers had dispersed. He sent Mam Smith home with Philip, then took Ginny's mother by the shoulders, forcing her to look into his face. After several minutes of persuasion she became calmer, and, looking utterly crushed, she walked home with them.

Deathly pale under the grime, young Arthur stood up as they went in and helped his mother into a chair. Sally, who had been sitting on the hearthrug, shuffled towards her to rest her head on her lap. Lizzie, who had been washing crockery, stood still.

'You've heard about your dad, I suppose?' Martin asked Arthur.

'Well, he's not got out. I can guess that much.'

'Did you know we found him alive?' Martin murmured. Arthur stared and shook his head. Martin went on, 'He was with young Joe Hood, behind a fall of roof. There was a bit of a gap at the top, so we shouted to them to crawl over. Your dad could have done it, but the lad was hurt that bad he couldn't move, and your dad wouldn't leave him. It was going to take us hours to shift the stone and coal to get them both out.'

'How can they block it up, knowing they might be alive?' cried Ginny's mother, tearing at her hair.

'They're not alive now, Mary Ann. They can't be. I've

explained that. They can't have escaped the afterdamp. It was rolling right towards them. We were lucky we weren't suffocated.' He turned again to Arthur. 'We felt all the air sucked away – it's a wonder it didn't put the lamps out. The rush came straight after. We thought at first the ventilation was interfered with, so we went a few hundred yards, and then we came on it. It was just the same as a cloud, bloody terrifying, man. We saw it before we got to it, rolling towards us and moving so fast we'd no choice but to pass through it. We crawled on our hands and knees towards the shaft, and when we'd got a fair way the air began to come right again; we could breathe. We saw Bob Dyer and some I didn't know, but they were all dead. Mr Vine would have been dead an' all, if me and Tom hadn't dragged him to the shaft.'

'I carried two of my marrers on stretchers to the cart shed today,' said young Arthur, 'two lads, not much older than me, with their hands just about burned off, as if the last thing they'd done was put them up to shield their faces.'

Their mother shrieked.

'That didn't happen to your man and Joe, Mary Ann,' Martin soothed. 'They died of the afterdamp. At least it's merciful.'

'I've carried two good lads to that cart shed today. I've seen what the explosion's done to them, and I've seen their families come and identify what's left, and I know this much,' said Arthur, looking directly at Ginny, 'I hate the owners, and I hate anybody that'll have anything to do with 'em.'

She flushed, and Martin put a protective arm around her. 'Ginny says she has nothing to do with the owners, and I believe her.'

'More bloody fool you, then,' said young Arthur.

Chapter Twenty-Three

Ginny sent a telegram to the Burns the very next day, and another to the impresario who had wanted to engage her after her last performance. Whilst awaiting an answer, she made herself useful at home and in the village. Her mother was in bed most of the time and fit to do nothing. 'I wish I could go to sleep and never wake up,' she kept saying, and reminders that she had children who needed her seemed to have no effect.

Young Arthur may not have wanted to demean himself by swallowing anything Ginny had bought, but within the space of two days she saw pride bow to hunger and, face taut, he silently fell to and ate as much of her providing as the rest of them.

The pit was not only blocked, but a channel was dug from Annsdale Beck to flood it and put out the fires. Those who had seen no bodies to convince them that their loved ones were dead had the fresh anguish of imagining them trapped and drowning. After that, few people were working in the village, and the able-bodied, Martin and young Arthur among them, were soon seeking work in neighbouring pits.

The trustees of the last disaster fund were predictably slow in coming forward with help from the residue of it, and people either too poor or too feckless to pay into union or provident society were soon in real want, sometimes relieved by help from family, neighbour, or private charity. The Board of Guardians began to give some outdoor relief for those in the last extremity. The workhouse loomed as a spectre to be shunned as long as possible.

Ginny went into the Co-op and cleared the slates of families in the deepest distress. She took Maudie and the baby under her wing, visiting them every day to make sure they wanted for nothing that practical kindness could supply. Maudie amply rewarded her with wholehearted gratitude.

The inquests were held at the Cock Inn. Emma soon came with the news that the landlord had seen a sharp rise in his profits, but he wasn't such a fool that he couldn't foresee an even sharper drop as soon as the coroner's business was finished and all the entourage left. The Cock was to go under the hammer and Emma would be without a job herself before very long.

'Never bother, you'll be all right. I told you I'll help you, and I will.'

Emma's face was taut. 'You can't help everybody for ever. Nobody's money stretches that far.'

Ginny shrugged, apparently unconcerned. 'Well, there's bound to be a new landlord, and he'll be glad of a good barmaid.'

'That's if there's enough left of the pit to pay anybody any wages.'

Martin was at the inquests almost every day, listening to scores of testimonies whenever he could get in, and hearing them second-hand whenever he couldn't.

'The place is packed,' he told them. 'The owners have got a QC, and the manager's got a separate one, just to represent him. There'll be no blame sticks to them if they can help it. The deputies and under managers hev a barrister, and we've got one to watch the case an' all. There's two Mines Inspectors there, the one for this county, and one from Yorkshire. And reporters, the place is rotten with them.'

Within the next few days a hundred and twelve numbered corpses were seen by the coroner and jury, and identified for the court by relatives and friends. The hundred and thirteenth still lay in the hospital mortuary, unclaimed, and the coroner and jury went to the hospital to see it there. Ginny asked Martin about him.

'His name's Andrea Lazlos. He's a Hungarian, or he was. He's lived in the pit yard for the past three months with two others. They had no other friends and no relatives; they were probably saving money to send home. That's all anybody seems to know about him.'

'An' that's all anybody seems to care,' she said.

'Aye, I suppose so,' he replied. 'Most people have enough trouble of their own without taking any on that doesn't belong to them.'

Lazlos. She could never forget him, burned and

delirious, crying out in his pain in the midst of strangers, with no one to understand his last utterances or speak a word of comfort to him in his own language.

'Mr Last Loss,' she remarked to Emma, 'lost his own country and his home and family, and finally lost his life in a strange land without a soul to mourn or bury him.'

'Aye, it's a bad job, but he doesn't belong to anybody here, so I suppose the parish'll bury him. And he's past feeling it now.' Emma was too preoccupied with her own troubles to spare much concern for the fate of Mr Lazlos's remains.

Remembering her own loneliness when she first went to London, Ginny could not dismiss him so easily from her mind. He haunted her. In the end, she went to see the priest.

'I will ask them. I promised I would, and I will. But I can't do it before Joe's requiem,' he said, as soon as his housekeeper had shown her inside.

She nodded. 'It's not that I've come about. It's Andrea Lazlos. I want him to have everything he'd have if his own family was here. A requiem, like, and a proper burial with a headstone.'

'He'll have a proper burial and a requiem anyway.'

She flushed, and the words burst out before she could check herself. 'You don't want to take my tainted money, that's what it is. You've heard a lot of talk about me and Charlie Parkinson.'

His look was open and serious. 'Nothing of the sort, but I do think any money you have would be better spent on the living. Especially your own family.'

'I want Mr Lazlos to have everything I said. I want him to have a headstone so if anybody comes looking for him, there'll be something to find.'

She arrived home to find a telegram waiting for her.

'I thought it was news of John, but I should have known that would be too good to be true. It's for you from your London friends, I suppose.' Her mother handed her the message and displayed no further interest in it.

Ginny read, ALL IN HAND. WILL WRITE LATER WITH DEFINITE ARRANGEMENTS. GEORGE.

When all the identifications were completed and the bodies released for burial, the court began in earnest to take testimony that might help them to determine the cause of the explosion. A QC arrived from London to observe the case on behalf of the Home Office, and to question witnesses as he saw fit. The court was hushed as Ginny watched Martin give evidence.

'Did you hear any shots fired before the first explosion?'

'I was too far from the dip to hear any shot fired that day, but I know shot-firing's done as a matter of course. It's caused fires before.'

'With the pit still full of men and boys?'

'Yes.'

'In direct contravention of the Mines and Quarries Act?'

'Yes.'

She heard him tell the story of his escape and his experiences with the rescue party, but nothing was as harrowing as hearing of him finding her father and young Joe Hood alive, then having to abandon them to save their own lives. 'We heard a rapping and came to a place where there was a fall of roof. We called out and Arthur Wilde answered us. We shouted to him to climb over the fall because there was a gap at the top he could just have got through, but he said one of the pony drivers lay injured with him and couldn't move, and Mr Wilde wouldn't leave him. We said we'd get back and free them both but we couldn't, because of the second explosion.'

They left after Martin had given his evidence. Outside, he looked grey and drawn. He took her hand. 'We could do nothing. I knew we were leaving them to their deaths. The last words your dad said were, "Tell Nance I'm sorry about our John and Ginny. Tell her I always loved her."'

Late that afternoon, whilst Emma was at the hospital and her mother was resting in bed, she answered the door to Charlie. Young Arthur looked towards them with a face like the wrath of God.

'The answer's no, Charlie, no to everything.' She made to close the door but he prevented her.

'I shall keep calling until you do me the courtesy of hearing me out. It will do me no harm, and it will be a kindness to your neighbours, give them something other than the disaster to spice their conversation. Come with me now, Ginny, and I promise that if I can't persuade you this time, I'll go back to London without you.'

'Wait there.'

She appeared at the door two minutes later with Lizzie at her side. The Vines' yellow Daimler almost blocked the street, and Ginny could feel a hundred spying eyes on her from neighbouring windows.

'We're not getting in that with you, Charlie,' she said. Lizzie pulled a face of disappointment. Instead, they walked out of the village, towards the Durham Road as Charlie talked incessantly of the brilliant career she had, the expectation of a more brilliant one still, the glamour of the halls, the adulation of the audience, the delights of London life and all the money she could make.

Lizzie listened entranced, eyes shining. 'Oh, I'd love that. That's just what I'd like to do!' Ginny caught the quick, bright glance and half-hidden smile flashed in Charlie's direction.

'Would you?' He smiled delightedly at her. 'Bravo! And no reason why you couldn't, with a little help. You're a clever girl, I'm sure, and I've no doubt you're talented. You must persuade Ginny to come back to London with me, and we can help you to get your start on the stage.'

'Will you, Ginny? Please? It sounds marvellous.'

'I loved the stage, Lizzie, but there's things here I love more, and I can't have both. So I shan't be going back to London. Not to stay, anyway.'

Charlie sighed, favouring Lizzie with his most caressing glances. 'That's a very great pity. I mean a pity that you, Lizzie, should be denied your chance. Your sister's very hard, but perhaps she'll relent in the end if you talk to her.'

'Don't look at her like that,' Ginny snapped. 'She's only eleven years old – she's not even in long frocks. Get on home, Lizzie, go now.'

Lizzie looked resentful. 'But you said you wanted me to come with you, Ginny.'

'Well, now I don't, so go home. Run all the way.' There was such an edge to her voice that Lizzie did run.

Charlie laughed. 'No need to be jealous of the child, Ginny. She is only a child.'

'Aye, she is only a child, so you remember that, and leave her alone.'

They walked on for a while. At length, Charlie broke the silence. 'I believe I forgot to offer you my condolences on the sad loss of your father. I'm sure it's a great grief to us both to be able to walk about the village unmolested, and I suppose your mother will miss her regular beatings.'

It was growing dark, but she saw the malicious gleam in his eyes. She turned heel and with a deft flick of her wrist lifted her skirt a bare inch above her ankle as she walked rapidly away, a gesture borrowed from the ladies of the Empire and one she had used many times on stage. She looked over her shoulder with a beguiling smile.

'Come on, Charlie,' she cooed, 'I'll show you the path I took through the woods that night I ran away from you after the races.'

He laughed and followed her. 'How unpredictable you

are. One never knows what you'll do next. You're insane to think of throwing yourself away on that fellow Jude, you know, Ginny. I know that's what you're about. He can never satisfy you now.'

Among the trees, and out of sight of the village she hitched up her skirts to her waist and threw the weight of them over her arm. Smiling eagerly up at him, she entwined her fingers in his hair and drew his head downwards until their lips met.

'But you can, can't you, Charlie? I long for the sort of satisfaction you can give me.'

She kissed him again, then with her fingers still gripping his hair, she drew his face ever downwards until it was level with her hips. She thought of her father and young Joe lying dead in the flooded mine, of her own dead baby and of Jubilee, and jerked her knee upwards with a right good will.

An instant later Charlie sprawled on his back, holding his nose and mouth. She let her skirts drop and leaned over him, hands on hips. 'I bet you never predicted that, Charlie. I'm a champion street fighter's daughter and I see I don't fail the breed. So there's a one from my father. He'd want his debts to you paid.'

He lay clutching his face, too stunned to reply, and for a second she was sorely tempted to pay her own debt to his friend with the toe of her boot, but she forbore and walked away, rubbing her knee.

She'd hardly gone twenty yards when she saw young Arthur leaning against a tree waiting for her. 'I wanted to know what you were doing with that bugger now Martin

Jude's making a bloody fool of himself over you, so I followed you. And now I do know, so that's all right,' he said.

Chapter Twenty-Four

'I come in the name of Him who bore our griefs and carried our sorrows, to speak a word of comfort to you,' the Methodist minister addressed them all. 'He took our mortal nature to become a "Man of Sorrows and acquainted with grief". He stood by the graveside as you do today, and Jesus wept. My pulpit is now the mounds of earth which have been dug out of these graves and my text is the open grave and the bodies of our dear brothers who lie sleeping there, mourned so bitterly by their dearest friends now gathered round them. Take comfort. There is one who has been down into the grave for us, and he has dispersed all its darkness and driven away all its gloom and he has hung up the lamp of his love, and we need not fear to go down to the place where they laid our Redeemer, because it is not the end. "I am the Resurrection and the Life, saith the Lord; he that believeth in me though he were dead, yet shall he live."'

Thousands of mourners and spectators witnessed thirty burials that day, and it seemed as if every village for miles around had been emptied of its inhabitants. There was a strong force of police in attendance, but their presence was unnecessary. The crowd was quiet, solemn and respectful. The largest proportion of people were pitmen with their wives and families, and their sympathy for the bereaved was heartfelt. It could hardly be helped with such vast numbers present, but Ginny was dismayed to see graves that had been carefully planted with flowers and shrubs trampled upon as people tried to get near enough to hear the services read.

Ginny's gaze was riveted on poor Maudie, who stood with her mother and sisters. She was listening intently to the minister's words, now seeming resigned to her catastrophe. As she stooped to pick up a handful of earth and cast it on to her husband's coffin, the babe in her arms began to cry. Her mother reached out to take him from her, but Maudie held him all the closer and turned away. Ginny clasped Martin's hand and held him tight.

The following day, in the Catholic part of the cemetery, the priest read the service over twelve victims, including thirty-three-year-old Andrea Lazlos. Martin was with her when Ginny herself threw the earth on his coffin, vowing that the names Ara Jera and Jan Staovsky should be inscribed along with his on the headstone.

Martin put an arm around her waist and drew her close to him as they walked home through a village wreathed in black crêpe. 'You're a good lass,' he told her.

She turned and kissed his cheek. 'And you're a better lad.'

For one long melancholy week, they saw cortège after cortège pass through the village. The sight of the mourners would have melted a heart of stone, but the people Ginny pitied most deeply were those like the Hoods and her mother, who had no body to lay to rest. Their grief could have no climax and no focus.

During that week Martin called to see them every day. He and Emma would sit at the kitchen table devouring the papers, reading the more striking or contentious passages aloud to the rest of them.

'Just listen to this,' he exclaimed one evening, reading from the *Chronicle*. '"Mr and Mrs Vine would like to express their sincere condolences to all the bereaved families and assure them that they mourn with them in their affliction."' He laughed bitterly. 'Aye, they're in mourning all right. They've killed the goose that laid the golden egg, and that's the only death they care about. The rest of us are too easily replaced.'

Ginny's mother and young Arthur nodded grim agreement, but Ginny pictured Mr Vine's joyless face and his sympathetic, bloodshot eyes. 'He must have cared something. He went down with the rescue parties. He nearly got killed an' all,' she said.

'He'd a good right to go down with the rescue parties. He was the cause of it all. The owners wanted the coal out fast and cheap, so he surrounded himself with men who hadn't the guts to object to breaches of the safety rules. Not to mention the fact they sometimes weren't fit to be in the pit after drinking with him,' Martin replied.

Ginny said no more, but thought of her days with Charlie, and the comfort she herself had found in drink.

Living with Charlie's sister couldn't be any easier than living with Charlie, and in her heart of hearts she pitied Robert Vine and blamed his wife and her brother's greed and ambition for driving him to drink and spurring him on to risk men's lives.

'Why, what about this, man?' Emma exploded, reading from a national daily. '"It is possible that the firing of a blast may have been coincident with the escape of sufficient gas to cause the explosion, but it will never be known whether a blast was fired or not. The only remaining suppositions are that a safety lamp had been damaged so that its flame was exposed or that one of the miners had used a naked light. So careless are some of these men that a miner has been known to make a hole through the gauze of his safety lamp to get a light for his pipe!"'

Martin's face was a picture of disgust. 'It's always the same. The blame's never fixed where it belongs. We get the papers full of Mr Vine's heroic attempts to rescue the men, and Mr Vine's hairbreadth escape from death, and Mr Vine's generosity to some of the bereaved families he's bought off for a pittance. They say nothing about him knowing perfectly well that gas was giving off in the broken workings and still bribing the men to use powder. The manager's the man with all the authority, and the responsibility's his, nobody else's; 1906, and they've learned nothing from the disasters of the past century. Or they have, but making money matters a lot more than keeping men alive. Oh, aye, and the fireman's reports have gone missing and that comes as no surprise. Ultimately, there's only one person to blame, and that's the manager.'

'It's not going to be pinned on him, though,' said Emma. 'It'll roll off his shoulders right down the ranking until it's saddled on some poor lad that's dead and buried, as like as not.'

There was a knock on the front door. Dreading it being Charlie again, Ginny moved to answer it, but young Arthur frowned and motioned her to sit down with a look of authority that was so like her father's that she obeyed before she had time to think. He answered the door himself, and a moment later ushered Tom Hood and his wife into the kitchen.

'We had the requiem for our Joe yesterday,' said Tom quietly, his face haggard. 'So we've come to see your mother, Emma. I think you'll know what it's about.'

'We've all a good idea what it's about,' said their mother.

'Well then, Arthur Wilde refused to desert our lad when he was injured and he ended up losing his own life. We'll never forget that, and we'll be proud to have Arthur's lass for our daughter-in-law. The only snag is, conscience won't let us agree to anything but a Catholic wedding.'

A look of scorn passed fleetingly over their mother's face. It was gone in a moment, and she nodded her agreement.

Emma was in transports. 'Does Jimmy know?'

'No. We wanted to ask your mam first. You can tell him yourself, and you'd better publish the banns.'

★

When the jury finally returned the verdict, Martin was outraged. He bought the hottest paper off the press and read it over and over again. '". . We are unable to attach blame to any single individual. At the same time the jury are of the unanimous opinion that the cause of the explosion was the unsafe working of the dip-board of the colliery. The jury consider that blasting with powder was highly injudicious and should not have been allowed by the under manager or prosecuted by the workmen." The under manager! Who the hell do they think he gets his orders from? I would love to write to the papers and tell them what really went on,' he exclaimed.

'Why don't you?' asked Ginny. Both Emma and Martin stared at her as if she were an imbecile.

'Because an anonymous letter's no good, and if I sign my name to it I'll be blacklisted,' he said. 'Why else do you think a deputy stands up and tells a pack of lies at the inquest? Because he knows if he tells the truth he'll never get another job and the owners'll try to throw the blame for the accident on him, so he denies on oath that any shot firing was authorized while the pit was full of men and boys. Nobody'll tell the truth, not where it counts anyway, because they all need their jobs – but they'll all chunter enough in the club and the Cock among themselves.' He paused, then added, 'And I'm as bad as the rest, otherwise I would write to the paper and tell them all there was shot firing with the pit full, and everybody knew about it, and the manager ordered it because the owners wanted it done.'

'Write, then. You could have a job managing me. I

could carry on working the halls,' said Ginny. His answer was exactly what she had anticipated.

'I've not sunk so low yet that I want to be living off a woman. When we get married, I'll earn the wages and you can look after the babies.'

'When we get married, Martin?' she asked.

'Aye, that's the plan. That's if I ever manage to get another job. I thought you knew,' he grinned.

She smiled. He was as unlike Charlie as any man could be. In Martin's world it was a man's duty to provide for his wife and no man worthy of the name would let it be otherwise. There would be no marriage until he could support her. Attempts to persuade him otherwise were doomed to failure, and she knew that to persist would demean him in his own eyes. Frustrating though it was, she loved him all the more for it.

'Write your letter,' she said. 'Something'll turn up, I know it will.'

'You sound like Mr Micawber,' said Emma. 'There's not much going to turn up round here until the pit's working again, and I don't see that happening for months, if not years.'

Ginny took Martin by the hands and stared earnestly into his face. 'You're probably blacklisted already for speaking out at the inquest, so write your letter, and send it to the papers. You'll never rest until you have.'

He turned back to the paper, and after several minutes' silence made up his mind. 'I will. I'll do it this minute. You can read it over before I send it, Em. Make sure it's all right, like.'

Lacking a stamp, he left the letter with Ginny for her to post, but the following day he was on the doorstep before the post office opened.

'I've been tossing and turning all night, going over it all in my mind. I want to send it, for the sake of everybody that got killed and their families, but I'll never get work in this county again if I do, so I don't know how we'll ever get wed.'

'We'll emigrate. I've heard California's a good place.'

He grimaced. 'I've thought about that too, but there's another thing. I don't want to leave Mam Smith. She's been as good as a mother to me, and I think Philip's all she lives for. If I took him away from her, it'd be the final straw. I think she'd give up the ghost.'

Ginny stiffened slightly, and he saw it. 'I know she's been a bit sharp with you, but she's a good heart at bottom, and she'll come round in the end.'

He gave her such a look of appeal that she softened and smiled reassurance. 'I'm going to post your letter, and it'll be all right. I know it will.' And that's the best lesson I ever learned from Charlie, she thought. If you want any luck, make your own.

Emma's face brightened. 'The landlord's got a buyer for the Cock. He says he'll be doing a flit in a month or so. The new owner's from London – just wants the place for an investment. He's looking for a manager.'

'There's a job would do for you, Martin,' said Ginny, suddenly animated. 'Why don't you go and see about it?'

'I know nothing about looking after pubs,' he protested, and Ginny looked crestfallen.

'There's not a great deal to it,' said Emma. 'If you keep me on, I'll teach you the ropes. You're used to managing the Union money, you should be all right keeping the books, and I can add up. The only thing I can't teach you is the cellar-work, how to keep a good pint, but you could easily learn that from the landlord before he goes.'

'You've nothing to lose,' Ginny cajoled, 'and at least if you get the job, our Emma'll still have hers. You can keep her on.'

'Go on, Martin. Get to the Cock now and find out where the agent is – I think it's a firm of solicitors in Wearham who're dealing with it. It might be a case of first come, first served, and you've nothing to lose by trying,' said Emma.

After he'd gone, Ginny read his letter over again, imagining what his feelings would be when he saw it in print. She slotted it back in its envelope and licked the glue. It might be fun to keep him in suspense for a while, to make his relief all the greater when the time came. On the other hand, there would be no marriage until he was sure he had a job, and what if he changed his mind in the meantime? She frowned as she reached for her coat, suddenly filled with nervous anticipation, unsure that she could bear much more suspense herself.

A brisk walk to the post office worked off some of her agitation. She stuck the stamp firmly on the envelope, and dropped it into the post box to hear it land with the knell of finality.

*

Later that morning young Arthur walked into the kitchen and dropped a couple of rabbits on the floor. 'We netted six, but I let the other lad take four. They're a lot worse off than us. I'll skin them when I've had a bite to eat. We spotted Parkinson and his sister in their yellow motor. I think he was on his way to the station. He's got a pair of real shiners.' He grinned at her, eyes dancing. 'Ginny man, I wish you'd seen 'em.'

'They've printed it!' Martin caught up with her as she was making her way home from Maudie's house the following Monday morning.

'You sound surprised,' Ginny smiled.

'I am, and it looks worse in the paper than it did when I wrote it. I shouldn't be surprised to hear from Mr Vine's solicitors. How will you like being bespoken by a jailbird?'

'They can't lock you up for telling the truth.'

'Even if they do, it'll be worth it. But what I do next, I don't know. I've tried for work at every pit for miles, and there's nothing.'

'You've heard nothing about the tenancy at the Cock, then?'

'That's the last job I expect to hear about, and that's saying something.'

Emma was in the yard possing a tubful of clothes when they walked through the back gate.

'Come on in and have a look at the paper. They've printed Martin's letter,' Ginny told her.

The house was full. Her mother was dressed and sitting

by the kitchen fire brushing her hair. Ginny was struck by the quantity of grey now mixed among the brown, and the many lines around her eyes and mouth. Lizzie was standing at the sink washing crockery. Martin handed Emma the paper folded back at the right page. Arthur, who for a wonder was polishing his own boots, looked up. 'Don't keep it to yourself, Em. Read it out.'

All eyes on her, and the atmosphere heavy with expectation, Emma read, '"Protest at the Verdict. I was engaged with others for nearly an hour in putting out a fire just a few days before the disaster. The use of gunpowder in the dip-boardgate posed great danger to the men employed in the colliery for several weeks before the disaster, and its continued use in blasting the coal after the danger had been so frequently demonstrated was a criminal neglect of reasonable care on the part of the managing partner, Mr Robert Vine. This neglect led to the deaths of a hundred and thirty-eight men and boys, and indirectly to the deaths of twelve men who attended the rescue."'

'That sums it up, and I'm glad somebody's had the guts to say it where it counts,' said young Arthur, black eyes glittering as he laid into his boots.

Their mother nodded. 'Well done, Martin.'

'Aye, that's what I thought, only now I can't get a job.'

'Neither can I,' said young Arthur, 'and I never sent any letter, so it doesn't seem to make much odds.'

'I've got a bit of news as well,' Ginny announced. 'I'm going to London on Thursday. I've got a benefit performance arranged in aid of a disaster fund for the bereaved families. I thought you could be a trustee, Martin. The show in London's just the start.'

The amazement on their faces was a memory to treasure. For a moment or two, nobody spoke.

'Can I come with you?' Lizzie was the first to break the silence, full of eager expectation. 'I would love to see the music hall.'

Ginny laughed, catching her excitement. 'You can. I want you all to come. I want you to meet two good friends of mine.' The thought of seeing Agnes and George again made her eyes shine, and her smile stretch from ear to ear.

Her mother gave her a sour look. 'The only thing Martin's letter doesn't say is that the owners sealed the pit and flooded it with men probably still alive down there. You look over-cheerful for a girl with a father dead in the mine and a brother lost at sea.'

Her smile faded in an instant. 'I'm sorry about me father, really sorry. But I don't believe John's dead. He'll come home before long. I know he will.'

Chapter Twenty-Five

Her mother was too ill and too low in spirits to travel, and wouldn't let them take Sally. Young Arthur refused point-blank to go, Emma wanted to stay near Jimmy, Mam Smith declined the invitation with cool thanks, and Martin decided that Philip should stay with his grandmother. It was as much as she could do to persuade Martin to accompany her. Only Lizzie was raring to go, and her wholehearted enthusiasm compensated Ginny for the rest.

They boarded the train at the crack of dawn and took their seats in a second-class carriage. Lizzie, so mad with excitement that Ginny laughed with pleasure to watch her, sat fidgeting beside her as green hills, fields, woodland and villages rushed by. Martin was looking more cheerful than she had ever seen him and he smiled at her whenever their eyes met. When Lizzie left the carriage to walk down the corridor, he said, 'I've had a bit of good news, bonny lass. I got a letter from the agent yesterday afternoon. You're looking at the tenant of the Cock Inn.'

Her eyebrows shot up. 'You've known since yesterday afternoon, and you didn't come and tell us?'

'I thought I'd save it for now. So what about a wedding?'

She laughed. 'If I'd known yesterday, I'd have had the banns up before we left. How can I wait another month?'

He pressed his lips against hers in long, melting kisses. Eventually she pushed him away, trembling.

'Ginny? What's the matter?'

'I'm scared. Oh, Martin, I'm not Maria, you know. I'm nothing like her.'

He sat back from her, blue eyes serious. 'I know that. You're not Maria, and you're nothing like her. I loved Maria and I laid her to rest. I've mourned her for three and a half years, and that's over. You're Ginny, and it's you I want now.'

'But what about . . .?' She couldn't bring herself to repeat the name of Charlie Parkinson. 'You might sometimes think about it when we're married. You might hold it against me.' She held her breath and a brief pause seemed to stretch into infinity.

'You were honest with me, Ginny, and I believed you. Now I'll be honest with you. I often used to think about you when you were away, worrying about you, like, but when we heard you were living with him, I hoped I might never see you again.'

She averted her face, tears springing to her eyes. He took her cheek in the palm of his hand, and with a gentle pressure turned her face towards his until she met his eyes.

'But when I did, I knew I loved you, even though I wished I didn't. I was terrified in that mine, Ginny, but it made me realize what matters and what doesn't. Pride doesn't matter, not now, not to me anyway. I love you, no matter what you've done, or who you've done it with. I love you, Ginny. I cannot help it.'

She rested her head on his shoulder and burst into tears, just as Lizzie re-entered the carriage.

'What's up?'

'We're going to get wed,' said Martin.

'Why that's nothing to cry for, is it?' asked Lizzie.

'You're the last on the programme, Ginny, with a one-hour spot to fill,' George told her as they sat round the supper table. 'There's been an amazing response to your appeal. You know most of the artistes, but there are two acts you've never seen, both from mining areas – the Salford Clog Dancers and a troupe of acrobats and tightrope walkers from Staffordshire. You've only got a couple of days to rehearse. Shall we run through any of your numbers tonight, or are you too tired?'

'Oh, go on, Ginny! I can't wait to hear them. You never sang any of them at home,' said Lizzie.

'I wonder why that might have been?' asked George, with a wry smile in Ginny's direction. Martin looked swiftly at him, and then at Lizzie.

'Have no fear, Martin,' murmured George, sensing his unease. 'The songs generally adapt themselves to the level of understanding of the listener. They put nothing in anybody's mind that wasn't there before, I promise you.'

The next couple of days were spent in rehearsals, arrangements for the sale of Ginny's house, and, what delighted Lizzie most of all, shopping in Bond Street, buying gifts for everybody at home. Martin looked more and more thoughtful. 'I knew you'd earned a bit of money, Ginny, but I'd no idea you were so well off.'

'I'm not so well off now. I've spent a fair bit these past few weeks, and earned nothing, so the house is about all I've got left.'

They ordered most of the purchases to be sent on and took a cab back to the Burns' house for another pleasant evening spent in rehearsals. After a little sightseeing the following day, stage clothes and make-up were packed into a trunk and they were off to the Majestic for the Benefit performance.

She took Martin into the dressing room with her, exchanging jokes and greetings with other artistes on the way. As they reached it, a troupe of acrobats of both sexes passed them, just coming off stage.

'They're not over-dressed, are they?' a stunned Martin commented after closing the door behind them.

Ginny laughed. 'They'd have a job trying to perform fully clothed.'

He discreetly turned his back whilst she changed into a red, figure-hugging gown trimmed with sequins, and watched in fascination as she applied greasepaint and finally pinned on a red feathered hat at a rakish angle.

'Five minutes, Mrs James.'

She checked her appearance in the mirror, dabbed on a little more lip-rouge, then linked arms with Martin and went to wait in the wings.

Ginny felt nervous, as always, but Martin was more nervous than she. As the buzz of excitement in the audience grew, they heard her introduction played. Up swung the house tabs. The theatre was suddenly hushed, the limes focused on the right-hand corner of the stage, and Martin looked agonized when she seemed to miss her cue.

'It's a good ploy to delay your entrance sometimes,' she whispered as they played her breezy intro again, 'creates maximum suspense.' She stepped into the spotlight and with a cocky, jaunty gait walked down to the footlights.

He watched her from the wings and the self-consciousness she felt at his watching kept her darting little glances in his direction as if needing his approval, but nerves and shyness soon dissipated as her alter ego claimed her and she became Ginny James. She gave the performance her heart and soul and took three encores at the end of it. The applause was thunderous as she finally ran off the stage in wild elation to throw her arms round Martin and kiss him fully on the lips.

'Marry me. Marry me now, Martin. I can't wait.'

Lizzie kept her awake for hours that night in the double bed they shared, chattering on and on about the show. 'I love the music hall, Ginny. The theatre's so big, and so grand! The acrobats, I couldn't believe my eyes! When they climbed up on each other to make a pyramid, I thought they'd touch the ceiling. My heart was in my mouth; I thought one of them would break his neck getting down again. And that clown! Did you see the size of his shoes? I nearly died laughing. I would love to be on stage. I don't know how you can bear to leave it. I never knew you were so good. You were the best singer, and you made the audience laugh, but you weren't as funny as the clown. Did you see us waving to you from the box? That box, it was bigger than our living room at home, I've never seen anything like it. I thought they'd never stop clapping and calling you back at the end. I wish you'd stay, and I could come and live with you, and go on the stage as soon as I'm old enough. George could write some songs for me.'

Ginny yawned. 'I can't. I'm going to marry Martin.'

Lizzie gave an exasperated groan. 'Martin. What's Martin, next to all this? It's magic, Ginny man. I know which I'd pick, and it wouldn't be Martin. All those men in the bar after the show, did you see the way they were looking at you? Some of them looked like real gentlemen. And what's Martin? Nothing but a pitman.' She gave these last words great emphasis.

'There's one thing I hope you learn as you get older – you can't always judge a book by its cover. If you knew the tricks some of those gentlemen get up to, it would make your blood run cold. Martin's more of a gentleman than any of them as far as I'm concerned. You'll understand when you're old enough to love somebody.'

'Oh, Ginny, you talk a lot of rubbish. If you're going to love somebody, why not a real gentleman, like Charlie? If it hadn't been for him, you'd never have got on the stage.'

Ginny pulled the blankets around her and turned over. 'You've a lot to learn, Lizzie, but not the hard way, I hope. Go to sleep. You've a busy day tomorrow if you want to see the sights.'

'This is the first time I've been able to get you on your own since we came. So what do you think to him?'

George was still in his dressing gown, lounging in full sunlight by the long windows in the drawing room, sipping hot coffee and reading the early morning paper. She sat beside him on the blue plush sofa and felt a quiver of apprehension as he folded his paper and laid it aside, to give her his full attention. 'He's quite different to anyone I ever met before, of course, and it's obvious that he wasn't born a gentleman.' He held up a hand to forestall the protests she opened her mouth to make. 'But he's something better, Ginny – he's one of nature's gentlemen. He's one of the most likeable men I've ever known and I can see the effect he has on you. You glow every time you look at him, and every time you think about him, judging by the look on your face just now.'

'Is it so obvious?' she smiled, delighted that Martin had the approval of her most valued friend.

'Painfully. It's tragic, though,' he sighed, 'that music hall's the loser in all this, and so are you. You'll sacrifice a good income along with your career, you know. But if you're determined to have him, you're right to sell your house. He would never transplant to London.'

'You're the second person to say that. Don't you think he could adapt? I did.'

'If his heart were in it, he might, but it isn't. I'm sure he'd find our way of life intolerably trivial. He's a crusader, Ginny, with dragons to slay. He has the fire of a cause in his belly. Go with him if you must, but make him laugh sometimes. Don't let him become too serious – too much of a fanatic. That would make Martin a very dull boy, and it wouldn't be much fun for you.'

She kissed his cheek. 'Did I ever tell you what a sweetheart you are, George?'

'Often. It's how you've managed to keep me twisted round your little finger for so long. We shall both miss you, Ginny.'

Breakfast was late, but over in time for them to take Lizzie to see Buckingham Palace and the changing of the guard. Agnes and George laughed to see the wonder on her face, taking pains to explain the ceremony to her, and tell her some of the history of the place. Ginny stood a little way apart from them, beside Martin. He was silent, seeming miles away. She sensed a dampening of his spirits, imagined he was thinking of the disaster, and tried to cheer him. 'We should have a good few hundred pounds to start the fund with. The theatre was sold out last night, and it seats two and a half thousand,' she told him, squeezing his hand.

'You've done well for us, bonny lass. I never realized how popular you are.'

'We had a lot of support from other artistes as well. And the impresario and the theatre manager. There are a lot of good-hearted people in the business. I'll have to write and thank them all.'

'Aye, and so will I. I'm grateful to them all, but I think you were the big attraction.' His smile belied the troubled look in his eyes.

'What's the matter, Martin? You looked like that when I came off stage last night. Is it because you don't like my act? Is it because some of my stuff's a bit too . . . um . . .?'

He shook his head. 'Your act's good, Ginny, really good. Some of the songs are a bit naughty, but George was right when he said they wouldn't put anything in anybody's mind that wasn't there before.'

'What's wrong, then?'

He sighed, that habitual droop at the corners of his mouth more pronounced than ever. 'I don't know what I thought your life was like in London, or what sort of theatres you played in, but I never imagined anything on this scale. I never realized how famous you are, how many people you have eating out of your hand when you're on the stage; and the stage suits you, Ginny, it fits you like a glove. You can earn more for yourself in a week than I could give you if I worked for a year. I've been thinking, and there's only one conclusion I can come to. We shouldn't get wed. I can only hinder you. You shouldn't sell your house. You should stay in London.'

She looked stricken. 'Stay with me then, and be my manager.'

He shook his head. 'No. For one thing, I wouldn't know where to start. For another, I couldn't live off my wife, Ginny, I just couldn't. And there are other things I need to do in Annsdale.'

She slipped an arm through his and held tight. 'If you were with me, I could live in London, but I've never been happy here on my own and I've had three years working on the halls. I liked the applause, and the glamour, and the drinks and gossip in the bar with other artistes, but it's not enough. It's not a proper life and touring's even worse. It's miserable most of the time.'

'But the audience loved you. They cheered you to the rafters.'

'Audiences have illusions about you. It's nothing to do with what you're really like. They seem to love you while you can give a good performance, and they turn on you if you can't. A lot of artistes are dead of drink at not much over fifty, and they usually start drinking to help them face audiences when they're not on top form. And nobody can be on top form all the time. I don't want that. What I want is a man, and there's only one who'll do for me. So I'm not staying if you won't stay with me. I'm coming back to Annsdale with you.'

'You'll be wasted in Annsdale, Ginny. You're good on the stage. Really good. It's what you're cut out for.'

'It's not. I'm cut out to be Mrs Jude and help you keep the Cock. You once said, "You've got to be where your sympathies are, lass." So I have, and my sympathies are with you.'

He hesitated, looking deep into her inky black eyes. 'Are you sure?'

She nodded. 'I can't be happy without you, Martin.'

Ignoring all the bystanders, he took her by her waist and lifted her off her feet, laughing up at her as he swung her round. 'Well, you know what I am, and what I've got to offer, and that's not much,' he said, setting her down again, 'so if you're set on swapping fame and fortune for Martin Jude, I can't stop you!'

On Tuesday morning, after a tearful dawn farewell to George and Agnes, Ginny followed Lizzie and Martin on to the train. Lizzie, exhausted, soon fell asleep. They travelled in silence for an hour or so, and then Martin cleared his throat.

'If I can't talk you out of marrying me, what would you think of buying the Cock with what you make on your house? We could be sure then that I'd never be out of a job again, and neither would Emma. I'll soon learn the trade, and I'll make a go of it.'

Ginny was silent, looking out of the carriage window, staring unseeing at the scudding clouds.

'You wouldn't be a loser, Ginny. I'll work like a slave and pay you back tenfold.'

'I know you would, Martin,' she said, quietly, 'but I was going to buy Mam a house with some of that money.'

'Aye, well, right enough, bonnie lass.' He was silent for a couple of minutes. 'The house your mam's in should be safe, you know. The owners'll let her stay on, with her man being killed in the pit.'

'I know that, Martin, but I wanted to buy her a nice little cottage in Annsdale.'

'Well, more credit to you for thinking of your mam, then. Although, a year or two in the Cock might get us enough money to buy her a one anyway.'

She deliberated for a few moments, chewing her lip. 'It's not only me mam. I just know the new owner wouldn't want to sell.'

His eyes widened in astonishment. 'You know who the owner is? You know more than anybody else, then. The agent wouldn't even give me his name. And you know him?'

She nodded, still staring out of the window. 'I know him very well.'

'Who is he, Ginny?'

She turned to face him. 'I'm looking at him.'

Martin's jaw dropped. 'You what?'

'I had all the same ideas you've just put to me. So when I knew you'd never get a job, and you wouldn't marry me until you had a one, I put a bid in for the Cock through an agent in Durham. It's yours already, Martin.'

Early on a bright April morning Emma was married to Jimmy in the little Catholic church, with as little ceremony as the church could desire for a mixed marriage.

'No flowers and no music. The bishop wasn't going to let it be much of a wedding for you if he could help it, Emma,' said their mother as the wedding party followed the bridal pair through the sombre streets afterwards, with Jimmy hobbling on a leg that still refused to heal.

'I don't care. I've got Jimmy, that's all I want. I'm happy.'

Jimmy gave his young wife a look of sheer admiration. 'And so am I. I've got the bonniest lass in Annsdale. She looks grand in that new frock, Ginny.'

A cheerful fire roared up the chimney in the best room at the Cock, where they sat down to breakfast. Ginny watched Martin look about him, seeming unable to believe his good fortune in stepping into such a property.

'Will you all toast the bridal pair in a glass of champagne?' the landlord asked after the remains of the meal had been cleared. 'To the best little barmaid I ever had, and her lucky husband. A long and happy life together.'

Ginny heaved a sigh of envy. It would be another two weeks before her wedding to Martin, and she hardly knew how to bear the wait.

It was a tight squeeze at home when Jimmy moved in. Ginny's mother let the bridal pair have the bed in the front room, and moved upstairs to sleep with her daughters. With her disgraced eldest soon to be a wife, and her pregnant daughter married, she seemed a little more cheerful. 'Although I don't know what sort of work he's going to find if that leg of his gets no better,' she told Ginny as they lay in bed that night.

Chapter Twenty-Six

When she saw Martin ready for their own wedding, Ginny's heart overflowed with gratitude and love. 'You do forgive me, don't you?' she whispered.

He took her into his arms and held her tight, and she was surprised to see tears in his eyes. 'It's not for me to forgive you, bonny lass. You must forgive me. I knew how much I was hurting you that first time I came to see you at your mam's, and I couldn't help myself. I wanted to punish you, and I'd no right. You didn't belong to me. All that's done with now, and I'll love you and cherish you for the rest of my days.'

She felt that sudden, secret thrill in the pit of her belly so intensely it made her catch her breath. 'And serve me?' she murmured.

His arms loosened their grasp on her. She could have bitten her tongue out. To say such a thing to him, something so coarse it couldn't help but force the most hideous remembrance of her life with Charlie Parkinson on him. She felt a pang of fear that she had disgusted him. An instant later she felt his arms tighten around her, pressing her closely, fiercely, to him until she could hardly breathe. She felt him shake, felt his breath on her ear. He was laughing.

'Better than you've ever been served in your life before, bonny lass.'

He held her a moment or two longer in a suffocating squeeze before his strong, honest man's hands were round her waist, and he was holding her at arm's length. His eyes danced, and the faintest blush appeared on his cheeks. 'An' I can do it an' all,' he laughed, 'so don't think I can't.'

They walked together through streets still hung with black crêpe towards the chapel, where Emma and Jimmy were waiting, and after the simplest wedding the village had ever seen they parted company from their witnesses and returned to Mam Smith's.

Martin went to the mantelpiece and took down the photograph of his dead wife, while Mam Smith and Philip looked on without protest. Ginny took the photograph from him. The smiling girl of her dream stared out at her; the girl who was caring for her baby in the land of the dead. Ginny carefully put the photograph back in its place.

'Let her stay where she is, where she can see us. When we get to the Cock, we'll have her up in the bar.' At the soft note in her voice, and the quick moistening of her eyes, Mam Smith and Martin exchanged curious glances. Philip hurled himself at her and wrapped his arms round her legs, squeezing her tight.

'I love you, Ginny,' he said.

She ruffled his curls. 'I love you, an' all.'

'You're a better lass than I took you for, Ginny,' said Mam Smith, 'but Maria's photo stops here with me. Come on, Philip, we'll go for a walk in the park and maybe drop in on Mary Ann. We'll be gone hours, three at the least.'

'In the midst of death, we are in life,' said Martin, as he waved them off. He locked the door after them and put the key ceremoniously in his pocket, then turned towards her, eyes twinkling and lips parted in a wide smile. 'There's no escape for you now, Ginny my lass, so get upstairs this minute and into bed, because if you don't, I'll make you Mrs Jude here on the clippy mat.'

He lunged towards her, eyes crossed and pleasing smile turning into a wolfish leer. She shrieked and slipped away from him, then dashed into the kitchen towards the stairs. He caught her halfway up, and they collapsed on the steps, giggling like children. He lifted her and, as if she weighed no more than a baby, carried her the rest of the way.

He was a lover. Knowing him as she did, how could she ever have doubted it? He made her feel clean, whole, cherished, guiltless. He had vowed, 'with my body I thee worship,' and slowly, tenderly, he showed her fully what he'd meant. His caresses and his murmurings of love warmed her heart and healed her soul. In the warm and happy afterglow of perfect lovemaking, she smiled up at him.

'You look like the cat that got the cream,' he teased.

'I got something a lot better than the cream. I got you.'

'And I got you.' He lay beside her and between kisses he murmured, 'And this between the two of us, well, if God made anything better, he kept it to Himself.'

'You said God was a Jewish fairy tale.'

'Aye, well, I'm not so sure now.'

'How could you live without it for three years, Martin?'

He shrugged. 'I don't know. I couldn't bear to string anybody along that I didn't really love. And I didn't want to get any lass with a bairn and have to marry her for the sake of it. I don't know. You just don't give way to it. I found plenty of work to do.'

'I'm glad you waited for me. I wish I could have waited for you. You're my one and only true love. You know that, don't you?'

'Aye. I know that,' he smiled. 'You've loved me for a long time.'

'I know I have. But how did you know?'

'You told me. When you helped me with Maria. When you asked me to take you to the dancing, when you fought to empty my bathwater, when you went away after your father kneed me in the face. When you stopped me at the pit to tell me it wasn't your fault. When you said, "I'll do anything you want, Martin," that first day you were back and I came to see you at your mother's. I was sick with jealousy and anger, but when you said that I wanted you so much I could have ripped the clothes off you and taken you there and then, and I might have if I hadn't got out. But most of all, when you said, "Oh, Martin, I'm so afraid. I wish you wouldn't go down again," and I could see you meant it. You've loved me for a long time, and I must have known for a long time, only I didn't realize it until you went away on the train. Then I started to love you back.'

'That was when you said, "Oh, Ginny, if only",' she said, kissing him again. 'I often used to wonder what you meant by that.'

'Everything and nothing. If only your dad was different, or Philip and Mam could have withstood him. If only I'd had more money and could have kept you, if only grieving for Maria hadn't been so new, then I could have thought of you. A lot of things.'

'I'm sorry I wasn't a virgin, Martin. I was frightened you wouldn't want me because of it.'

He returned her kisses. 'I want you all right, and I always will. You're mine now and we love each other. That's all that matters.'

He drew her towards him to begin more fond and gentle lovemaking. Later, lying in his arms, she had a sense that they were safe from all hurt, as if they were cradled in the palm of God's hand. At length, she said, 'It must be a sin to be so happy when so many people are in mourning.'

'I know. It's terrible, terrible to say it, but every time I got out of that pit, and when I saw them all stretched out in death, all I could think was, "My God, I'm still alive," and all I could feel was glad, glad that that cup of bitterness had passed from my lips. We'll do everything we can for everybody, but don't ask me to begrudge us the happiness we've got. They've got their grieving to do and we cannot do it for them. Us being miserable'll not make them any happier.'

'I suppose you're right, and like Mam says, a bit of help's worth a lot of pity. All the same . . .'

'I know. All the same. We'll do what we can.'

Chapter Twenty-Seven

Strolling arm in arm with Martin along the riverbank with the fresh moist autumn air in her nostrils and birds soaring overhead wild and free, Ginny drank in the beauty of her beloved North Country. The red and gold of the leaves which rustled underfoot and floated gently on the river heralded again the dying, mournful time of year, but now a deep contentment left no room in her heart for either pain or regret.

Turning for home, they heard the strains of a lament on Northumberland pipes, a sound unheard in the village since Bob Dyer had been sealed in the pit six months earlier. The thought of old Bob sitting playing made the hair stand up on the back of her neck. They walked briskly on to find the musician waiting patiently on the bench outside the Cock. Not Bob, but a stranger. Leaving Martin to open the bar, Ginny ran upstairs to wash and tidy herself, then, looking every inch the young landlady, she joined her husband and their new customer.

'Aye, the new owners might be all right. It's not very likely, but they might run against the general grain of owners, and I hope they do; but it still won't hurt to bargain from a position of strength, and the only strength for the pitmen is unity. Join the Union; it's the only way to get decent treatment for everybody. No weak links in the chain. Any man willing to trade his own safety for company favour, or to take less than a fair rate for the job makes conditions worse for himself and everybody else.'

She looked at him fondly, Martin Jude, the Union's most zealous evangelist. The newcomer was obviously getting more than the beer he had bargained for. Ginny's fondness didn't blind her to the effect Martin's intensity of feeling had on people who didn't know him – it was apt to make them flee. The man began to look hunted, overwhelmed by this deluge of persuasion from such an unexpected source as the landlord of a well-kept inn. She went to his rescue.

'Give him a chance, Martin. Let him have his pint in peace, at least. He might become one of our regulars if you don't drive him away before he can enjoy it.'

The customer shot her a look of gratitude. 'Thanks, missus.' He took a long, appreciative draught of the best beer for miles around, then, wiping the froth from his lip with the back of his hand, asked, in accents more northerly than Wearham's, 'Any idea where I can get decent lodgings?'

Ginny appraised him. Late forties maybe, greying, average height and well made, clean, but down at heel and shabby. He carried his belongings in a canvas bag, but the pride in his bearing commanded respect and his manners were good.

'Will you be bringing your family here once you get settled?' she asked.

He shook his head. 'I'm a widower. Only got three kids, all married. We've all moved about a bit. Pits open, pits shut, you move on to get work. If there's enough here, I'll let me lads know. They might want to come.'

'Why, there's plenty of lodgings round here. At nearly every other house there's some poor woman lost her man, or her lads. Any of 'em might be glad of a lodger,' said Martin, voice laden with bitterness against those who had made it so.

'I'll give you a good address,' said Ginny, taking an instant liking to the man. 'She's a proper lady, mind, and if she can't help you, she'll put you on to somebody who can. Go to number eleven Snowdrop Terrace, and see Mrs Smith. Say Ginny sent you.'

Martin looked startled, then said, 'I don't think that's a good idea, Ginny.'

'Let Mrs Smith be the judge of that. She'll send him somewhere as good if it's not.'

The Vines and their partners had gone. The pit had fallen into the hands of a Mr Woolfe, another mining engineer cum speculative investor, who astutely bought it at a knock-down price in view of its condition and the fervent wish of its former owners to be quit of it and the district.

In the long term, its rich seams and the ready availability of the skilled labour necessary to exploit them promised amply to repay his outlay. Mr Woolfe was a man of energy and enterprise, and had set men to the tasks of repairing the shafts, pumping out water, and surveying the mine. It was now restored to a safe enough condition to be worked. He was recruiting labour, and migrant miners were beginning to arrive from neighbouring villages and further afield.

'Why didn't you send him to your own mother's?' asked Martin, when he'd served the handful of midday customers and the piper had left the bar.

'Her new house is a lot bigger than the old one, I know, but it's still full with her own three and our Emma and Jimmy and the baby. Besides, I don't think she's in the humour for a new husband yet. Maybe in another eighteen months or so, I'll send somebody along,' smiled Ginny with a twinkle in her eye.

Martin gaped. 'What makes you think Mam Smith wants a new husband? She's never shown any sign of it to me.'

'She probably didn't want one while she had you and Philip to look after, but now I think she's lonely. I see the way she looks at the two of us sometimes. Wistful, like.'

'You daft ha'p'orth. She doesn't get the chance to be lonely. Philip's there more than he's here.'

'He's at school and out playing more than he's at either place. And visiting's not the same. A bit of extra money never hurts, and she needs somebody to look after. A nice, tidy widower who can play her a tune on his pipe – just the thing to put the sparkle back in any widow's eyes.'

Martin laughed at the sly expression on her face and hit

her with the bar-cloth. 'I hope we don't get wrong for sending him, that's all.'

She eventually bolted the door on the last daytime customer and helped him clear up, then took him by the hand, a wicked gleam in her eye. 'Come on. All this talk about needing husbands reminds me how much I need mine.'

Along with Tom Hood and a couple of others, Martin was a trustee of the distress fund. He did most of the administration and the beneficiaries of the fund called at the Cock on Friday mornings for their entitlement. Although there was little likelihood he would ever work in a pit again, Martin still did most of the secretarial work for the Union and the Cock assumed a new role; that of the regular Union meeting place. Asserting the rights of the working man and fostering political enlightenment were objectives dear to the landlord's heart. Ginny cared little for politics, but made an ideal publican's wife, witty, sociable, and, when playing the landlady, always good-humoured. It was his little firebrand of a barmaid who endorsed all Martin's views on politics and unionism, with a fervour that matched his own.

Emma arrived early that evening. 'That sore on Jimmy's leg's broken down again,' she told them, 'I don't know when it's ever going to heal properly. It seems all right for a bit, then it starts weeping again, and it smells. He keeps saying it'll be all right, but I can tell he's in pain with it.'

'He's the best little feller I've ever known,' said Martin. 'You never hear a word of complaint from him. He ought to have had more compensation for that. He'll never be fit for hewing again.'

'We're hoping for the best,' said Emma, taking off her hat and coat, 'and at least he's got a job in the engine room. He might not want to work at the face again, once he gets used to it.'

'Not as much money, though.'

'But at least he's safe. I just wish his leg would heal.'

'How's me mam?'

'Better than anybody can remember. I think it's the first time in me life I've seen her without bruises.'

'Aye,' Ginny sighed, 'and who'd ever have thought he'd die a hero's death in the end?'

'I don't think anybody ever thought he was a coward, but he was a bad old bugger to us all the same.'

Martin looked mildly disapproving but, unable to refute the truth of Emma's last statement, he reversed it. 'He was a bad old so-and-so to you, but he died a hero's death in the end. You two stop up here and have a bit chat for half an hour. I'll go and open up.'

'Poor soul, he looks weary,' commented Emma once Martin was out of earshot. 'You'll wear him out faster than the pub or the Union will. I bet you never leave him alone. You're happy now you've a licence to romp in bed with him all night.'

'Half the day as well. Love and lust. Marriage is marvellous. It gives you a right to pester a man to death.'

'You're bloody awful, our Ginny. I can't wait to see you with a bairn to keep you awake half the night. Let's see how keen you are then,' Emma laughed.

'You might not have long to wait.'

Emma laughed all the more. 'How far on? Half an hour?'

Still laughing, they walked downstairs and into the bar. Another stranger stood there talking to Martin.

'John!'

'I can't believe it! I thought we'd never see you again. We had a telegram saying you were lost. Why didn't you write?' demanded Emma.

He shrugged, looking sheepish. 'I just got out of the habit. I'd no idea the daft buggers had sent you a telegram. I've been at death's door, though; they put me ashore in Cape Town with typhoid, and I stayed in South Africa longer than I needed to, because I like it there, and I've got a bonny little Dutch lass waiting for me. I'm going back as soon as I can afford to. I think I'll trek up to Kimberley, see if I can get a job in the gold mines. We licked old Kruger. I might as well see a bit of the benefit.'

'Don't talk about going again, you've only just got here. Have you seen me mam?' demanded Emma.

'That I've not. When I got home, she wasn't living there any more. I just came to get a pint before walking on to Old Annsdale. By, the pub looks grand. You're a lucky man, Martin. You've done all right for yourself.'

'Ginny's made my luck. She's done all right for us all, and I intend to do the same for her before I've finished,' said Martin, face serious, 'but there's plenty weren't so lucky. There's a few of your old marrers you'll never see again.'

*

The Cock was going from strength to strength. They threw it open at minimal cost for weddings, christenings and any other excuse for a celebration. Ginny installed a piano in the best room, and persuaded Miss Carr to teach Jimmy to play. He hadn't hewed long enough for his fingers to lose all sensitivity, and he was an enthusiastic learner.

As soon as the last of the black crêpe disappeared from village windows, Ginny started to give concerts on Pay Fridays. People came from Old Annsdale and all the surrounding villages to hear her and to pass good money over the bar. They agreed that a fifth of the profits should go to the distress fund. Most people in the village recognized her open-handed generosity, but there were a few who would never accept her, she knew that. Those upright people, whose greatest delight in life was holier-than-thou conversation along the lines of 'I thank thee, Lord, that I am not as this Publican', were unlikely ever to relinquish so rewarding a target as the landlady of the Cock Inn. Ginny laughed at them. She would live exactly as she wanted to live, and defy provincial prudery.

'I've got the name, so I might as well have the game,' she told Emma. 'London's got its faults, but at least the working class there are a bit more broad-minded. I'm soon going to give everybody something to talk about, friend and foe alike.'

When the swelling of her belly was barely visible, she sang a folk song it had amused George to adapt for her, in front of a packed house. She saw Emma and Martin busy behind the bar, and Maudie standing beside him, furiously washing glasses. John was sitting at a table in company with their mother, whose health and good looks had been improved beyond recognition by a little peace and prosperity, and the return of her adored first-born. Mam Smith and her new lodger sat close together, seeming happy in each other's company.

All looked expectantly towards Ginny. Feeling as nervous as she ever had in the grandest theatres in London, and knowing that fear would add spice to her performance, she gave the nod to the pianist and stood completely still, hands clasped demurely in front of her. After a few introductory bars, she began:

A traveller for many long years I have been,
But I never went over to France.
Most cities and all market towns I've been in,
From Berwick-on-Tweed to Penzance.
Many hotels and taverns I've been in in my
  time
And many good landlords have seen,
But of all the great heroes who others outshine
Give me the brave widower, the valiant
  widower,
The stout-hearted widower who keeps the
  Cock Inn.

She saw Emma nudge Martin, who looked across at her and smiled. She sang on, as if butter wouldn't have melted in her mouth until she got to the last verse:

Then here's to the brave-hearted hewer I prize
In a bumper now filled to the brim,
For who could resist such a pair of blue eyes,
Such a face, such a smile, such a him?
Away, then away with my single girl's vow,
My hand then in his with the ring;
Because he was willing to take me in tow,
I married the widower, the stout-hearted widower,
I married the widower, and we keep the Cock Inn.

She gave a ghost of a smile, and the mere hint of a wink, and saw Martin pushing his way through the throng towards her as she drew breath to repeat the last two lines:

For I love the widower, the stout-hearted widower,
Yes, I love the widower and I love the . . .

He managed to clap a hand over her mouth just in time to stop her, but couldn't prevent the rest of the company roaring, 'Cock Inn!'

A sea of laughing faces surrounded them. Amid a riot of cheering and clapping and stamping, Martin held up an admonishing finger and looked at her severely. 'Now you really hev gone too far. I can see I'll hev to rein you in.'

She opened her eyes wide, a picture of injured innocence. 'But I cannot help people's minds, Martin!'

'No, but you know what people's minds are. And that's the last time you sing that,' he warned.

With every eye expectantly on them, Ginny solemnly lowered her gaze and nodded in perfect wifely submission, but when he clasped her to him and held her head against his chest, she knew it was to hide a smile. As he hurried back to his customers, still carefully hiding his face from her, she pressed both her hands to her lips. With the bright flame of love that burned in her heart for him shining in her eyes, she spread her arms wide to scatter kisses after him, before treating the audience to a final, impudent, wink.

A Dorset Girl

Janet Woods

When her mother and stepfather perish in a fire, Siana Lewis finds herself destitute, with a younger brother and sister to support. Although her prospects seem bleak, Siana's beauty and intelligence will attract the attention of three men.

Daniel, her first love – the man who will betray her.

Francis Matheson, the village doctor, who admires Siana's determination and thirst for knowledge.

And Edward Forbes, the local squire. A sensual and devious man, Edward is used to getting what he wants. He desires the beautiful peasant girl from the moment he sets eyes on her – and he's determined to have her. Whatever it takes.

'A thoroughly enjoyable saga with a delightful heroine and vivid characters' Anna Jacobs

PRICE £6.99

ISBN 0 7434-6799-X

Beyond the Plough

Janet Woods

Now a wealthy young widow, former peasant girl Siana Forbes has overcome her humble beginnings to become mistress of Cheverton Manor, the handsome estate which her infant son, Ashley, will one day inherit. When the man she has always loved, country doctor Francis Matheson, asks for her hand in marriage, it seems her happiness is complete.

But trouble lies ahead. An unexpected tragedy means Francis must leave for Australia – a land where danger and hardship await. Left behind to raise a growing family, Siana too has problems when a sinister figure from her past emerges, determined to cause havoc. And a terrible ordeal suffered by her stepdaughter on the night of the harvest supper leaves Siana with a heartbreaking choice. Will she be able to overcome the odds stacked against her and keep her family together? And will she ever be reunited with her beloved Francis?

PRICE £6.99

ISBN 0 7434-6800-7